KISS MY CUPCAKE

HELENA HUNTING

PIATKUS

PIATKUS

First published in the US in 2020 by Forever,
an imprint of Grand Central Publishing, a division of Hachette Book Group, Inc

First published in Great Britain in 2020 by Piatkus

1 3 5 7 9 10 8 6 4 2

A CIP catalogue record for this book is available from the British Library.

ISBN 978-0-349-42648-8

Printed and bound in Great Britain by Clays Ltd, Elcograf S.p.A.

Papers used by Piatkus are from well-managed forests
and other responsible sources.

Piatkus
An imprint of
Little, Brown Book Group
Carmelite House
50 Victoria Embankment
London EC4Y 0DZ

An Hachette UK Company
www.hachette.co.uk

www.littlebrown.co.uk

For the outliers who are willing to choose the road less traveled over the easier path

KISS MY CUPCAKE

chapter one

JUST A BIG OLD PILE OF CRAP

Blaire

I have a fantastic idea for your little cupcake shop, Care Blaire!"

I cringe at the nickname, how ridiculously loud my dad is, and the reference to my first ever solo entrepreneurial endeavor as my "little cupcake shop." He doesn't mean for it to sound condescending, although it does.

My first inclination is to throw some sarcasm at him, but I'm aware he's trying to be helpful in his own misguided way, and the conversation will be over that much sooner if I play along. "What's this fantastic idea that has you so excited?"

"The café right beside Decadence is going out of business at the end of the year. I'd be happy to pick up the lease on that building and you could open up shop right next door to us! Wouldn't that be wonderful? And so much more practical than what you're doing right now."

I hold my phone away from my ear and breathe in and out

to the count of four so I don't snap at him. "My current lease is a year, Dad."

"Can't you break it?"

"Not without a penalty, no."

"Hmm. Well, I could cover that for you. I don't think it hurts for you to give this a go on your own for a few months, but then you can come back home and be part of the family business. And obviously I'd provide you with the financial capital if you decided to make the transition."

And there's the braised carrot I was waiting for him to dangle. "Can I think about it?" There is absolutely zero chance that I'm going to take him up on his offer. It's not that I don't want the financial help. It's all the strings that come along with it that I'm not interested in dealing with.

"Of course, of course. It's a great opportunity and I wouldn't want you to miss out on it. Why don't we talk later in the week?"

"Sure. Sounds good."

"Love you, Care Blaire!"

"Love you, too, Dad." I end the call on a frustrated sigh and then nearly do a face plant into the concrete trying to sidestep a pile of dog poop. I also come perilously close to dropping my Tupperware container full of buttercream-topped delights. The dog doody happens to be decorating the sidewalk right out front of my "little cupcake shop." I mentally shake a fist at the thoughtless dog owner who left it there as a special surprise.

This better not be a sign.

I glance around, looking for something to...remove the visual and olfactory offense, but the sidewalk is trash free. Normally I would be happy about the lack of old newspapers or takeout food wrappers blowing down the street, but today it's rather inconvenient. The last thing I want is a stinky mess sitting front and center outside of my not-yet-open storefront. As a helpful warning to other passersby, I pluck a yellow flower from one of the planters brightening the entrance to my brand new cocktail café/bakery, aptly named Buttercream and Booze—scheduled to open in just one week—and stick the stem in the fresh pile. I'll come back out and get rid of it so no one else suffers the same almost-fate.

Even the nearly craptastic accident and my conversation with my dad don't dim my good spirits for long. I rummage through my purse in search of my keys—they always migrate to the bottom of my purse. I finally snag them, slide the key into the lock and push the door open. It tinkles cheerily, an auditory accompaniment to the vibrant, clean interior.

I wanted simple, fresh, and chic without being overly bubblegum adorable. So I nixed any pink from the décor that doesn't include cupcake frosting. Instead I went with pale hardwood flooring, simple white tables and luxurious chairs upholstered in pale gray, easy-to-clean faux leather. Pops of vibrant yellows, pale blue, and silver accent each table's centerpiece. The windows are sparkling and streak-free, the signage across the front of the café is clean, simple, and classy in eye-catching gray with a metallic sheen.

I inhale deeply as I step inside, the faint scent of fresh paint and bleach almost entirely eclipsed by the lemon oil diffusing in the corner, and the lingering smell of the real vanilla candles from yesterday.

I forget all about cleaning up the poopy present and shriek when I notice the box sitting on the bar. I set my purse and Tupperware on the closest table and my coffee on the bar. Despite my excitement, I take a moment to wash my hands prior to nabbing a pair of scissors. I carefully drag the tip along the seam to slice through the tape.

"I thought I heard you making sex noises out here." My best friend Daphne appears at the end of the hall, scaring the heck out of me.

The scissors slip and catch my finger. "Ow! Crap!" A bead of blood wells from the cut and I suck the end of my thumb, the metallic tang making me slightly woozy. I'm a bit of a baby when it comes to the sight of blood.

"I'm so sorry." Daphne rushes across the café, heels clipping on the hardwood. She nabs the small first-aid kit behind the bar, flips it open, and retrieves a bandage.

"It's okay. I'm just clumsy this morning, and jittery."

"Everything okay?" Her expression shifts to concern as she quickly covers the wound with a Band-Aid.

"Oh yeah, you know how it is. I woke up at three because I needed to use the bathroom and my brain wouldn't shut off. Then I got another idea for opening day cupcakes so I figured I'd make a test batch while drinking an entire pot of coffee."

She glances at the adorable cupcake clock on the wall. "So you've been up since three?"

"Mm hmm. And of course my dad called this morning with another one of his amazing ideas."

She grimaces. "Oh no."

"Oh yes."

"What wonderful suggestions did he have this time?" Daphne is aware of my parents' constant push for me to join the family business. I love them, and they've worked hard to get where they are, but their dreams and mine don't line up. They love sautéing and roasting and hobnobbing with the rich and famous. I love butter and sugar and vanilla and *not* hobnobbing.

I give her the abridged version.

"And how did the conversation end?"

"All I said was that I'd think about it."

"You did not!"

I hold up a hand. "I'm not honestly going to think about it, Daph, but I also didn't feel like listening to an hour-long lecture on why being part of the family business would be better for me. I know exactly what will happen if I go back to working with my family. I won't have a say in anything. They'll take over the whole thing and change it from my cocktails and cupcakes theme into something ridiculous and highbrow. They'll strip me of all decision-making power, pooh-pooh all of my ideas, and I'll get to watch my dream go up in flames." It sounds dramatic, but it's not. My family is well-intentioned but pushy. "I didn't work this hard just to go back to kobe beef and duck fat truffle fries." Not that there's anything wrong with either. I enjoy eating both, but I don't enjoy preparing them the way my family does.

"Okay. That's good. I was worried there for a second." Daphne sheds her thin cardigan and hops lithely up onto the bar top. I finally notice her outfit; she's dressed in a pair of pale yellow jeans and a light-gray shirt with Buttercream and Booze in silver and blue letters across her chest.

"Oh my God! The shirts came in!" My volume is far too loud for the early hour, but my excitement cannot be contained. "I need to take a picture." I pat my hips, but my phone is in my purse, which is sitting on the table where I left it. I raise a single finger. "Hold on! I need my phone. Or maybe I should get the good camera. And we need a cupcake. Actually, we should stage a bunch of photos."

"Blaire." Daphne grabs my wrist. "Take a breath or six and chill the eff out."

"But we need a picture. One for our Instagram. Oh! We should host a T-shirt giveaway!"

"Done and done. I posted half an hour ago and it's already in our stories and on our Facebook page and posted to the website. Social media managed." She says the last part with a British accent, mimicking "mischief managed" from *Harry Potter*. We're both huge fans. Sometimes we have weekend movie marathons despite having seen the films quite literally a hundred times. Don't judge. There are worse addictions.

Daphne is a photographer and has her own business a

couple of blocks down. She opened her studio last year and I was right there with her, helping in whatever way I could. Unlike B&B, her place didn't need too much work, but I was there with a paintbrush and moral support. I even brought the Cupcakes to Go! truck on opening day to help entice new clients with sweet treats.

Daphne's actually the person who told me about this place. She's also been kind enough to help get all of my social media up and running. Currently, I pay her in cupcakes since I can't afford much else in the way of compensation. She's assured me this is a great addition to her portfolio and if Buttercream and Booze takes off she'll most definitely benefit. I squeeze her hand. "You are so amazing."

"I know. It's one of the many reasons I'm your bestie." She winks. "Now open the damn box so we can get excited about something else and you can freak out about more potential Insta posts."

"Right! Yes!" I take one of those deep breaths Daphne suggested because I'm speaking like I've mainlined cocaine after drinking seventeen Red Bulls and everything I say is punctuated with an exclamation mark. "Calming myself before I get more excited," I mutter as I open the flaps. That calm lasts about a quarter of a second and then I'm back to excited freak-out.

"They are so much fun!" I gently free one of the unicorn martini glasses from the box. "Aren't they the most adorable thing you've ever seen?"

"They are absolutely the most adorable things I have seen." Daphne bites her lip, obviously fighting laughter.

"Well, I think they're perfect." I can already imagine the specialty martini and the cupcakes I'll make to go with them. The glasses were a little expensive, and slightly outside of my budget, but they're so much fun and they'll look amazing in photos for social media posts.

"I wholeheartedly agree. You should display a few up there." She motions to the shelf adjacent to the bar that showcases a row of candy-inspired martini glasses.

"Ohhh! Great idea!" I carefully free two more unicorn glasses from the box and round the counter.

Daphne hops down off the bar. "I'll be right back."

I *mm-hmm*, too consumed with rearranging the shelf to be concerned with where Daphne is going.

Daphne returns as I finish positioning the glassware. She's grinning and her hands are clasped behind her back. "Close your eyes."

I slam my lids together. "They're closed."

"Arms up."

I raise them over my head and Daphne laughs. "Just to the side, like you're halfway into a jumping jack."

I lower them so they're out in a T. "Oh my God. What do you have? What came?"

"Stop jumping around and you'll find out."

I didn't even realize I was bouncing with excitement. I still and wait while Daphne drapes something over my head.

When she ties it at my waist behind my back I start bouncing again. "It's my apron, isn't it?"

"Stop moving and don't you dare peek." She smacks my butt.

"Ow!"

"It was a tap, you sucky baby."

"It was unexpected." And the most action I've had in a long time. Opening one's own business means I have very little time for anything but work, more work, and limited sleep.

"Eyes closed until I tell you." She takes me by the shoulders and pushes me forward. "Okay. You can open them."

I pry one lid open, and then the other. Daphne has moved me to the center of the café, where a massive mirror with the Buttercream and Booze decal hangs from the wall. I'm off to the right, so I can see my brand new apron without the obstruction of opaque letters cutting through it.

My hands start flapping without my permission, so I ball them into fists and hide them behind my back for a moment while I search for some calm. "It's just so perfect, isn't it?" I'm halfway to tears, I'm so elated.

But then, that's what this place reduces me to: tears and excitement. I've worked my tushy off to get here.

"It is." Daphne, being the awesome friend that she is, hands me a tissue before I even have to ask. "You've come a long way from weekend markets and a cupcake truck."

I survey the product of all my hard work. "It's been a journey, hasn't it?"

"An uphill battle to the top of cupcake mountain, really," Daphne agrees.

"I'd rather take the hard road than compromise my dream." I run my fingertips over the letters that spell out Buttercream and Booze. My phone chimes from inside my purse, signaling a call. The ringtone, which is "The Addams Family" theme song, means it's my mother.

Daphne and I look at my purse and then each other. "I'm letting that go to voicemail. I one hundred percent guarantee my mom is calling to try to argue my dad's case."

Daphne sighs. "They really don't get it, do they?"

"Nope."

"Have you told them when your grand opening is?"

"Absolutely not." I do not need them showing up on opening day throwing advice at me. And honestly, it wouldn't be that difficult for them to find the information on their own if they had the wherewithal to check out social media, but I've been extremely vague about the whole thing.

"It's too bad they can't just support you without taking everything over."

"They have the best of intentions and a complete lack of chill." Two traits I'm not unfamiliar with.

"Truer words have never been spoken." Daphne blows out a breath. "It'd be nice if they would let you access your trust without forcing their opinions on you."

"They really love the concept of conditional independence." My family owns some of the most highly regarded, exclusive fine dining establishments in the Pacific Northwest. The expectation was always that I, too, would become a chef and carry on the family legacy.

She taps on the edge of the counter. "It's just frustrating to *know* you have the money, but if you use it there are all kinds of stupid stipulations that go along with it. Sort of defeats the whole purpose of having a trust in the first place, doesn't it?"

Daphne's family is well off, too. We went to the same prep school and have been friends since we were kids. The main difference is that her family has backed every single dream she's ever had an inkling to pursue, whereas mine keeps trying to hammer the square peg that is me into a round hole of their design. "Hence the reason the money is staying where it is until this place is established and I've proven I can make it work."

Fingers crossed that's what happens. For the past several years I've been squirreling away money and living in a crap apartment because I'm determined to make a go of this, on my own merit. So I put the research in, found a storefront I could afford in an area where I thought I could be successful, worked up my business plan, secured the financing, and now here I am, opening my own place, without my family's input, much to their chagrin.

Daphne motions to the shop. "How much more proof do they need?"

"Running a successful cupcake truck business isn't quite the same as having a storefront." I run my finger around the rim of a martini glass.

Daphne taps on the counter. "I actually think the cupcake truck was probably the more difficult of the two. The crap you had to deal with on a regular basis was insane. At least you don't have to worry about slashed tires anymore."

"Thank goodness for that." The food truck business is no joke. It's wildly competitive, territorial and exceptionally cut-throat. The number of times I had to replace my tires because some jealous competitor wanted to take down Cupcakes to Go! was ridiculous.

My family was always worried for my safety. Regardless, it was my first attempt at being an independent business owner. Now here I am with my own storefront and no intention of ever working for my family again if I can help it.

Back when I was younger and still trying to appease my parents, I went to culinary school and apprenticed under re-nowned chef Raphael Du Beouf. He was talented, handsome, and suave. I was naïve, impressionable, and smitten. I fell for his sexy accent, his ridiculously capable hands, and his lines. So of course, like many stupid twentysomethings, I soaked up the attention and praise he lavished on me, and eventually we started sleeping together. I thought I was in love, while he thought I wouldn't find out that he was sleeping with three other aspiring chefs on the side.

Brokenhearted and totally disenchanted, I let my parents—who felt partly responsible since they were the ones who pushed us together in the first place after he started working at one of their restaurants—fund a year abroad for me in Paris. I got over Raphael and fell in love with everything pastry and deca-dence. I returned with a new plan that—much to my family's shock—did not include taking my place in their business.

So I made connections of my own and started from the ground up. I rented a booth at the local street market and sold cupcakes every weekend while working back of house at a high-end bakery. Which is where I met my friend and eventual business partner, Paul. He also worked the local street market circuit and eventually we pooled our resources, bought a food truck, and launched our mobile cupcake shop, Cupcakes to Go! On the weekends we would still hit the local markets, but during the week we made our rounds and delivered our delicious, decadent wares.

So as much as I rue my relationship with Raphael, his womanizing ways set me on this path. No regrets.

I shake off my trip down memory lane and motion to my apron-clad self. "Shall we take some Insta-worthy pics?"

"Yes!" Daphne jumps to her feet and grabs her camera—it's pretty much an additional appendage.

She poses me in various locations around the shop, holding all manner of props, including the cupcakes I baked prior to my arrival. "You look like the love child of Betty Crocker and Ward Cleaver," she mumbles as she moves around me, snapping shot after shot.

I'm a big fan of fifties-style dresses with full skirts and up-dos reminiscent of the same era. It's not meant to be a gimmick; it's just my thing. I pluck one of the decorative martini glasses from the counter display and am about to take a fake sip when a massive bang shakes the entire store, making the windows rattle and the bottles on the bar tinkle. I almost drop the martini glass. It's plastic, so it wouldn't be a tragedy if I did, but still.

"What the heck was that?" I set the glass on the closest table and rush to the front window, surveying the street. I don't know what I expect to find. A tank? A wrecking ball?

"I don't know, but it felt like an earthquake."

I spin around to face Daphne. "When was the last time Seattle had an earthquake?"

She doesn't even hesitate. "2001, I think."

"Why would you even know that?"

Daphne shrugs and then covers her head with her hands when another violent bang rattles the martini glasses—the real ones—so badly, one of my new unicorn glasses falls off the shelf and shatters on the floor.

"Oh no!" Daphne slaps a palm over her mouth.

We regard the sparkly puddle with mutual horror; the gold horn sticks straight up, the eyeballs peer wonkily at us from the carnage.

"Save the unicorns!" I shout.

We scramble over to the shelf, carefully grabbing the rest of the stemware before it can meet the same sad fate. I cradle them to my chest, collecting as many as I can.

The next bang isn't as unexpected, but it's still jarring. I jump and nearly lose my hold on a unicorn. As it is, I have a horn poking me in the boob. At least the glasses are no longer at risk of falling off the shelf.

"I think it might be coming from next door." Daphne carefully sets her armload of glasses on the counter.

"What the hell is over there? A portal to another dimension?" I prop my fist on my hip and glare at the wall, as if my angry face is going to make the banging on the other side stop.

"An old bar I think?" Daphne and I both cringe with the next loud slam. "I've never really paid much attention to it, to be honest."

"It sounds like they're coming through the freaking wall! I'm going over there to see what's going on."

I grab the empty box and carefully put the shattered unicorn martini glass pieces inside. Whoever is over there needs to see what they've done.

"I'll be right back." I rush outside and manage to sidestep the doggy doo again as I stalk over to the run-down bar next door. I glance up at the faded, peeling sign above the store-front: THE KNIGHT CAP. I reluctantly admit, in my head, that it's a clever play on words.

The windows are covered with brown paper, as is the door, but another loud bang comes from inside. I knock quite vigor-ously and shout hello, but I'm sure no one can hear me over the ridiculous racket coming from inside. I also catch the faint pounding of bass.

I decide my best bet is to poke my head in and see what the heck is going on. I yank on the door and it opens an inch, then slams closed again, as if there's a poltergeist on the other side holding it shut. I try again, struggling with the door, which shouldn't be this heavy. There's some kind of wind vortex trying to suck it closed again, but I finally manage to pry it open and slide my body through the gap, still clutching my box with the broken unicorn martini glass. My dress nearly gets caught, but I yank it free before I get stuck in the door.

I cough a few times, breathing in sawdust. The place is absolutely filthy and a wreck. It's deceptively large and long, and the entire back of the pub is covered in plywood. Now that I'm inside, I can make out more of the song booming through the sound system, causing the floor to vibrate. It's some rock tune with heavy guitar riffs and a lot of drums.

"Hello!" I shout and take a few cautious steps across the dusty hardwood. When no one answers, I call out a second time.

A large, somewhat hulking figure appears in the doorway between the old, dusty bar and the new plywood enclosure. The garish lights behind him eclipse his face in shadow until he takes another step forward, bringing him into view.

Standing about twenty feet away is a well-built man wearing a pair of paint-splattered jeans, scuffed-up work boots, and a red-and-black plaid shirt. The sleeves are rolled up to his elbows, showing off vibrantly colored tattoos that cover both of his forearms and disappear under the sleeves. His hair is cut short and styled with some kind of product so it's perfectly smooth, not a strand out of place. An intentional, curated messiness. And he's holding an axe.

Why is this guy holding an axe?

I take an uncertain step back toward the door, because, as I was saying, *he's holding a freaking axe*.

I prop my fist on my hip and tip my chin up as axe man's gaze sweeps over me. Judging. Assessing. His left eyebrow quirks up. He has eyes the color of bourbon, high cheekbones, full lips and a rugged, square jaw with a lovely five o'clock shadow, despite it barely being eight in the morning.

"What the heck is going on here?" I motion to the mess of a bar.

That quirked eyebrow rises higher. "Excuse me?"

"What is this?" I snap.

Axe man's full lips pull up into a grin. "It's called a bar, and judging from the look of it, I think you fell down the wrong rabbit hole, Alice. Wonderland isn't here."

@buttercreamandbooze:

Without the horn a unicorn is just a horse, and without frosting a cupcake is just a muffin!

chapter two

HOT LUMBERJERK

Blaire

My name is Blaire, not Alice, thank you very much." I want to smack myself for that terrible, unimpressive comeback. I blame my inability to come up with something—anything—better on thinking we were in the middle of an earthquake, the loss of one of my precious unicorn martini glasses that I honestly cannot afford to replace, and this axe-wielding hipster. Oh, did I forget to mention that beyond the fact that he's filthy and dressed like some kind of *GQ* lumberjack, he's also incredibly good-looking?

"Well, *Blaire*, you're standing in the middle of a construction zone, and I'm pretty sure those shoes don't meet the required code, so you can march them right back out the door." He uses the axe handle to point to my heels—which are adorable and surprisingly comfortable.

I take a step back. "Pointing is rude." *Where the hell has my quick wit disappeared to?*

"So is trespassing."

"I knocked, more than once, but with all the racket going on in here it's not really a surprise that no one heard me, is it?" I'm irritated and gathering steam, thanks to my embarrassment, residual fear, and frustration over the problems this guy is causing me. I can't afford setbacks—there's too much on the line for me. Plus this guy has insulted my outfit. True, I may be silently judging him for his own wardrobe choices, but I'm certainly not going to voice them. *Yet.* "I own the café next door and all your banging around in here is making my life impossible."

"You mean the cupcake shop?" Once again, he uses the handle of the axe to point in the direction of my café. It makes his tattooed forearm flex enticingly. I don't even like tattoos. Well, that's not entirely true. I don't not-like tattoos. I just don't understand how anyone can sit through hours of being stabbed with needles for the sake of wearing art that could very easily be hung on a wall instead—pain free.

"It's not a cupcake shop. It's a *cocktail* and cupcake café." *Damn it wit, I need you!*

"Right. My bad. A cupcake and cocktail café isn't the same as a cupcake shop." His sarcasm bleeds through in his dry, day-old scone tone.

I ignore the dig, because trying to explain the difference to a flannel-wearing hipster is pointless. He's clearly the opposite of my target market. "What's happening back there?" I motion to the plywood room behind him. "Is that even legal?"

"It's called an axe-throwing enclosure, and yeah, it's legal." He pulls a piece of paper out of his back pocket and shakes it out so it unfolds, then holds it up in front of my face. When I try to grab it from him he snatches it away. "No touching, looking only."

I pin him with an unimpressed glare, uncertain as to whether that's what makes his cheek tic, and raise my hands in mock surrender. "I wouldn't want to soil your precious paper with my frosting fingers."

He lowers the paper so I can see that it's a permit for an axe-throwing enclosure. "See, Alice, totally legal."

I glare at him. "It's Blaire, and you need to move this enclosure thing because all that banging around is making my glassware fall off the shelves."

Axe man's eyebrows pop. "Uh yeah, that's not going to happen."

I flail a hand toward the mess of plywood. "One of my brand new unicorn martini glasses broke because of you, and they're expensive."

"Unicorn what?"

"Martini glasses. It's a martini glass with a unicorn face on it, and a horn. They're adorable and they weren't cheap and all your banging caused one to fall off the shelf and break." I hold out the box so he can see the damage he's responsible for.

He peeks inside, but makes no move to take the box. "Can't you just move your glasses?" His completely unaffected, blasé attitude is driving me crazy.

I set the box on the bar rather aggressively, making the glass inside tinkle. "I'll have to move an entire shelf. Maybe more than one." I continue to flail my arms all over the place. I'm sure I resemble an octopus on some kind of hallucinogenic stimulant. All the caffeine I've consumed today was obviously a terrible idea because it's making me edgy and discomposed.

"Okay." He hooks his thumb in his pocket, obviously not understanding the difficulty this axe-throwing room of his is going to be for me and my business. He's completely self-centered as well as condescending. I hate him already. Forever. Like a kindergartner.

"It's not okay at all. Moving a shelf will offset the entire layout of the wall. You can't just take a shelf down without there being any design consequences," I tell him. "It disturbs the continuity and interrupts the flow. The whole vibe will be thrown off!"

And now he's looking at me like I'm crazy. "Well, I'm sorry that taking a shelf down is going to mess with the cup-cake vibe, or whatever, *Blaire*, but unless you'd like to foot the bill to uninstall and reinstall all of this." He thumbs over his shoulder. "I'm thinking moving a shelf is probably your best bet if you don't want any more shattered unicorn dreams."

I huff my irritation, because although he has a point, the only person inconvenienced is me. And all this noise is going to make concentrating impossible today. I avoid responding, because I don't want to give in and agree with him. "How long is this going to go on for?"

"We can stop arguing about you moving a shelf anytime you want."

I've already filed this guy under Jerks I Want to Junk Punch. I hope someone puts Veet in his shampoo and all that luxurious, thick hair falls out. The thought of that alone makes me feel better. "I mean the noise, smartass."

The corners of his mouth turn up slowly until he's full on smiling. Dammit. Of course he has great teeth and a beautiful smile to go with his stupidly handsome face. All he probably has to do is flash that smile and people move shelves for him without a second thought. They probably move entire walls. And drop their damn panties, too.

He lifts a shoulder in a careless shrug. "I guess it depends on how long you want to stand here, bickering with me. I could do this all day, but that means I'm not working, and if I'm not working the enclosure isn't getting built. So it's entirely up to you how long it takes." His smile widens, likely at my appalled expression. "I'd offer to set you up with a pair of safety boots so you can keep having a go at me, but I'm not all that interested in putting a saw or a nail gun in your hands. I have a feeling it might be me you'd try to nail to the wall."

I flash him a less than friendly smile. "I meant how long do you expect these renovations to take?" I don't want them to interfere with my grand opening next week.

"Dunno. I'd say at least a couple of weeks, but it all depends on how often you decide to come over and give me shit."

"So now you're the one being inconvenienced, is that it?"

All he does is stand there with his arms crossed, wearing a telling smirk.

"Well thanks so much for making more work for me. It's not like I don't have enough to do right now. And I sincerely hope you're insulating that wall because I sure don't want an axe coming through it like some kind of B-rated horror movie!"

I spin on my heel and try to yank the door open with a dramatic flair, but of course the stupid wind-suction means I have to use both hands, which completely ruins the impact.

Once the suction seal is broken, the door flies open and I stumble back, almost landing on the filthy floor. I don't look back as I regain my composure, straighten my spine and exit his crappy pub.

"It was really nice to meet you, Blaire," he calls out after me, voice dripping sarcasm. "I'm Ronan Knight, by the way, thanks for asking, and for being so understanding about the renos!"

Well, now the name of the bar makes sense. Of course he has a super hipster, but also highly masculine name that's just as sexy as he is. Jerk.

He rattles the box with the broken glass. "Hey! You forgot your unicorn dreams!"

I consider flipping him the bird, but that would mean stooping to his level and I'm unwilling to play his game. "Kiss my cupcake!" I shout over my shoulder, wishing my wit had kicked in earlier. I stalk angrily down the sidewalk and nearly lose my footing for what seems like the hundredth time this morning when I step in something slippery. I glance down and gag, then tip my chin up to the sky. "Seriously?"

Of course I stepped in the dog-doo.

Because today hasn't been ruined enough by my new jerk of a neighbor.

I remove the offending shoe—the yellow flower is stuck to the bottom—and try not to breathe in the noxious odor. Daphne looks up from the bar where she's currently on her phone posting photos when I hobble back into my shop, my soiled shoe dangling from my finger.

Daphne's expression is somewhere between incredulous and questioning as she gives me a quick once-over. "Who are you and what have you done with my friend Blaire?"

"What?"

"Since when do you go around confronting complete strangers?"

She makes a good point. "Since I don't have enough money to replace that stupid glass. Everything I have is tied up in here." I wave my poopy shoe around. "I need this place to do well, Daph. I want to prove I can succeed on my own—with your help, obviously, and Paul's—but this needs to work out. I can't go to my family for help. They're too..."

"Crazy? Meddling? Impossible to deal with?" Daphne suggests.

"Exactly."

"Well, I gotta say, this new, bolder you is something I can definitely get used to. You're finally growing into your lady balls." She grins and nods to the shoe still dangling from my finger. "What happened?"

"I stepped in crap. Literally."

"Next door?"

"No. Out there." I motion to the sidewalk and hobble-weave my way through the tables all the way to the back door. I throw it open angrily and debate whether I should toss the shoe. I leave it outside, fairly confident no one is going to touch it.

I wash my hands before I return barefoot and still very much annoyed. Especially when the banging starts up again, and it seems like it's even more vigorous than it was before.

"So what's going on over there?"

"The lumberjerk next door is putting in an axe-throwing enclosure."

Daphne's eyes flare. "Lumberjerk?"

"He was wearing a plaid flannel shirt, wandering around with an axe. And get this: His name is Ronan, totally a hipster, right? He probably changed it from something far more pedestrian, like Robert or Bill. His hair looks like it's styled with pomade. All he was missing was the lumber-beard and the black-rimmed glasses."

Daphne holds up a hand. "Wait. Flannel in August?" Daphne asks. I'm glad she seems appropriately horrified by that fashion travesty.

"Or maybe it was plaid and I'm making up the flannel part. Regardless, he was wearing a plaid long-sleeved shirt with another shirt under it. In August. Totally ridiculous. And he's a completely condescending jerk! Can you believe he had the nerve to tell me I should move my shelf because he's putting in an axe-throwing enclosure? Who even likes throwing axes other than barbarians?"

"Uh, axe throwing is pretty popular these days."

I give her a look that tells her how much I don't appreciate her opinion on this. Or the fact that she is most certainly correct. "That's not the point. The point is he's inconveniencing me by using our adjoining wall for his freaking axe throwing! Why should I have to move my glassware for him? Moving that shelf means I'll have to adjust the entire layout. What a selfish bastard."

"Or do you mean shelf-ish bastard?" Daphne grins, and I fight one of my own.

"That was ridiculously lame."

"And yet, still funny."

I roll my eyes. "I need to tackle the shelf."

"Leave the shelf where it is."

"Why? We can't even put anything on it. Or hang stuff from that freaking wall if Lumberjerk is going to be throwing axes at it. And there's still a bar in there! How can they serve alcohol and wield axes? That seems outlandishly unsafe."

"There's protocol. And inspections."

I tap my lip, considering my options. "Inspections?"

Daphne shakes her head and raises a hand. "Don't start a war before you've even opened your doors, Blaire."

"You didn't meet him. He's a grade-A a-hole extraordinaire."

Although, she does have a point. "I'll tuck that piece of information in my pocket in case I need it."

Later, when I'm heading home for the day, I find a flyer tucked under my windshield wipers, which is odd, since I'm parked in the alley behind all the shops, where only the owners and employees are allowed. I lift the wiper and flip it over, curious and hoping that I don't have to fight a parking ticket I can't afford. It's definitely not a ticket, but it's dusk, and shadowy back here, so I climb into my SUV and toss it on the seat beside me.

It isn't until I get home and the interior light comes on that I finally realize what's on the flyer. It's an advertisement for anger-management therapy. At the top, in semi-legible man-scrawl is a note:

> *I'd invite you over for a little axe throwing to get out some of your latent aggression, but I'm not sure that's a good idea. Maybe this will help your vibe.*
>
> *~ your friendly neighborhood bar owner*

"What a jerk!" I ball it up and toss it in the trash. I don't have to wonder how he knew it was my SUV since I have a Buttercream and Booze magnetic decal stuck to the side panel.

@buttercreamandbooze:

Got a problem with me? Kiss my cupcake.

chapter three

THIS MEANS WAR

Blaire

Two days later I arrive at the shop after nine in the morning. I'm meeting Paul, my cupcake truck business partner and friend. My goal had always been to set up a storefront, while Paul really enjoyed being on the move and networking in new areas. He wanted to travel, and I wanted a home base.

We made a deal that he gets to keep the cupcake truck and the rights to the business. Instead of buying me out completely, he's agreed to continue to bake the cupcakes and I'll continue to decorate them for both of us while I get Buttercream and Booze up and running. That way he doesn't have to find someone else to partner up with, and neither of us has to hire someone to help.

I met Paul upon my return from Paris, while I was selling desserts in a booth at a local street market. Like me, Paul had his own cupcake and pastry booth, and we were right across from each other. Realizing that it would benefit us to work together—and save on booth rental costs—we ended up pooling our resources and our creativity. Having been on the street market circuit for a couple of years, Paul took me under his wing and showed me the ropes. He baked the cakes and I decorated them. We were a great team in the kitchen. Within a year we'd saved up enough to buy a food truck, and Cupcakes to Go! was born. At first Cupcakes to Go! was great and I loved having a partner. But Paul and I started butting heads since we both wanted to be in control of the business side, and by then I knew it was time to move on. It was always a temporary business venture, but it was a great learning experience.

This morning he's stopping by so he can try my newest cupcake creation and we can decide if there need to be any adjustments to the cake flavor and texture. The Cupcakes to Go! truck is parked out front on the street when I pass. The back door to my shop is already propped open with a wedge, which is considerate. It means I don't have to search my purse for my keys.

I'm busy juggling the cupcakes, my purse, and my travel mug, so I almost step in another pile of poop right in front of the door. "What the hell?" I grumble, looking around. Who would walk their dog in the back alley where there's all kinds of garbage? And who would leave their freaking dog poop behind? Maybe whoever it is has some kind of beef with the previous storeowner. Or maybe they have something against buttercream icing and booze.

The possibility that I've already made potential enemies and I haven't even opened my doors to the public unnerves me. I shake my head. I'm being paranoid. This isn't the food truck business. No one is going to slash my tires here.

I sidestep the poop and set the cupcakes inside, out of harm's way. This time I hunt down an old plastic bag immediately so I don't forget about it and no one accidentally steps in it. I make a face as I crouch down to pick it up, expecting the noxious odors to hit me, but strangely enough all I get is the faint stench of garbage. I also expect it to be squishy and gross, but it's unusually firm. Completely solid, in fact.

Once it's safely in the bag I try to lob it into the dumpster, but my aim sucks and it hits the side with a low thud and *thwang*.

I frown, because dog poop should not make that kind of sound when it hits metal. I don't know what gets into me, other than curiosity, but I open the bag and peek inside. Which is when I realize that it's not *real* poop. It's plastic.

I glance over at The Knight Cap and narrow my eyes. He must've seen me step in the poop the other day and this is his idea of being funny. "What a jerk."

Paul pokes his head out the back door. "I thought I heard someone back here. What's going on?"

I pull the fake poop out of the bag. "My neighbor is a turd, that's what's going on."

Paul makes a face. "Is that . . ."

"It's fake." I stalk over to the service entrance of The Knight

Cap. The door is propped open with a wooden wedge. The sound of a circular saw and the loud strains of rock music come from inside. I replace the wedge with the fake poop and as an afterthought, I take the wedge with me, because screw him.

"What was that all about?" Paul asks as I scoop up the box of cupcakes and he follows me down the hall.

"Apparently my new neighbor has the maturity of a twelve-year-old and thinks he's a comedian."

"Making friends already, huh?" Paul chuckles.

"Haha. As you can clearly hear, he's not the quietest, most conscientious neighbor." I set the Tupperware on the counter and wash my hands before I open it up to display my late-night endeavors.

"Oh, wow!" Paul wafts his hand over the container, inhaling deeply. "Is that maple? And bourbon? And bacon?"

"It is. Try one and tell me what you think. I'm not sure if the maple flavor is too overpowering in the icing." I tap on the counter, trying to be patient while he peels the wrapper and takes a healthy bite of the cupcake.

He closes his eyes and chews, nodding slightly. "The bourbon cream in the center balances out the maple perfectly. I wouldn't change a thing."

"Really?"

"They're decadent, Blaire. People are going to fall in love with them. Can you email me the recipe and I'll make a test batch tomorrow so I can be sure I get it right?" He glances inside the Tupperware and taps the top of two small containers labeled *icing* and *filling*, nestled among the cakes. "You're so on top of things. We're still doing the lemon drop cupcakes as well?"

"Yes, definitely. Plus the usual flavors, and the morning glory cupcakes. I have everything I need for the buttercream."

"Okay, great. Then I think we're all set. You're doing a fabulous job, Blaire." Paul gives me a kind smile.

"Thanks, I really appreciate your help."

"Well, it's mutually beneficial, isn't it? You honestly put together the most amazing flavor combinations."

I wave off the compliment, getting emotional about the whole thing. While I'm not going to miss the cramped quarters of the cupcake truck, we've been working together for a long time and he's been a good friend and partner.

He gives me a side hug, grabs the Tupperware and heads out. I'll see him at the crack of dawn on opening morning so I can decorate the cupcakes and make sure everything is picture perfect.

A few hours later, Lumberjerk passes by my front window, waving jovially.

Such a jerk.

As the week progresses I decide that my disdain for Ronan is completely justified. He's a dick. A giant, stupidly attractive dick who always wears long-sleeved plaid shirts—yes, I totally made up the flannel part—rolled up to his elbows with another shirt underneath it. And jeans. And work boots. Every damn day.

How do I know this?

Because every single day he passes my storefront at some point and makes a big show of waving exuberantly while shouting hello.

And yesterday he was wearing a pair of black, thick-rimmed glasses. It's all too much. And annoying.

Especially since he seems to love getting under my skin.

Every day I find a flyer tucked into one of my flowerpots for some kind of class or session to help "calm the restless soul." One has a coupon for three free yoga sessions, which I'd be tempted to use if I actually had time for yoga. The next day he leaves me a brochure warning me about the effects of too much sugar and caffeine. It's even accompanied with lavender oil.

But what really takes the cupcake are the contents of the cardboard box I find sitting in front of my door this morning. I'm hesitant to open it, assuming something is going to jump out at me. I'm relieved to find nothing living, or dead, inside the box. That relief is short-lived, though, because inside the box is my unicorn martini glass. Except it's been reassembled ass backward—quite literally. There are now plaid accents and a little logo with a guy in a suit of armor wearing one of those old-school nightcaps where its eyes used to be. Also, the horn is sticking out of its butt.

Half of me is annoyed and the other half is impressed that

he took the time to do this to needle me. Again. It's a hideous, yet quite amazing work of art. Not that I would ever admit that to his face.

On the upside, the constant banging seems to have stopped. The paper is still on the windows, so I'm assuming it's going to be a while before the place opens. Although a new sign was put up yesterday boasting the name THE KNIGHT CAP in masculine gold letters. I'm almost surprised there isn't some kind of plaid on the signage. I'm sure there will be loads of it making the interior extra gaudy.

But today I could care less about Lumberjerk, because it's my grand opening and it's going to be amazing. My Instagram following is already over one thousand, my Facebook page has double that. More than two hundred and fifty coupons have been downloaded.

I've been here since four in the morning frosting and decorating cupcakes. We have hundreds ready to roll, and Paul has a contingency plan should I be a little too hopeful about opening day. The display case is perfectly organized and prepared; the specials board is a work of art.

I make sure today's featured cupcakes and drinks are front and center in the showcase: a lemon drop cupcake with lemon curd filling and a tangy lemon buttercream complemented by a delicious, tart, lemon drop martini. Its counterpart is a bourbon bacon cupcake with maple buttercream icing paired with a smoky bourbon old-fashioned topped with a strip of maple candy bacon. Yes, I've already Instagrammed them.

The sandwich menu is simple, yet the variety is pleasing enough for every palate and the array of savory and sweet scones, plus coffee and tea options, make this the only cupcake cocktail café of its kind.

I step outside and set up my A-frame sign boasting today's specials and my quote of the day:

"WHEN LIFE GIVES YOU LEMONS MAKE LEMON DROP MARTINIS!"

I double and triple check that the bar is stocked, the coffee is ready to be poured, the hot water is prepped for tea and Callie is comfortable with her counter duties. She's my only employee—because one person is all I can reasonably afford to pay. I'm hoping we can handle whatever gets thrown at us. She looks adorable in her Buttercream and Booze shirt, and her shoes have a lemon wedge print on them, which is beyond perfect. Thankfully, Daphne's agreed to help out this morning and not to take photos. I'm so freaking lucky to have her as a friend.

I clap my hands excitedly, smooth my palms over my apron and adjust the hem of my dress. Today I'm wearing an off-white dress with a huge lemon slice pattern. I added a temporary lemon slice tattoo on my cheek, decorated with a tiny yellow jewel.

I give Callie a brief rundown of the specials. While I expect the majority of my business to cater to the lunch, afternoon, and cocktail hour crowd, it seems spiked coffees might very well be a hit this morning, considering the line of people waiting for the doors to officially open.

We're only a few blocks from the university, and there are several student-centric apartment buildings close by, as well as plenty of local businesses.

The first hour is mayhem of the most delicious sort. It doesn't matter that it's not even noon—almost everyone seems to want cupcakes and coffee or tea. The college crowd and the Saturday shoppers fill the café in the early afternoon, the two-for-one cupcake coupons are piling up, and I'm kept busy making martinis and bourbon old-fashioneds while Callie works the cash. Daphne sticks around since we're far busier than I anticipated, which is not a bad problem to have.

Around three in the afternoon the door tinkles and Lumberjerk weaves his way through the tables, making every single woman in the place—college students, mothers, grandmothers—and a good percentage of the men do a double take.

Daphne whistles low under her breath. "Holy crap I think my panties just lit themselves on fire."

I shoot her a look. "He's not that hot."

She gives me her *seriously* face but she doesn't have a chance to respond because he's already standing in front of us. I plaster on a smile. "I think you're in the wrong place. Axe throwing is next door."

"Blaire." Daphne elbows me in the side.

He smiles back, widely. As if he knows exactly the effect he's having on me and every damn woman in here. "I thought I'd stop by and grab one of those cupcakes everyone seems to be freaking out over." He pulls a two-for-one cupcake coupon out of his back pocket. Where it's been curved around his tight ass.

Not that I've noticed how tight it is over the past week. Okay. I've totally noticed. Every single time he's walked past the front window.

He passes me the coupon and I snatch it from him with more aggression than necessary, which makes that smile of his widen even more. Damn him and his perfect teeth and his sexy eye-crinkles. I motion to the display case of cupcakes, each tray labeled based on flavor with a description of the cake and frosting combination. "What tickles your fancy?" I cringe internally at my terrible choice of wording.

Ronan tips his head to the side and his tongue peeks out of the corner of his mouth. I want to shove it back in—with a mixing spoon.

He shrugs. "What you do recommend?"

"How about some Death by Chocolate?"

He chuckles. "I'm not really a fan of chocolate cake, or death."

"Not a fan? Obviously you've been eating the wrong cake." Daphne's voice is smoky and low, like she's thinking about eating one of those Death by Chocolate cupcakes off his naked chest, while riding him.

"Maybe." He shuffles over a few steps and leans in, peering

at the options. He taps on the front of the case, leaving behind a fingerprint. "Bourbon bacon cupcake with maple buttercream? That sounds good. I'll try one of those."

"Would you like it to go?" Yes, I'm trying to get him out of my shop as quickly as possible since his mere presence is a gray cloud hanging over what's supposed to be a sunshiny day.

His gaze lifts, wry smile firmly in place. "Nah, I'll sample the goods right here, but thanks."

I slip my hand into a pale pink non-latex glove and pluck one of the cupcakes from the display case, then wait for him to decide on his second one.

"The lemon drop cupcake is a featured special today if you'd like to give it a try."

"Hmm. Is it sour?" The *like you* is clearly intimated, though unspoken.

"It has some pucker power, if that's what you mean. It's a good balance of sweet and tart."

"So exactly like its creator, then?"

Daphne chokes on a cough and turns away so she can help the next customer while I finish up with Ronan. He hems and haws for another minute before he finally decides to go with the lemon drop cupcake.

"Would you like anything to drink with that?" I set the plate on top of the glass display counter.

"Nah, just the cupcakes, thanks." He passes over a five-dollar bill.

He braces a forearm on the glass case, despite the fact that there's a sweet little sign that reads DO NOT TOUCH THE GLASS. Peeling the pale yellow wrapper from the lemon cupcake, he jams half of it into his mouth in one bite, making a small noise of surprise—likely a result of the sweet-tart combination of flavors. Cake crumbs litter the glass top and there's now a small line of customers waiting.

Instead of moving aside, he continues to devour the cupcake in a less than polite manner, while leaning on the display case, making it impossible for anyone else to check out what's available. Not that any of the waiting customers are particularly upset about it, considering the way many of them are eyeing him, probably wishing they're that freaking cupcake he's mowing down on.

He eats the first one in three bites and licks the icing from his fingers before he starts in on the bourbon bacon and maple one. His brows pull down on the first bite, and a deep groan follows. He chews quickly, his Adam's apple bobbing as he swallows. "Holy fuck, that's awesome. It's like sweet, but not? Savory, but...decadent?" He jams the rest of it into his mouth, leaving more crumbs on the glass top counter and making a general mess.

He also groans his way through the mouthful. It's ridiculous. "Wow. That was amazing. They both were, but the bacon is the winner for me. Can I buy half a dozen of those?"

"Of course you can!" Callie appears out of nowhere. "I can help, Blaire, and you can take care of the new customers." She gives me a slightly manic, bright smile.

"That'd be great. Thanks."

Ronan glances at what has now become a significant line. "Oh shit. I'm kinda holding things up, aren't I?" He winks at the waiting customers, who all happen to be women. "Sorry, ladies."

There's a collective murmur of "it's okay" and "no problem" and I'm pretty sure someone says "marry me."

I let Callie take over his order since she's already loading up a box for him.

His little performance seems to have an impact on the rest of the customers standing in line, because every single one of them orders a bourbon bacon maple cupcake.

On his way out, he stops at a couple of tables to chat with some of the customers. I eye him suspiciously, but I don't have time to contemplate it much since he's created quite the backlog.

"You failed to mention Lumberjerk is also a super hottie," Daphne mutters as she bumps my hip so she can get to the cupcakes.

"That's because his personality ruins all the pretty," I reply. But that's not entirely true, because despite the jerkiness, I can still definitely appreciate how nice he is to look at, unfortunately.

"I don't know. Is he really that bad? He came in to support you, and now everyone is ordering cupcakes by the half-dozen, so it's not like he's bad for business."

I grunt instead of answering, because she might be right, but admitting it is against my current moral standards.

We run out of bourbon cupcakes so I have to run to the back to restock the display case while Callie and Daphne manage the front counter.

It's nearly four thirty before things calm down and I can finally take a breath. I move through the tables, checking on customers. I pause to clear some plates at a two-top with a pair of women in their mid-twenties and notice a couple of pieces of paper sitting beside an empty coffee cup. Upon closer inspection, I realize it's a coupon. For half-price wings and beer at The Knight Cap. And it's for today.

As if on cue, the low rumble of bass coming from next door makes the floor vibrate under my feet.

I plaster on what I hope is a pleasant smile and tap the coupon. "Do you mind if I ask where you got this?"

"That super hot guy who orgasm-moaned his way through his cupcake at the display case dropped it off at our table on the way out," she offers.

"I'm stuffed, but I would totally pretend to sip a beer so I could stare at him for a while." Her friend pats her belly.

They both laugh and I join in, although I sound like I'm choking on a squeaky toy, or like I've swallowed the Wicked Witch of the West. "Do you mind if I take one of these?"

"Go right ahead! I say you should treat yourself after you close up for the night and enjoy some eye candy." She pushes one of the coupons toward me.

"I might do that." I wink and slide the coupon into my apron pocket, then clear their empty plates and cups.

After I drop them in the bus bin, I sidle up to Daphne at the till and slap the coupon on the counter. "Looks like our neighbor wasn't being quite so supportive."

Daphne scans the coupon. "Where'd you get this?"

"He gave it to our customers on his way out. Invited them to his Grand Opening. So kind and thoughtful, huh?"

"But you said that place was a construction site last week. How could it be ready to open so soon?"

"Who the hell knows?" I glance at the tables and notice that there are several women holding the same damn coupon. *That slimy bastard.* "But I'm going over there to confront him. Hold down the fort." I grab the coupon, stalk around the counter and head for the door, my anger gaining steam as I step outside and notice the giant GRAND OPENING banner plastered to his storefront and the sign that looks almost exactly like mine, but reads DONE WITH TEA AND CAKES? NEED A BREAK FROM WONDERLAND? HALF-PRICE BEER IS HERE!

"Sonofdouchecanoe!" I mutter and stomp my way up the front steps. I yank on the door, expecting the same suction vacuum as last time. However, the problem must have been fixed last week because it opens surprisingly easily, almost sending me flying backward. Again, but for the opposite reason.

I recover before I end up sprawled out over the sidewalk and step inside the low-lit pub. It's the exact opposite of my bright, airy café. However, I can easily pick out at least six tables with familiar faces—because they were all recently patrons of mine before they defected here.

I loathe to admit that in the week since I stepped foot in this place, it's come together quite nicely. Despite the dim lighting, I can see the tables are pale pine, and the décor, although lacking in sophistication, is cozy and comfortable. And, as I predicted, there's a red-and-black plaid theme throughout.

Perfectly publike. It's a great place to sit back, drink beers, eat wings and hang out with other hipsters while getting your axe throw on. Which is exactly what's happening in the back half of the pub.

It's even manned by a huge, ominous-looking bouncer who doesn't let anyone through the door without first signing a waiver and passing a sobriety test.

I drag my attention away from the axe-throwing enclosure and search the bar for the backstabbing turd who owns the place. I find him behind the bar, a black towel thrown over his shoulder, matching his black-rimmed glasses.

I cross the hardwood floor, noting that it's been freshly varnished, and step up to the bar as Ronan places a pint in front of one of his customers with a wink. She also happens to have recently been a customer of mine.

He grins when he sees me and props his thick, gloriously tattooed forearms on the bar. *Gloriously tattooed*? What is wrong with me? "You taking a break from Wonderland to join the madness, Alice?"

"I'd like to talk to you."

"I'm a little busy." He motions to the already crowded pub.

"But you can pull up a stool and tell me all your woes over a pint." He winks.

I want to poke him in the eye.

I ignore his semi-flirtatious behavior, aware that these are probably the lines he uses on every single woman who bats her lashes at him, which I don't do. Instead, I slap the coupon on the bar. "Would you care to explain this?"

"It's a coupon for half price beer and wings. Not sure you're much of a wing eater since that would mean getting your fingers dirty." And there's that smile again. So condescending.

"I know it's a coupon and I know what it's for, thanks. I'm fully capable of reading. What I'd like to know is what the hell you think you're doing coming into *my* café under the guise of being supportive, when really, you were planning to steal my customers."

His smile drops. "I wasn't trying to steal them."

"Oh, really?" I wave the coupon in front of his face. My voice continues to rise over the thumping bass. "So you just happened to stop by and drop a handful of coupons at my patrons' tables inviting them to leave my place and go to *your* Grand Opening, which you also happened to schedule the same day as *mine*?"

He bites his bottom lip, glancing at the women sitting at the bar to his right, who all recently came from my café. "Can we talk over here?" He tips his head to the end of the bar.

I follow his lead and meet him at the other end. He uses his hip to open the swinging half door that separates the bar from the rest of the pub and motions me down a short hall. Old, framed photographs line the wall, a few of them slightly askew, as if someone has brushed them with their shoulder on the way past and tried to right them, but only ended up setting them even more out of line. For some reason it's endearing, annoyingly so. He ushers me into a small office, which was clearly left out of the renovations based on the ancient desk and the rolling chair that looks like it's from the seventies.

He leaves the door slightly ajar. In this confined space I'm noticing how big he is compared to me. At five-five I'm not exactly fun-sized, and my heels put me at a solid five-eight, but Ronan is well over six feet.

Not that I'll allow his size to intimidate me.

I toss the coupon on his desk—it's messy and there is a pile of them scattered all over it—and cross my arms. "Real dick move, hijacking my Grand Opening, Ronan. You said your place wouldn't be ready for at least a couple of weeks. It somehow miraculously came together in one?"

His brows pop. "It's not like we're appealing to the same client base. You serve fruity drinks and cupcakes, and I serve beer and bar food."

"That might've been a decent argument if you hadn't come by pretending to be all nice-nice, putting on a great show for my customers, having yourself a foodgasm in front of them, buttering them all up and stealing them right from under my nose with this." I stab at the coupon.

He half-rolls his eyes. "I didn't steal them."

"Like hell you didn't!" I throw my hands up in the air, agitated, and nearly hit him in the face since there isn't much room for flailing in here. "More than half the women lining your bar were in my café before you pillaged them."

"Okay, *pillaged* intimates something a lot more sinister than handing over a coupon and inviting them to stop by when they were *done* at your place."

"They might have stayed longer, had another drink, ordered some cupcakes to go if you hadn't stopped by and flashed your pretty smile and special offers at them." I flick his glasses, which is admittedly crossing the invisible *don't-touch* line, veering into assault territory, but I'm really fired up and we're less than a foot apart so it's almost impossible to not touch him. "Are these even real or are they a prop? What about your tattoos? I'd hardly be surprised if you ordered those fake sleeves online so you can look more hipster than you are." I don't know what it is about this guy, but he brings out a side of me that I didn't even know existed. Sure I can get worked up about things, but not usually to this degree.

"So I can...What?" He shakes his head and holds up his hands, maybe to prevent me from flicking him again. "I've been pulling twenty-hour days for the past week, and if I wear my contacts it feels like I have sand under them. The glasses are real, and so are the tattoos."

"So you're a legit thieving hipster. Good to know."

He purses his lips. "I'm not trying to steal your business."

"And I'm supposed to believe you after you drop by and flirt with all my customers and leave these coupons for them?"

"I wasn't flirting with them."

"Oh my God! Yes you most certainly were with the smiles and the banter and the damn winking."

"I don't wink."

"Oh yes you do."

"I do not."

I hold a hand up, unwilling to argue about this. "The winking isn't the point. The point is that you're a lying, conniving bastard and I'm on to you."

I reach for the doorknob at the same time he does, so his fingers skim the back of my hand. I jolt from the contact, because it honestly feels a little like I've been electrocuted. Not in an *I'm going to die* kind of way, but more of an unexpected stimulating way. I'm not sure which is worse, actually.

He raises both hands in the air and adopts a contrite expression. "My intention wasn't to steal your customers, Alice."

"It's Blaire, not Alice!" Of course he's still making fun of me. "As if I'm going to believe that after you leave fake poop in front of my back door and all the anger management, get Zen with yourself flyers! Not to mention what you did to my poor unicorn martini glass!"

He rolls his eyes. "Oh, come on, I was playing around and you have to admit the unicorn glass looks way cooler now."

"It's an abomination! And of course it's funny to you since you're the one doing the pranking!"

His expression sobers. "Look, it's too bad you took it the wrong way, but you came in here that first day guns blazing and I figured it might lighten you up. Obviously I was way wrong about that. As for the grand opening, I just thought it would be better for both of us if they happened on the same day, more like a two-for-one kind of deal, you know?"

"You mean you thought it would be better for *you* since I'd already done the work to bring people to the area. If you really thought it would be better for both of us you should've approached me, but you didn't."

He crosses his arms. "Well maybe I would have if you'd been more approachable."

I prop a fist on my hip. "And you think playing pranks on me would accomplish that."

"Okay. So I should've told you my plan—"

I cut him off, triumphant that he's finally admitted he's wrong. "Of course you'll admit it was a mistake now, when the damage is already done."

His eyes go wide, as if he's trying to look innocent. "I can see how this might look to you, but I really wasn't trying to steal your customers. Besides, it's not like people can survive on cupcakes and alcohol indefinitely—"

He did not just say that. "Do not try and justify your actions to me." I point a finger at his face. "I see right through you. Just remember, Ronan, you threw the first axe."

"What? I didn't throw anything."

"It's an expression." I roll my eyes. "I'm being cheeky. You threw the first stone, took the first shot. It's on." And with that I yank open the door. "You may have started the war, but I'll be the one taking you down, one sweet treat at a time." I wink and sashay through the bar, slipping my hand into my apron. I pull out a handful of my own coupons and toss them on tables, inviting customers to stop by before they head home so they can bring their loved ones something delightful to sink their teeth into.

@buttercreamandbooze:

I BAKE the world a better place.

♡ ✉ ✎   ☆

chapter four

I'M NUMBER ONE

Blaire

Things heat up with my neighbor post–grand opening. A little not-quite-friendly competition, so to speak. Things like, when Ronan has a special, I try to make mine better. On Friday night I hand out two-for-one cocktail coupons to combat his half-price draft beer and house wine. Everyone knows that house wine is the cheap crappy stuff.

So what if the two-for-one martinis aren't made with the premium vodka? They're also full of things like crème de cacao and other sweet, minty, chocolaty, or fruity booze and juice, so it hides the taste and does the trick.

Twentysomething-year-old guys might not mind cheap draft beer, but most women in their late twenties would much rather sip a pretty martini over a cheap glass of wine any day of the week. How do I know this? I polled my followers, of course.

And don't think Ronan is an innocent. His prankster ways

continue—this week I stepped in what I believed was poop—again—but it just happened to be poop-shaped Play-Doh. It also contained sparkles, which I got on my hands and which subsequently were all over everything I own for the next three days.

In addition to the fake sparkle poop, Ronan has taken to dropping off a daily coupon for me, except they're modified to whatever it is he's been serving to customers that day. He always includes some kind of tongue-in-cheek comment about what he regards as my less-than-friendly personality. I am friendly. Just not with him. Today's coupon was for half-priced salt-and-vinegar fish and chips and some honey lager—which I hate to admit sounds kind of yummy. He scrawled a note on the back about drawing more flies with honey than vinegar.

Two weeks in, and things are going well on the business end. Better than well, actually. We're busy throughout the day, we have orders for pickup and takeout all the time, the cupcakes are flying off the shelves and people love our daily cupcake cocktail themes. My social media feeds are full of tags and picture perfect photos of B&B, of groups of friends gathered together in the café, and of delighted smiles and rave reviews.

Even so, I'm barely eking by right now. On the upside, I'm close to being able to cover my expenses without digging too deeply into my line of credit. Am I eating a lot of leftover cupcakes and close-to-the-expiration-date sandwiches that would otherwise be destined for the garbage? Most definitely. But I knew finances were going to be tough at the beginning.

It can take up to three years for a business to grow its legs and with the way things are looking, there is a chance I'll be able to turn a profit within the next few years. Notwithstanding an annoying neighbor who is taking some of my business.

"This is amazing. You must be on top of the world right now!" Daphne sips her salted caramel martini while scrolling through the Instagram feed.

The last customer left about twenty minutes ago, probably heading next door for whatever Lumberjerk has planned for tonight. I closed up shop and made us a drink and now we're relaxing at the back of the café, stretched out on the comfy couches and chairs.

Daphne snaps a photo of me lounging on the couch and Paul returns from the bathroom in time to peek over her shoulder. "Definitely post that."

"Right? It'll get tons of likes," Daphne agrees.

Paul comes by first thing in the mornings to drop off the cupcakes for the day, giving me plenty of time to decorate them before opening. But tomorrow he has an out of town event, so he dropped everything off this evening and I convinced him to stay for a drink. There's no way I could've made this work without his help and I'm eternally grateful for his friendship over the past several years.

I wait for Daphne to pass her camera over. "Can I at least see it before you post it? What if I look like a shrew?"

"As if I would post a bad picture of you." Daphne is appropriately offended; she and I have spent a ridiculous amount of time perfecting posed photos over the past several weeks.

I hold my hands up in supplication. "I know. It's a conditioned response. I got a message earlier in the week from my sister telling me she thinks my right side is more flattering."

Daphne's lip curls in disdain. "I hope you told her to suck it."

"It's her way of trying to be helpful."

"It's her way of being a bitch," Daphne argues.

I shrug. Maddy is pretty much always a bitch. I've spent my entire life dealing with her, so her random comments are nothing in comparison to some of her other antics.

"Anyway, the only time I've seen you possess shrewlike qualities was when you and Raphael broke up," Daphne continues.

I glare at her. "We do not talk about Raphael."

"Raphael? How come I've never heard of this guy?" Paul asks.

"You have. He's more commonly known as The Douche."

"Oh. You mean the guy who was boning you and three other chefs at the same time?" Paul drops into the chair beside mine.

"The one and only. And can we not discuss him, please? It was years ago, before you came along and made me realize there's more to life than kobe beef and truffle fries. Unlike you, he was more interested in showing me his bratwurst than he was in teaching me anything of value." I pat Paul on the arm. One of the things I appreciate most about Paul is the fact that our relationship has always been strictly professional and platonic. Which was what I needed after the nightmare that was Raphael.

"Back when you were still trying to please Mummy and Daddy." He takes a swig of his Manhattan.

"Those days are long gone." I take another, deeper sip of my martini. It's more like a gulp. I love my family, but they are ridiculously highbrow in their approach to the food industry. They're also crazy.

I have no desire to serve people who think it's reasonable to spend two thousand dollars on a burger. I don't care if God himself blessed the freaking cow and then dusted it in edible gold.

"Have they seen this place yet?" Paul asks.

"Uh no, they haven't." And if I can prevent it, I'm hoping they won't ever manage to make the trip out here to my "little cupcake shop." They chose their side the day it became clear they were more concerned with the success of their business and keeping star chef Raphael happy than with my own broken heart. At least I'd gotten my trip to France out of the deal.

While I've been lost in my head, thinking about my family, Daphne and Paul have been chatting. Paul reaches over and pinches my arm, almost causing me to spill my martini on my dress. "Ow! What the hell?"

"Did you hear anything Daphne just said?" He gives me a look.

"Sorry, I was thinking. What'd I miss?"

"You know Tori Taylor the famous YouTuber?" Daphne asks.

"Sure. What about her?" I know the very vaguest basics about Tori. She has an insane number of subscribers and has made a career out of "Best of" videos. Last year alone she put at least ten small businesses on the map. The second she promotes something, thousands of people are right there, buying whatever it is, or going to whatever location she deems popular. She has incredible influence.

"Check this out." Daphne hands me her phone so I can watch the video she has cued up. Tori appears on the screen, makeup on point, looking stunning as usual, name dropping the brands she's currently wearing, citing the discount code you can use to get the same look/purse/shirt/shoes before she pans out to show her viewers the cool interior of her favorite local bar in LA.

"I've been coming here since I was legal to drink." She winks. "Every time I come home this is the place I go to meet up with friends. It has the perfect ambiance. It's quirky, cool and has the most amazing drinks." She goes on to talk about the special cocktail she's currently drinking, and her love of jalapeño-infused margaritas. "So it got me thinking, I have this road trip coming up and I need to know where the best bars are in the Pacific Northwest. What are the funkiest places, the ones with the best drink menus, the coolest vibe, the best food between San Francisco and Seattle? I want the bars that have it all. Drop your nominations in the comments and make sure you link their social media so I can check them out! And don't forget to use the hashtag 'toritaylorbestbars!' Maybe your favorite bar will be a stop on my road trip! And best of all, the winner will not only be featured on my channel, but I've made a deal with the Food and Drink network to showcase the best bar! Check my site for more details!" She makes a heart with her hands, kissy lips the screen, winks and signs off.

"You have to enter this!" Daphne declares. "We need to get everyone we know to nominate Buttercream and Booze for best bar! Can you even imagine how amazing it would be for business if you were featured on Tori's channel, let alone on Food and Drink?"

"It could make your career." Paul starts scrolling through the comments. "This video has been up for an hour and there are thousands of nominations. What's the name of the pub next door?"

"The Knight Cap," Daphne and I say at the same time.

"It's already in here a bunch of times." Paul shows me his phone.

"Of course it is." I roll my eyes. "I'm sure Lumberjerk held everyone at axe point until they gave him a raving review."

Daphne slides her chair closer, pulls up The Knight Cap's social media and starts comparing our social media posts, because that's her specialty. I'm getting better at staging photos, but since Daphne is still building her portfolio, she's happy to give me advice when I need it.

"You have twice as many followers as The Knight Cap. And your posts are way prettier. Although, I have to admit, the Lumberjerk isn't hard to look at."

Paul makes a face. "Man, this guy wears a lot of plaid."

I throw my hands up in the air. "Yes! Exactly! Every freaking day it's plaid, plaid, and more plaid!"

"Well that's the uniform over there, isn't it?" Daphne says.

"Don't defend the plaid."

Daphne shrugs. "It kinda works for him, though."

"You're supposed to be on my side!"

"I am on your side, but I'm also allowed to appreciate a hottie, and this guy is smokin', with or without the plaid. I will say, though, it's clear that he doesn't have a professional helping him with this. All of these pictures are candid and based on the number of selfies from the bartender I'm going to hazard a guess that he's the one posting most of this stuff." Daphne shows me an image of a younger guy, smirking at the camera while Ronan pours a pint in the background.

"Let's hope they don't hire anyone then, because I'd like to keep the social media leg up on him. And hot or not, we need to do better than the whole axe-throwing thing he's got going on over there."

"Mmm, it's a double draw, isn't it? Hot guys and axe throwing in a college town is high on the yes-please scale."

As if they can hear us talking through the wall—which they can't, the plywood is thick and the music is loud enough that the low thump of bass makes the floor vibrate—a thud, followed by shouts of approval and some muffled chanting, makes all of us jump. "Someone hit the target." And based on the chanting, it was the resident Lumberjerk.

Daphne taps her lip with a manicured nail. "You know what we need to do?"

"Steal all of the axes and break off the handles?" Paul suggests.

"Axes can be replaced and theft isn't a good way to get ahead. We need to fight axes with cupcakes." Daphne makes a face and waves that comment away. "What I mean is that we should roll the cupcake-drink theme into events."

"You want to have a salted caramel event?" I ask.

"No. Well, yes. Kind of. Like we come up with different theme nights to draw in new customers the same way we have theme cupcakes and drinks every day. We need something buzz-worthy that's going to help us get more nominations."

"Okay. So what can we do that's better than axe throwing? And I don't want to do something that's super dangerous." The last thing I want is someone chopping off a vital body part. I can barely handle a paper cut without getting woozy.

"We could hold a cupcake-decorating contest. Winner gets a fifty-dollar gift card? That way the money goes back into Buttercream and Booze."

"Ooooh! I like this. That could be super fun."

"Exactly!" Daphne agrees. "I don't know that we need to try to compete with The Knight Cap. Your clientele is during the day and into the evening, where Lumberjerk caters to the evening and late night crowd. So I think we need to focus on what attracts people here and what we can do to keep them entertained for as long as possible."

"Okay, so we need to poll our customers and find out what other kinds of events they'd be interested in. Karaoke is always a winner, and trivia nights are super fun. I always loved a good poetry slam night back when I was in college."

Paul scoffs.

I cross my arms. "What? Poetry slams are fun."

Paul cocks a brow. "I'm sure for you they are."

"What is that supposed to mean?"

"You look like a cross between a librarian and a fifties pinup girl. The fact that poetry slams excite you isn't even a remote surprise."

"Whatever. You just wait, my poetry slam nights are going to make axe throwing seem like a trip on a snooze cruise."

"Gettin' your rhyme on already?" Daphne smirks.

"It must be the booze."

They chuckle and groan.

"But seriously, when it comes to poetry slams, I never lose."

@buttercreamandbooze:

YOU'RE A GREAT SINGER. ~love, Wine

chapter five

POKE THE AGITATED ALICE

Ronan

"The books look good so far." My grandfather pushes his glasses up his nose, bushy white eyebrows furrowed, shoulders hunched as he leans in close and leafs through the printed reports. Being in his eighties means everything gets lost in translation when he's looking at a computer screen with the exact same numbers, so I print things out for him, even though it makes forests cry.

He rolls his shoulders back, sitting up straighter as he looks around the bar. His eyes crinkle in the corners, the lines in his face deepening with his wistful smile. "The renovations look good, too."

I lean on the bar, pride choking me up, so my reply comes out a little gruff. "Thanks Gramps." It was hard for him when I started changing things, so he hadn't come in much for a while, but he's back to popping in almost every other day.

He pats my arm with his big, knobby fingers. Gramps and

I are about the same height, although he's lost a couple of inches with age. His white shock of hair is slicked back and styled neatly, and as usual he's wearing a white button-down and a pair of black dress pants. "Back in my day the only guys who decorated their skin were the ones who were in the Navy or spent some time behind bars." He tells me this pretty much every single time he sees me, which is often, especially now that I'm helping run his bar. Mostly it's a joke. Although the first time he saw my sleeves he asked me why I couldn't hang my art on my walls like regular people.

"I can make you an appointment, get you set up with your own art if you're jealous of mine. We could get matching ones."

Gramps snorts a laugh. "I don't even like it when a pretty nurse takes my blood. Not gonna have some guy coming at me with a bunch o' buzzing needles."

I rap on the bar and point a finger at him. "Just remember that when you tell a nurse she's pretty nowadays it's called sexual harassment."

"It's really a woman's world, isn't it? Can't say we didn't have it comin' or that Dottie didn't tell me it would happen. God rest her soul." He makes the sign of the cross, and I do the same.

Grams passed away a little over a year ago, and for a while there I was worried Gramps was going to follow in her footsteps. They'd been together for more than sixty years and had been working side by side every single day since they met. In all the time they'd been married, they'd never spent a night apart. Sure, Gramps would go out with his friends and play poker, and Grams would have "knitting" nights with her friends—which were really gin martini socials with a few balls of wool and sets of knitting needles lying around for decoration—but there wasn't a single night in over sixty years that they didn't sleep beside each other.

I'm not sure if I'd consider that romantic, clingy, or an extreme case of codependency. Regardless, they loved and bickered fiercely. So when Gramps woke one morning to find that she'd passed in her sleep, I wasn't so sure he was going to be able to manage the world without her. And more selfishly, I worried about how I would handle it if Gramps couldn't deal with the loss.

My dad—his oldest son—and my mom were killed in a car accident when I was twenty. I was old enough to survive on my own, but it still shook the foundation of my life. I'd always been close to my grandparents, so they stepped into the role of surrogate parents. Which is how I ended up back here, running the show instead of just bussing tables and tending bar—although I still do those things, too.

I'd been working my way up the ladder in finance, because that's where the money is, but it isn't my passion. Not even close. It was a nine-to-five grind that lined my pockets but gave me zero in the way of job satisfaction.

For the past several years I've wanted to open my own brewery, but to do that I need cash. So I went to Gramps for a loan, hoping to circumvent the bank's high interest rates.

Having immigrated from Scotland to America as a kid and growing up in a middle-class family that sometimes struggled to make ends meet when they first came to America, he's a big fan of working for what you get. Which means he didn't just hand over the money. Not a big surprise.

However, he offered me an opportunity. The Knight Cap has been in our family for three generations, and he can no longer handle the responsibility of managing the place on his own. Plus, it was in serious need of an overhaul. He would fund the renovations and if I could breathe some life back into the pub, he would loan me the start-up money for the brewery—no interest. It would give me the experience I needed running a business and hopefully keep his pride and joy from going belly up.

So far, I'm keeping up my end of the bargain.

"I have to admit, I wasn't real keen on the axe-throwing business, but it looks like once the renovations are paid off, you'll be turning a real profit there, as long as no one hacks off an arm, anyway." He winks. "It's a real good start, son."

"Thanks. And there are some pretty strict rules around the axe throwing, so everyone's limbs should stay safely attached to their bodies."

"That's generally where ya want them, eh?" He drums his fingers on the bar top, his grin wry. "And I appreciate that ya kept the wall o' photographs. Means a lot to this old man."

"Well, I might not have been there for all of them, but they mean a lot to me, too." I know it's been hard for Gramps to have to step down from running the bar. It's been his second home for most of his life, and all the memories in it contain Grams.

My phone lights up with new social media alerts. We both glance at the screen.

"What's that all about? You get yourself a new girlfriend? You started dating one of the ladies you hired?" His expression brightens and I laugh.

"Once again, asking my employees out is on the list of no-no's these days. Too many potential complications."

Gramps throws his hands in the air. "Dottie and I would n'er 'ave gotten married if we'd worried about complications, now would we?"

"This is true. However, my employees are college students."

"Ah well, you're bound to meet a lass eventually, especially working 'ere."

I decide to veer the topic away from my dating life, since it's not very exciting these days. Besides, if I let him keep going he'll eventually get on me about settling down before I'm too old.

It's not that I don't want a partner, but from what I've seen, you can't be married to your job and married to another person unless you're like my Gramps and Grams who worked together. Otherwise, the career or the partner ends up neglected.

And right now, my career is paramount. I have an obligation to Gramps, and the brewery is actually within my grasp.

Besides, I haven't been able to meet anyone since I'm always at The Knight Cap.

At least this is the justification I give anyone who asks about my relationship status. Honestly, losing my parents at twenty was rough, and that was a kind of pain I wanted to avoid. It didn't help that I'd had a girlfriend when they passed away, and that relationship hit some major turbulence, eventually crashing and burning because I couldn't handle the loss and she didn't know how to help me grieve. It wasn't her fault, we were college kids, but it sure did have an impact.

Relationships make a person vulnerable to pain, and losing my parents and the end of that relationship was more anguish than I could deal with. Watching Gramps degrade quickly after Grams passed was another reason to avoid getting serious with anyone.

"For now I'll focus on the pub, which reminds me, I haven't told you about the golden opportunity that might put us on the map and make it rain."

His mouth turns down. "Is this some young person slang I don't understand?"

"Uh yeah. 'Make it rain' means make lots of money. There's this huge YouTuber—"

"YouTuber?" More frowning ensues.

"Yeah, it's a woman who makes videos—"

"Videos?" Gramps's eyes go wide, and he gives me a disapproving look. "Not the dirty kind. Ya won't be using my Dottie's bar to be makin' those naughty films."

I choke back a mouthful of coffee and cough into my elbow. "No, Gramps. Just videos, not of sex. Why in the world would you think I'd do something like that?"

His eyes shift away and he shrugs, then takes a big gulp of his beer. "I was looking something up on the computer this morning and you know how it likes to fill in words for you sometimes. Well, it took me to a site with all kinds of things no one should be looking at at nine in the morning. Felt like I needed to go to confession after that."

"Not the best way to start the day, huh?"

He shakes his head. "Those images get stuck in the brain, they do. Anyway, you were saying something about this YouTuber?"

"Right, yes." I smack the bar, happy to move the subject away from my grandfather accidentally stumbling on a porn site. "She has a channel."

"Like a TV channel?"

"Yeah, kinda. I mean, they even have commercials that you have to watch—"

"Can't you DVR and fast-forward through the junk?"

I introduced Gramps to DVR back when I lived with him and Grams after my parents passed and it's probably his favorite thing in the world. Apart from this bar and the memory of Grams. "Not on YouTube. Anyway, this woman, Tori Taylor—"

"Sounds like one of those dirty film stars."

"I promise she's not a dirty film star. Anyway, she has a channel with over ten million subscribers."

"Geez, that's a lot of people. She do neat tricks or something? Is she a dancer?"

"No, Gramps. She's not a dancer. Just let me finish." I wait to see if he's going to interrupt again, but he stays silent, for now. "Anyway, she runs a 'Best of' feature on her channel. Best products, best places to visit, that kind of thing. She's running a Best Bar in the Pacific Northwest competition and The Knight Cap is entered." I pull up the video on my phone and play it for Gramps, then show him The Knight Cap nominations before I shift to Instagram where he can check out all the other bars that have been nominated, too.

He pauses my scroll a few pictures down. "Isn't that the place next door? Buttercream and Booze?"

"Yup. Sure is." Of course she's been nominated, likely by every single human being she knows. And despite her super prickly attitude, apparently she has a lot of friends because she's clogging up the feed with all the damn nominations.

Gramps takes my phone and starts scrolling. Then he hits her profile link and keeps on flipping through pictures. He lets out a low whistle and holds the phone out two inches from my face. "Have you met her?"

"Sure have."

"She's quite the looker," Gramps mutters.

"I guess, if you like the whole June Cleaver get-up."

Gramps cocks a brow. "Does nae matter what she's wearing. Could be a burlap sack and she'd still have the face of an angel."

Gramps isn't wrong. She's stunning in a very classic,

wholesome way. I have to admit, as unconventional as her clothing choices may be, they also make her alluring. She's a mass of contradictions. Her entire look screams sweet and retro, but she's a real take-no-prisoners spitfire. And I have to admit I kind of like how easy it is to get under her skin. It's addicting, really.

The flyers were meant to be a joke and so was the fake poop. I'd watched her step in it the day before and thought the best way to clear the air would be to make light of it. Apparently Alice and I have very different ideas as to what is funny and what isn't. She didn't seem to appreciate the fake turd. Or the anger management flyer, or the lavender oil—who doesn't love the smell of that? And I didn't so much as get a thank you or a chuckle over the reconfigured unicorn martini glass. Which I put a lot of time and effort into for my own personal satisfaction.

I thought she'd laugh and soften up, but that isn't at all what's happened. Then again, what would I expect of someone who'd rather mix drinks with fourteen freaking ingredients instead of pouring a nice hoppy beer instead.

"Does she own the place next door, or just work there?" Gramps asks.

"I think it's hers? She runs it, that much I know."

"Well, it's been empty a long time. Every single business that crops up there ends up going under within the year. Here's hoping she's got better luck than the rest. I'm guessing she got a deal on the rent with all the bad juju coming outta that place."

I'm not a big believer in things like "bad juju" or luck. Places fail or succeed for a lot of reasons, not because the businesses that occupied the same location prior tanked. Regardless, the fact that she probably got a deal on rent tells me something about grumpy Alice in Wonderland. She's clearly a fighter and savvy. I've got my work cut out for me if I'm going to beat her as The Best Bar in the Pacific Northwest.

Was it the smartest way to handle things by piggybacking on her Grand Opening? Probably not, and I hadn't intentionally copied her, but it definitely ended up working in my favor. Good thing I like friendly competition.

"Live bands, they're always popular." Lars, my fulltime bartender, polishes a glass while checking out his reflection in the mirror. "I'd be happy to be the first live performance if you can get Lana to bartend."

He's good at his job, and the women love him, which is why I deal with his inflated ego. He's also my twenty-three-year-old cousin who's still waiting for his big break to rock stardom, hence the bartending gig. "So you can serenade her with songs you've written professing your undying love?"

"Women eat that shit up."

"Too bad you can't date her since you work with her." It's more of a reminder than anything.

"Why are you always such a buzzkill? This is a bar, not some office."

"Why are you always such a fuckboy?"

He smirks. "I'm surprised you even know what that means, old man."

"I'm thirty, not collecting my pension."

"Whatever. I'm in my sexual prime and I plan to capitalize on that for as long as my dick will allow."

"Just not with any of the women who work here and preferably not the patrons, either."

He rolls his eyes. "What's the point of being a bartender if I can't use it to get laid?"

It's my turn to give him a look. "Okay, first of all, think about what you're saying, Lars. Do you really want to entice drunk, not fully coherent women into your bed? Consider the potential ramifications of that. Carefully."

His entire face scrunches up. "When you put it that way..."

"Consent is best sought when sober." I'm aware that I am, in fact, being a huge buzzkill—but for good reason. Serving alcohol is a big responsibility, especially in an establishment that has been in my family for years. I'm all for having fun... within reason. And twenty-one-year-olds aren't known for high-level thinking skills when they're under the influence.

If Lars and Lana end up dating, there's really not much I can do about it, but by telling them a no-dating-coworkers-and-customers policy exists, I figure I'm at least putting the fear of unemployment into them. Although, I will say that as much of a player as Lars presents himself to be, he doesn't like to disappoint people. So I'm banking on that to keep him in line.

I rap on the bar top. "Anyway, back to live bands. Won't we need sound equipment for that?"

"Yeah, but I have two sets at home, so I can bring one to keep here if you want. Most bands have their own equipment, but they're not all created equal." He smirks. "Plus, we can host a karaoke night. Everyone thinks they're a singer when they're drunk."

"Hell yes, they do," I agree. And I can just imagine Alice in Wonderland throwing an epic fit over it.

"Look at how excited you are." Lars mirrors what I'm assuming is my wide smile. "You win this thing and you definitely better credit me with some of the ideas, man."

"It's a long shot. Literally hundreds of bars have been nominated."

"Yeah, but this one has history and a great story. I vote we start posting about our grandparents. Tori Taylor ships pretty much every famous couple out there."

I frown, feeling like I'm missing something. "Ships what?"

"She's always posting about couple goals. Anyways, it's something else we can post about if we need to, you know, to pull in the lady crowd."

"Right, yeah." I don't want to have to worry about things like couple goals and romance. I just want laid-back and easygoing. A nice chilled-out environment where people come and drink pints and enjoy conversation or sports or whatever, as opposed to my uptight neighbor and her perfect prissy cupcakes and fruity drinks. "I'll get some graphics made so we can start promoting the live band. You think this Saturday will work for you?"

"Yeah man, I can get the guys together for Saturday."

"And you'll be ready to perform?"

The bell over the door chimes, and a group of women who look to be in their early twenties walk in.

"I was born ready." Lars winks and turns to the group of women. "Evening, ladies. Looking thirsty."

I shake my head and leave him to his flirting. It's after seven and I have yet to make a stop next door for my daily dose of sweet and sour. My neighbor might be an annoying pain in the ass, but those cupcakes are addictive. I'm starting to wonder if they're laced with something.

I stop by every night before closing—she shuts down around nine, but stays open later on Friday and Saturday. It has to make for insanely long days for her. But her hours aren't my problem. Besides, I pull long days, too.

I nab a coupon from behind the bar. "I'll be back in a few," I call out as I pass Lars chatting up the group of women who now span the four barstools directly in front of the draft taps.

He tips his chin up at me and goes back to checking IDs as I push through the door and step outside in the waning evening sunshine. It's still warm and balmy for early September. I miss the nights where I used to have time to sit outside on my balcony and enjoy watching the sun set. Now I'm always here, at the bar, watching the light fade through the windows.

I'll get that back someday, though. For now, I remind myself that there's a bigger plan and a few missed sunsets aren't the end of the world if I'm able to pursue my dream.

When I was young—in my teens, and long before I was of legal drinking age—my dad used to dabble in home brewing. I learned from a very early age to appreciate the science behind creating superior craft beers. It had always been a hobby for my dad and somewhere along the way it became a passion for me. Now, aside from my grandfather, it's the final connection I have with my dad, the one thing I don't want to give up, especially as the memories of him continue to fade.

For a while money mattered more than dreams, but when Grams passed, it shifted my perspective. I needed the memories to stay fresh and I needed time with Gramps, so here I am.

I glance up at the sign I had custom made, expensive but worth it. Your storefront is your main source of advertising for passersby, and the more alluring it is the more likely people are to come in. I snicker as I pass Alice in Wonderland's sidewalk sign. Today it reads: DON'T BE BITTER. TREAT YOURSELF TO SOMETHING SWEET!

I open the door and survey the shop. Despite it being a Tuesday, the café is busy, almost every table occupied by latte- and martini-drinking women. In the corners, young couples huddle, their textbooks lying open but ignored as their owners pick at cupcakes, their feet intertwined under the tables while they flirt.

Alice-Blaire is behind the counter, hands propped on her hips, bottom lip caught between her teeth. Her dress is pale pink with a huge rainbow swirl lollipop print. The skirt flares wide; obviously there's some kind of material underneath to make it so... poofy. It accentuates her lush, curvy figure. Her hair is pulled into some kind of intricate up-do, making her look like she's stepped straight off the set of a fifties-era sitcom. She sure is an interesting woman.

Her head turns and her welcoming smile turns saccharine. "Well, if it isn't my favorite neighbor." She bats her lashes. "I've been expecting you."

My own grin widens with genuine happiness. For reasons I don't quite understand, part of me really enjoys the daily dose of snark I get from Blaire.

"Miss me, then?" I lean on the glass display case. Yes, I'm very aware it says I shouldn't. I'm also aware that the second I leave she'll be out with some environmentally friendly, lemony-smelling glass cleaner, wiping away the mark my forearm leaves behind.

She makes a guttural sound, rolls her eyes, and mutters something under her breath. I don't quite catch all of it, but I swear it sounds sexual.

I probably need to get laid.

"What was that?"

"Nothing." She keeps that smile plastered on her face, but

her cheeks have flushed pink. "What can I get for you today, Ronan?"

"Dunno, what'd you recommend?"

"I'd recommend Death by Chocolate again, but we're fresh out and you always seem opposed." She taps her pink-glossed lips and *hmm*s. They're full. A little pouty. Probably perfect for kissing.

Yup, definitely need to get laid.

"Oh! Actually, I have something special for you today."

"Special?"

"Mmm." She arches a brow and spins around, her skirt flaring impressively. There's a bow knotted at the center of her back. Even her apron is tied perfectly, which seems impossible since she can't see the back of it. Unless she has someone do it for her.

She's in the middle of retrieving something—not from the cupcake case—when a lanky guy wearing a polo that reads CUPCAKES TO GO! over his left pec appears from the back of the café.

"All set for tomorrow morning. You need anything else before I take off?" He runs a hand through his thinning hair.

She abandons the box, which I'm assuming is for me, and takes a few steps in his direction. "Thanks so much for taking care of all of this tonight instead of tomorrow morning, Paul. I know it's going to be a busy day for you."

"Well, I wasn't going to leave you hanging." His shoulders roll back and his smile oozes pride and satisfaction.

"You're a godsend." She puts a manicured hand on his forearm. "I would've been here all night if I'd tried to pull that off on my own."

That smile of his widens further and he tips his chin down as she tips hers up. "Can't have you turning into a zombie on me."

"I appreciate your concern for my well-being and my non-zombie status." She gives his arm a squeeze and steps back. "Now you should go because it's getting late, and I don't want *you* to be the zombie on account of being here so late."

She turns away from Paul and his gaze follows her. She crosses over to the sink, turns on the tap, and lathers up her hands. She hums a tune under her breath as she rubs her palms together. She also does a hip shake.

He glances at me as he takes a step back and his expression shifts to hostility. Huh. That's interesting.

He knocks into the bussing cart, which gets Blaire's attention.

"Oh! Thank you so much for taking that to the back, Paul. Callie has been running off her feet all day and we'll both definitely appreciate the help."

"Oh, right, yeah, of course. Have a good night, Blaire."

"You, too."

He backs down the hall, throwing me one final glare before he disappears. I wonder if she's mentioned me to him, and if so, I'm guessing whatever she said wasn't all that pleasant. Blaire sashays across the small space, holding a plate with a single cupcake. She sets it down on the counter and pushes it toward me. "Here you go. I made this one special for you." She winks.

I glance down at the cake. There's a tiny cookie-shaped decoration on top with the phrase EAT ME in block capital letters.

I lift my gaze to hers. "You made this for me?"

She blinks once—that same, almost unnervingly placid smile plastered on her gorgeous face. Wait. *Gorgeous*? Since when do I find her and her odd fashion sense attractive?

"I did," she replies.

I glance back down at the cake, assessing the details more carefully. The tiny cookie looks like it's made out of candy and the letters have been painted on with an incredibly steady hand. I touch the edge, gently and with care. "What about this? Did you make this?"

"Yup. It's not laced with arsenic or anything. You can eat it without worrying about your health."

"I wasn't until you said that."

"I wouldn't risk the welfare of my entire business over you." She's still smiling, but there's a sharp edge to her tone, like a razorblade slice.

I laugh a little. "You're killing me with your kindness, Blaire."

"Are you gonna eat it or what?" She leans against the edge of the counter.

Obviously I've reached the limit to her patience, which is exactly what I've been waiting for. I love it when she gets sour with me. Like one of her lemon curd-filled cupcakes.

"You gonna jam it in my mouth for me if I don't?"

"Maybe." Her lips twitch.

"Don't you want me to savor the experience?" I pluck the tiny candy cookie from the top. "It doesn't say devour me, it says EAT ME. Slow or fast is always the question. Slow is usually better, though, don't you think?" What in the actual fuck am I doing? Am I using sexual innuendos?

The design on the cupcake is clearly an *Alice in Wonderland* reference, not an actual invitation to eat her. And why am I suddenly thinking about what that would be like? Is she quiet or loud? I bet she's demanding. Probably bossy. And there's nothing sexier than a woman who tells you exactly what she wants.

I pop the tiny candy into my mouth, to make sure none of the thoughts floating around in my head ends up coming out of my mouth, and also to get this over with. Because I need to get out of here instead of continuing this conversation. She's my competition in the Best Bar challenge, not a prospective date.

Fast is how it's going to be, apparently.

Except that tiny little candy dissolves on my tongue, fizzing unexpectedly. And the flavor is familiar.

Blaire smirks and clasps her hands behind her, rocking back on her heels.

I peel the wrapper from the cake and drop it on the plate. I bring it to my nose and sniff it. "Is that . . . coffee?"

"Just take a bite," she snaps.

Her tone, however, doesn't match her expression, which I realize she's trying to keep neutral, but is failing at quite painfully. Her gaze is trained on my face—eager, expectant. She bounces a couple of times and I glance at the reflection in the mirrored bar behind her, lined with bottles of top-shelf spirits and liqueurs. She's wringing her clasped hands behind her back, but trying to keep them hidden.

I take a bite, not as big as I originally intended, because that's probably what she expects and I want to prolong the agony of her anticipation as much as I humanly can. I intend to tell her it's just okay, but the moment the flavors hit my tongue I groan. Loudly. "Oh my God," I mumble, crumbs tumble out of my mouth and sprinkle all over the counter. Which I realize is disgusting.

But Blaire doesn't seem to care. She grins widely, satisfaction and triumph making her face even more stunning. I consider asking what this is, but decide I don't care enough to stop eating it. There's coffee in the icing, but it's not overly sweet, it's light and buttery and decadently creamy. The cake practically melts in my mouth, hints of... whiskey, cocoa, and vanilla and with the next bite I get a hit of creamy custard with a gentle hint of... almond.

Blaire doesn't seem to notice the mess I'm making. At all. She's sucking on her bottom lip and bouncing on the balls of her feet. Her lip pops free, teeth marks still evident. "Enjoying yourself." It's not a question, more of an accusation.

I want to shove the rest of it in my face instead of answering, but I lift my hand to cover my mouth so I can ask a question instead of affirm what she clearly already knows. "What is it?"

A slow smirk spreads across her lips.

She doesn't say anything right away, so I jam the rest of it in my mouth. Half of me wants to beg her for more, but I know if I do, then somehow I've managed to give her the upper hand. Which is ridiculous. It's just a cupcake, and regardless of what she thinks, we're not really competing with each other. For the YouTube thing sure, but I don't see how she can win against me and my kickass cool bar and the axe throwing. And now the whole live bands idea and karaoke.

The cupcakes-and-cocktails theme is cute. But that's about all it is.

I try to keep my groan in this time, but a sound of contentment slips out.

"So you like my screaming orgasms?" she asks.

Which is when I start coughing. I also try to inhale with food in my mouth and choke. And cough some more. Blaire takes a step back since I'm spraying the counter with half-chewed cupcake. It's a travesty because I want that all in my belly and not on the counter.

"Are you okay?" she asks when I continue to cough for another solid fifteen seconds.

"Yeah." *Cough*. "I just"—*cough*—"didn't expect that."

"It's the name of the cupcake," she informs me.

"I figured, since you didn't scream even once."

"I'm not a screamer." Her eyes flare, as if she didn't mean for that to slip out.

Now it's my turn to smirk. "Is that right?"

She spins around, but I can see her face in the mirrored wall in front of her. Her ears have gone red and she mutters something to herself, nabbing the box from the bar behind her. She rolls her shoulders back and turns to face me again. Her cheeks are the same color as her ears. She drops the box unceremoniously on the counter. "I figured you'd want more than one."

"Yes. Definitely." I nod.

"Multiples really are the best." Her cheek tics, and the tips of her ears look as if they're going to light on fire and take all her hair with it. I wonder how much product she uses to keep it looking so perfect and if it's soft to the touch or not.

"I love multiples." Both the giving and the receiving. I leave that part out, because I would prefer to eat the cupcakes, not wear them, and I feel like we're suddenly treading a very fine line. Either that or we've already jumped right over it. I shake my head to clear it. "Uh, what do I owe you?"

"Those are on the house. Enjoy your night."

Blaire usually happily charges me full price for my cupcake addiction. Although she does tend to toss in an extra one for good measure. I'm tempted to ask if I'm going to end up hogtied in the trunk of a car if I eat the rest of these, but I figure that might be pushing it. "I can't imagine anyone has ever said no to free multiple screaming orgasms."

She gives me a patronizing look. "Okay, Ronan, the joke is over. Off you go." She shoos me away. "I have customers to serve and they want what you had."

I leave the cupcake shop feeling a lot like I lost that round. I even forgot to pass her a coupon for free beer and fried pickles.

Lars has moved on from flirting with the group of women so he can serve other customers. I round the bar and flip the box open, intent on eating another one of the cupcakes. I shake my head when I see the rest of them. Each one has a message written on tiny sugary cookies: EAT ME, BITE ME, SUCK IT and there's one rogue Death by Chocolate cupcake, complete with skull and crossbones.

Huh, looks like Alice has a sense of humor after all.

@the_knightcap:

Stop trying to make everyone happy. You're not beer.

chapter six

SO HILARIOUS

Blaire

My customer poll shows me that poetry slams are not quite as popular as I thought. So my plan to open our events with one is vetoed by Daphne and Paul in favor of Comedy Night.

It took all of two days, a few social media posts and two hours of auditions to secure our night of entertainment—I will say that there are a lot of people out there who think they're funny but are not. We're paying our entertainment in free cupcakes and booze, and even with the entry fee, which I was originally on the fence about, the café is packed. We have a fabulous selection of drinks, cakes, and savory treats. And Daphne has offered to make a few video clips of the entertainment to post on YouTube, which is amazing since I'll be too busy mixing cocktails to handle something like that.

I fully believe nothing can ruin this night. That belief is naïve and likely shortsighted.

However, since the EAT ME cupcake incident, there's been a shift with Ronan. One I'm not sure how to take. Yes, I still think he's an asshole. Yes, I'm still wary. Yes, we still stand outside on Friday afternoons and toss coupons at customers, trying to get them to spend their money on our wares. But he's addicted to my cupcakes. He comes in here every single night to get a hit of my special treats, and he can't even hide his excitement or his enjoyment.

Normally I charge him, but that night I was feeling extra generous because he's inadvertently sparked my cupcake creativity. I knew I had a winner on my hands, and that his reaction would inspire customers to buy what he was getting off on.

Every time he puts on a performance, I usually sell out of whatever's left in specialty cupcakes, so the initial out of pocket was totally worth it. Is it annoying that he constantly leaves me coupons for wings and asks me if I'm ready for a "big girl drink"? Sure, but toying with him is as much fun as watching him scarf down my cupcakes while grudgingly moaning his delight.

He hasn't made his daily stop yet, although generally he comes in later, within a couple hours of closing and after his dinner rush. I give my head a shake, because fixating on when Ronan stops in for cupcakes is unhelpful when I should be focused on my event.

Twenty minutes later, the opening act hits our small makeshift stage. Chairs and tables have been rearranged so everyone has a great view. At first I'm worried, because the guy is clearly nervous, but as the jokes start flowing and the crowd begins to chuckle and then laugh boisterously, he gains confidence. He finishes to a huge round of applause, and the bar is flooded with orders between the acts. Three comedians are scheduled tonight, which is perfect. It means rounds of drinks, appetizers, snacks, and desserts come in waves, which we're prepared for.

Everything is going as smooth as buttercream frosting until the final comedian sets up. It's almost nine and the sound of bass and feedback filters through the wall I share with Ronan's bar, making the floors vibrate.

As the final act begins, she's rudely interrupted by the sudden, very loud banging of... drums? It's followed by equally loud guitar riffs, and a growly voice belting out lyrics, which eclipse the comedian entirely for a few seconds.

It stops as abruptly as it begins and the performer makes a joke, setting off a round of nervous chuckling. Unfortunately, not thirty seconds later it happens again. "Dammit." I drop a stack of plates into the bus bin. The clatter would be loud if the noise coming from next door didn't drown it out, along with Karen the Comedian. She tries speaking louder, but it doesn't help. "I'm going over there."

Daphne, who's been filming and taking photos, makes a face. "Maybe I should go."

I give her the hairy eyeball. "So you can drool all over Ronan and forget to ask him to tone it the hell down?"

She arches a brow. Whatever. It's the truth, even if me calling her out on it in a less than pleasant manner is probably unwarranted. But this is my first event, and he's ruining it with whatever he has going on over there. People always remember what happened at the beginning or the end of an event the best. So my customers are going to remember the fun start to their evening and how it was ruined because a loud band drowned out the last damn act.

I rush over to Ronan's bar in time for the really loud music to start. Pounding bass, drums, and excessively aggressive guitar riffs blare through the sound system. The place is packed, bodies crowding the small stage positioned to the right. No wonder it's so loud in my café—the band is pretty much playing right against our adjoining wall. I notice that it's the young bartender up onstage. I think his name is Larry or something. He starts scream-singing. It's pretty unpleasant, not that I think scream-singing is ever really all that appealing.

I scan the dimly lit bar, searching for Ronan in a sea of black rim glasses-wearing twentysomethings. I finally spot him, in all his plaid glory, behind the bar, pouring pints. It takes me forever to squeeze my way through the crowd, but when I get to the bar the lineup is three deep. I try to edge my way between waiting customers, but it proves impossible.

Annoyed and frustrated, and frankly, grossed out by the number of sweaty bodies pressing up on me, I do another cursory scan of the bar and notice an opening a ways down.

I settle my hands on some guy's hips, trying to skirt around him. Unfortunately he takes it as a sign that I want to dance—or make out.

He spins around, eyes flaring as he takes me in. I'm glad I'm wearing heels because I'm not particularly tall and he certainly is. A slow smile spreads across his face. His cheeks are baby smooth, indicating he's probably just old enough to be here legally.

"Sorry, excuse me. I'm just trying to get to the bar. I need to talk to the bartender."

"You can talk to me while you wait if you want," he shouts over the noise.

I'm not sure how that would even be possible because it's too loud to hear myself think, let alone have any kind of meaningful conversation. I tap my ear to indicate that I can't hear him.

"We don't have to talk." He winds an arm around my waist, catching me off guard as he pulls me closer. "I'm totally into cougars."

"Cougar?" I slap my palms on his chest—which is ridiculously bony—and turn my head as he leans in.

"Yeah, you're like, close to thirty, right? That's hot."

I am seriously going to throttle Ronan. It might not be his fault that this clueless git is suddenly mauling me, but I'm blaming him since he's the reason I had to come here in the first place. I purposely step on his foot with my pointy heel.

He lets me go with a yelp. *Such a baby.* I elbow my way

through the crowd, done with the *excuse me*s and *sorry*s. I decide the only way to get to Ronan is by going behind the bar, which means shoving my way all the way down the line of thrashing and waiting customers. I finally free myself from the wave of bodies—I might go out the back door and brave the stench of garbage to get back to the café in lieu of having to fight the throng a second time—and try to wave Ronan down at the end of the bar.

He glances in my direction, tips his chin up and goes back to pouring pints. *Bastard*. There's no way I'm going to let Ronan ignore me. I unlatch the waist-high door and slip in behind the bar. I tread carefully across the honeycomb mat, waiting while Ronan slides two pints over the bar and rings the money through the till before I tug on his sleeve.

I feel very much like a kid seeking the attention of someone who definitely doesn't want to give it to me.

Ronan startles at the contact and frowns when he realizes it's me and not one of his employees. "What the hell, Blaire? You can't be back here."

"I need to talk to you!" I say, just as another particularly loud aggressive drum solo starts up.

He motions to his ear, signaling he can't hear me.

I pin him with an unimpressed glare and he rolls his eyes. I grab his arm, digging my nails in and try to pull him down so I can shout directly in his ear.

He gives me a look like I'm insane. "I'm kinda busy here." He points to the sea of bodies.

"You're ruining my Comedy Night with this!" I gesture in the direction of the band.

He huffs and shakes his head while he tries to pry my hand free from his arm. I stumble back a step, heel caught in the honeycomb mat meant to keep the bartenders from slipping on spilled beer. "You're gonna get hurt back here. You gotta go." He points to the end of the bar.

"Not until we talk."

"For fuck's sake, Blaire. I don't have time for this shit tonight." He circles my waist with one arm and hauls me up against him.

I gasp and flail, forced to hug his neck as he stalks the length of the bar. I don't want to notice how firm all of him is, or how good he smells when he's this close. "What the hell are you doing? Put me down! You can't manhandle me like this!"

"I can when you're behind my bar, wearing fucking heels, and at risk of spraining your damn ankle," he shouts, his minty breath washing over my cheek, lips brushing the shell of my ear.

"You're ruining my night."

"Maybe your comedians suck. Ever think of that?"

Instead of opening the waist-high door, he swings me up, catching me fireman style under the knees, his cold palm wrapping around my thigh briefly as he lifts me over it and then unceremoniously dumps me back on my feet on the other side.

"My comedians don't suck! Your scream-o band is the problem." I keep flailing, which is frustrating because it makes me look like more of a lunatic.

"I need to work." He turns and starts to walk away.

"I'm not done with you!" I call after him.

He motions to his ear again.

Ugh. I hate him. I flip him the double bird. "How's that? Can you hear that?" I shout.

He has the audacity to salute me, gives me his back and leans on the bar, turning his head so some scantily dressed college girl can yell her beer order in his ear. He really is a jerk.

By the time I get back to B&B the last comedian has given up on account of the noise and the crowd is starting to clear out. Probably heading next door to enjoy the stupid band. I apologize to Karen, and while she's understanding I don't think there's much of a chance that she'll come back anytime soon, if ever.

I start to clean up with the help of Daphne, who hasn't asked what happened yet, likely because I'm so angry it's a wonder there isn't steam coming out of my ears. Only a few diehard customers are left in the place and I'm pretty sure the only reason they're hanging around is the possibility of half-price cupcakes.

I offer them the deal and they polish off what's left of their martinis, pick a half-dozen each and take off, muttering about stopping at their car before they head over to The Knight Cap to check out the band, leaving my place totally empty. I'd planned to stay open until ten tonight, but it looks like I don't have to anymore.

I flip the bird at the wall between our two bars as yet another bass-pounding song starts, and then box up the few remaining cupcakes.

Daphne dumps what's left in the coffee carafe down the drain. "Guess the talk with Ronan didn't go all that well, huh?"

"He's a dick."

"What'd he say?"

"He pretended he couldn't hear me and then man-handled me."

She sets the carafe down. "He did *what*?"

"He was behind the bar, ignoring me, so I went back there to confront him and he picked me up and carried me back out!" My cheeks heat as I recall exactly how forceful he was, and how strong, and also how easy it was for him to carry me. I'm not particularly petite.

Daphne's eyebrows rise. "Can't say I'd be all that upset if it was me he was manhandling."

"He ruined the night!"

"Well, to be fair, he only ruined the last act and I'll be honest: She was the weakest of the three, so maybe it was a blessing in disguise. Plus you do usually close at nine, so maybe he didn't realize you were still open?"

"She was distracted, and do not defend him. It's thoughtless of him to schedule a live band on the same night as our first event. He couldn't have not known about it. We had signs and flyers out all week. He should've consulted me!"

Daphne crosses her arms. "Because you two are clearly besties."

"It's common courtesy!"

"Which would hold some water if you two were actually on some kind of friendly terms, but all you do is push each other's buttons. I'll honestly be surprised if you don't either kill each other or end up boning each other's brains out."

I scoff. "Not in a million years."

Daphne grins. "Want to put some money on that?"

"You know I don't gamble."

"Uh huh. However you want to play it, Blaire. But I see the cupcakes you set aside for him every single day, and there's an awful lot of effort going into something for someone you supposedly hate."

I glance at the box still sitting on the counter with the cupcakes I decorated and specifically set aside for Ronan. "I do it because it's satisfying to watch him helplessly devour them."

"Okay."

"It's true."

"Uh huh."

I dump the box in the trash to prove my point, but it feels a lot like I've proven hers instead.

The next morning, once the brunch rush is over I steel my resolve and head to The Knight Cap to talk to Ronan about last night before he opens. I can see him through the window, leaning on the bar, wearing one of his plaid shirts, thick fore-arms exposed.

I bet it's purposeful so he can show off his tattoos. I take a deep breath, determined to keep my cool and try to open the door, but it's still locked. I knock on the window and he glances my way, pushing his black-rimmed glasses up his nose.

Stupid sexy hipster glasses.

I rattle the doorknob to demonstrate that I can't get in.

He lifts his left arm and taps his watch. It's very old school, something I would like to *not* find endearing and generally don't, especially since he doesn't make a move to come out from behind the bar and let me in.

So I keep knocking. And knocking. And knocking some more. In fact I start knocking out the rhythm of a song. He shakes his head, tosses his pen down on the bar top, and shambles slowly to the end of the bar. He stops three times on the way to the door to adjust stools and once more to fix a picture that's hanging askew on the wall. His back is to me, and he strokes his chin, tipping his head to the right before he readjusts the picture in the opposite direction. I take the opportunity to stare at his butt, which I would like to smack and also kick with my pointy heel. I'm not sure what would be more satisfying, although I do know what would be most embarrassing. For me.

He finally saunters over to the door and taps the sign with the opening times posted on it. "We don't open for another fifteen minutes."

I bite back a bitchy retort because as he's pointed out before, you don't attract flies with vinegar. "Can we please talk?"

He jams a thumb in his pocket and rolls back on his heels. "You seemed to communicate just fine with hand signals last night."

I clasp my hands behind my back and fire the middle finger at him from there, while I plaster a smile on my face. Immature? Yes. Does it make me feel better? Marginally. "You manhandled me."

"You shouldn't have been behind my bar with heels on. You were a distraction and a liability." His gaze moves over me in a slow sweep. It's not unappreciative.

"Can we please do this without a door between us?" It's demeaning to be kept out here on the street, speaking loudly to be heard through the pane of glass.

"Are you gonna try to maim me with your talons again?"

"Maim you?" What in the world is he talking about?

He flicks the lock and steps back, not bothering with chivalry. I open the door and slip in out of the cold as he unbuttons his plaid shirt and pulls the collar aside.

"What are you doing?"

"Showing you the evidence."

"Of what?"

He bends, bringing his shoulder down to my level. There are crescent-shaped nail marks in his skin defined by bruises.

"I did not do that."

"You sure did."

"I'm sure that was from whatever college girl you had a quickie with in your office when you took a five-minute break last night, not from me."

He blinks a few times, inked forearms flexing when he crosses them. The right one is covered in beautiful flowers, and the left is some kind of landscape. I can't see enough of it to figure out what exactly it is. One of those arms was against my bare thigh last night when he picked me up. "First of all, I have no interest in college girls."

I scoff and mirror his pose. "Could've fooled me with the way you were eyeing them last night."

"I was tending bar. My job is to be friendly when I'm serving booze. Secondly, I don't fuck where I work, and third, the word *quickie* isn't in my vocabulary. I'm an all-or-nothing kind of guy."

I fight to hold my smile. "So you're saying you like to savor instead of devour."

"That's exactly what I'm saying."

I have to tip my head up to meet his gaze. His caramel-colored eyes are hot, burning like a shot of whiskey. "You treat sex the opposite of how you treat my cupcakes."

He licks his lips and swallows thickly, like he's tasting the memory of one right now. "I devour the first one and savor the rest when I'm alone."

"Hey, Ronan, sorry I'm a bit la—" Ronan's usual bartender—and the screamer from last night—is at the end of the bar, hands in the air as he takes deliberate steps backward and thumbs over his shoulder. "Oh, sorry, man, I didn't, uh...I'll go grab a couple cases of beer or something." He disappears around the corner.

I don't understand what that was all about until Ronan's attention returns to me. We're literally inches apart, and his arms are no longer crossed. He takes a step back and so do I, bumping into the door.

I clear my throat. "We need to set a schedule for our events. You ruined the last act of my comedy night with your live band."

"I'm sure it wasn't that bad."

"It was." On many levels. "Look, you're open until two and I'm only open until nine most nights, ten when I have entertainment on the weekends. You can hold your band until nine thirty, can't you? How much could that possibly hurt your business?"

"Why should I have to be the one to make concessions?"

"I already moved all my glasses and had to adjust my entire interior wall that adjoins your bar. The least you can do is give me an extra half hour."

"What're you gonna do for me?"

"I can start my comedy nights at seven instead of seven thirty. It's only half an hour and then we can both benefit. My customers can move over to your place and I can close when you have live bands." I don't want to bend, but I realize compromise is the only way to win this. I need him to be willing to work with me so I don't keep losing out. "Unless one of us switches days?"

"Live bands are best on Saturday nights." And he's back to crossing his arms.

"And comedians usually have nine-to-five jobs." Or they're booked somewhere better than a café in downtown Seattle.

"Unless they're actually good." It's like he's living in my damn head.

"They were good." I'm extra defensive, which is frustrating, especially since it makes him smile. "And the last one would have been a whole lot better if not for the noise over here."

We stare each other down for several long seconds that slowly turn heavy and uncomfortable. He finally sighs and runs a palm down his face. "You're not going to leave unless I agree to this, are you?"

"That's correct."

"Okay. I can push back live bands until nine thirty, but make sure you wrap up the yukkity-yuks by nine so you're not back here next Sunday griping at me for something else."

"Do you have anything else planned for this week?"

"Do you?" he shoots back.

I roll my eyes. "I'm trying to be proactive."

"If that's what you want to call it. Maybe you're trying to steal my ideas."

"So far you've been the one piggybacking me, not the other way around."

He leans in and lowers his voice. "Except last night when you were clinging to me like I was carrying you on a tightrope, not across a bar, one you weren't supposed to be behind in the first place."

I open my mouth and snap it shut. He's goading me. On purpose. I brush a wayward curl from my forehead with my middle finger and spin around, yanking the door open.

His laughter follows me all the way back to my café.

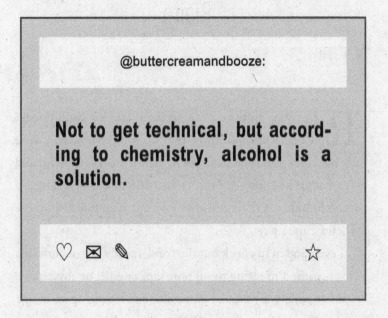

@buttercreamandbooze:

Not to get technical, but according to chemistry, alcohol is a solution.

chapter seven

WHAT HOUSE ARE YOU?

Blaire

Ronan stays true to our agreement and his band doesn't go on until nine thirty the following Saturday, giving my last comedian time to finish his act. It works out well, and it's great for business—Ronan's more than mine, since it means a good chunk of my customers end up migrating over there when I close up.

I even pop in to check out the band, mostly out of curiosity. Not because I'm trying to support him or ogle, or anything.

After polling my regular customers and setting up an online survey, Harry Potter Trivia Night is born. The winner gets a dozen HP-inspired cupcakes and a round of drinks for them and three friends.

I'm a huge Harry Potter fan. I've read all the books, listened to the entire series on audio more than once, and I own all the movies. I also saw every single one in the theater on opening night. "Big fan" is an understatement. I'm pretty proud of the fact that I didn't need to go online to research tough questions since I'm so well versed already.

I've gone all out. Every drink and cupcake is HP themed. My posts are getting a record amount of likes, and we have twenty individuals entered in the contest. It's going to be fabulous.

I'm decked out in my Gryffindor dress, wielding my Hermione wand and wearing my Hogwarts cape. It's almost like a pre-Halloween party. If this event gets the same amount of attention as the comedy nights do, trivia night will become another monthly staple at B&B. I'm thinking *Stranger Things* deserves its own event, too.

At seven, the café begins to fill with entrants and their friends. Callie is kept busy behind the counter, Daphne is helping with drinks, and the hardcore HP fans are dressed in their house garb, devouring cupcakes and house-themed drinks.

I call out the names of the competitors and am completely shocked when Ronan walks into the café dressed in a Slytherin hoodie. The Slytherin part isn't much of a surprise—he definitely fits the profile with his dark hair, less-than-aboveboard business tactics, and prankster ways, but the fact that he's an HP fan is unexpected. Unless he borrowed the hoodie from one of his employees. I wouldn't put it past him to use it as an opportunity to piggyback on another one of my ideas.

"You're a Harry Potter fan?" I ask when he approaches the counter to register.

"Hell yeah."

"The movies or the books?" I demand.

He scoffs and makes a face like he can't believe I'd ask such a thing. "The books, of course. I own all the first-edition hard-covers and the soft ones, too. Plus Jim Dale nails the audio."

"Oh my God, I love his voice!" The audio books are amazing, and I listen to them all the time when I'm at home, testing cupcake recipes.

We grin at each other, and for half a second I dislike him a little less. I register him to play, and he grabs a drink before he takes a seat at the table up front where all his fellow HP competitors are already waiting.

There's a sizable crowd of non-entrants lining the fringe of the café as we get ready for the contest to begin.

Word to the wise: HP fans are ultracompetitive. The first three rounds of trivia weed out the *I saw the movie but never bothered to read the books* crowd. By eight we've narrowed it down to the best six contestants. Ronan manages to stay in the top three.

He nails the rapid-question round, putting him in the finals. His adversary is Shanna, a twenty-two-year-old lit major at the local college who's writing her thesis paper on Harry Potter lore, so he has his work cut out for him.

I pull the final question, which has been selected randomly, and whistle into the microphone. "Wow, this one's a doozy. For the title of Harry Potter Trivia Champion, a dozen of my magi-cally delicious cupcakes and drinks for you and three friends, name every ingredient contained in Polyjuice Potion."

Ronan and Shanna both slap their hands on the buzzer at the same time, but Shanna gets there a fraction of a second sooner, the red light bathing her face in a sinister glow.

"Shanna, what's your answer for the win?"

She leans in to the microphone, closing her eyes—it's how she's answered every single question. "Lacewing flies, leeches, knotgrass, fluxweed..." Her brow furrows and she hesitates for a second before continuing. "Shredded Boomslang skin and a bit of the person you want to turn into." Her eyes pop open and she smiles triumphantly.

"Is that your final answer?" I prompt.

"Yes. That's my final answer."

I admit, I'm disappointed when I have to say, "I'm sorry, but that is incorrect." Shannon's face falls like a pile of crumbling bricks.

"Ronan, would you like to respond and try to steal or would you like a new question?"

"I'll try to steal, thanks." He clears his throat, eyes fixed on mine as he leans in, lips almost touching the mic. His voice is a low, confident rumble. "The ingredients in Polyjuice Potion are lacewing flies, leeches, knotgrass, fluxweed, shredded Boomslang skin, a bit of the person you want to turn into *and*..." He pauses for dramatic effect. "Powdered Bicorn horn."

I have to bite the inside of my cheek to keep from smiling. "Is that your final answer?"

A cocky grin spreads lazily across his face. "Yes, Blaire, it's my final answer."

"You're sure?" I arch a brow.

His smile doesn't waver. "Absolutely."

"You are correct. We have a winner!"

"Hell yeah!" Ronan jumps to his feet and raises both fists into the air as if he's won a round in the boxing ring. He turns to me and in what I can only assume is an impulsive show of victory, he wraps his arms around my waist, picks me up off the floor, and swings me around in a circle.

When he sets me down, I take a dizzy step back. He keeps his hands on my waist to prevent me from falling off the makeshift stage. "I gotta head back to the bar, but I'll take a raincheck on the drinks." He winks, jumps off the stage, and fist bumps his way to the front door.

The brief warm and fuzzies disappear the following night when Ronan hosts a Beer Pong Tournament. The loudest beer pong tournament in the history of the universe, apparently, because every thirty seconds there's a collective "ooooooh" or "yeeeahhhhh" coming from his place.

It takes everything in me not to go over and check it out after I close up. And even then I peek through the window, just to see. It looks ridiculously fun. But I know if I go in there Ronan will find a way to make me participate, and I have terrible aim. I'm guaranteed to lose, which would also mean drinking beer. I have an early morning tomorrow, so I back away slowly and head home, where it's mostly quiet and there are no twenty-one-year-olds playing beer pong in the apartment next door to mine.

Over the next several weeks my competition with Ronan heats up, both of us trying to outdo each other with new events, particularly since we've both made it through to the top one hundred bars from the over five hundred who were initially nominated for Tori Taylor's Best Bar contest. The next round will bring us down to the top fifty, and both of our bars are currently hovering in the thirties thanks to social media votes. After that, the competition is going to get steeper with the quarterfinals, taking us down to the top twenty-five bars. I don't want to get cocky or complacent though, since we still have a long way to go to number one.

I hold a poetry slam night and despite the initial lack of excitement, it turns out to be a totally popular event, especially with the drama students at the college.

Unfortunately, Ronan plans another one of his loud events—all his events are loud—on the same night, so we're forced to wrap it up early. I should really know better by now.

On the upside, every new, fun event I host does better than the last. We hold a Halloween cookie-decorating contest and sell a ridiculous number of gory cupcakes and fun, horrifying drinks. Orders for cupcakes for the local businesses continue to pour in, which means I'm endlessly busy and still managing not to dig too far into my line of credit. It also means I'm light on sleep, but I can deal with being tired as long as B&B is staying afloat.

Tonight I have a bachelorette cupcake and cookie-decorating party. It's actually one of Daphne's engagement photo shoot clients who came back looking to secure her for additional dates—including the wedding. When Daphne suggested the bachelorette party I absolutely ran with it, with her input, of course. It gives her another opportunity to take some fun candid photos to add to their engagement and wedding albums and I have the opportunity to do something new and different.

Daphne came in earlier to snap some shots of the setup, and then popped back in before the bride and her wedding party were scheduled to arrive.

The bride's sister arranged the event and rented out the entire café. Customers can still come in and purchase cupcakes to go, but there's a warning on the door and the entire place is full of women decorating treats.

We decided the cupcakes are fun, but you can't make interesting shapes the way you can with a cookie. We start with a cupcake-decorating tutorial—Daphne records that part—but that's quickly devolved into turning cupcakes into vaginas. And the cookies...well, those are just as entertaining. Once the debauched decorating begins, Daphne takes off back to her studio, half apologizing for not being able to stay. I wave her off; honestly, this is the most fun I've had with a decorating class.

At eight Ronan pops by—he still makes a daily stop for a cupcake—and gets a gander at the penis cookies the ladies are working on.

The entire wedding party stops to watch him cross the café.

"Ooooh! Hey there, cutie, you can come sit with me!" The bride's sister—Stephanie—is on her third martini and lost her filter an hour ago. The drinks aren't even that strong. Every time she decorates a cookie, she ends up taking a picture of her biting into it and then she forces her friends to send her the picture. She then promptly posts it to all her social media accounts. She's also tagged the café in every single post. I should probably mention that the cookies she's most fond of posting are the penis ones.

I consider untagging the café, but decide that based on the number of likes the posts are getting it doesn't hurt to let it ride. Who knows, it could become another new revenue stream.

"What're you ladies up to?" He shoots a smile and wink in my direction—the wink is probably unconscious—and veers toward the women.

"We're decorating cookies. See!" Stephanie holds up her most recent work of art. A very orange penis, complete with pubic hair. It looks like it was decorated by a six-year-old. Or a drunk woman, the latter of which is accurate.

Ronan's eyes go wide and he coughs into his fist. "That's very convincing."

"I even gave it pubes! They're made out of licorice."

"I manscaped mine," one of the other bridesmaids declares and holds up her less orange, much more aesthetically appealing bald-balled cookie.

Stephanie's eyes rake over Ronan, pausing at his crotch. "Do you manscape?"

"Uhhh—"

"Ladies, this is Ronan, owner of the bar next door. When you're done here, you should drop by. You must have some kind of special drink promotion you can offer these lovely ladies, right, Ronan? And don't you have some kind of event going on? Is it a live band?" I know it's not because I stalk his IG profile. I don't follow him, because I don't want him to know I'm watching him, but after the loud, live entertainment started I needed to know ahead of time what I was facing every week.

His gaze moves from the penis cookie two inches from his face to me. He looks like he's plotting my murder. I can completely understand why. These ladies are already halfway to rowdy drunk. They're all on some ridiculous pre-wedding keto diet—which died a sad, necessary death once I told them the cookie calories don't count tonight—and they've been sipping martinis for the past two hours. They'll fit in perfectly next door.

"Ooooh! You own The Knight Cap?" Stephanie puts her hand on his forearm, leaving icing smears on his tattooed skin. She's definitely on the prowl based on the way she's eyeing Ronan's crotch the same way he eyes my cupcakes.

Ronan either chooses to ignore her or maybe he's too busy giving me the death glare and missed her simpering question. She strokes his forearm, rubbing in the icing. I'm sure it's sticking to his arm hair.

"He does, don't you, Ronan?"

"I don't actually own it, I just run it. It's my grandfather's—"

"Oh, wow, isn't that sweet? You work with your grandpa? I love guys who are close to their families. I'm close to my family, too." Stephanie is still petting his arm. Still holding her penis cookie up in the air, as if she's waiting for Ronan to praise her efforts.

The rest of the women are watching the one-sided exchange with something between fascination and mortification. Mostly it's fascination, though.

The woman on Stephanie's right snorts. "You haven't talked to your mom in three years."

"I'm close with the rest of my family, though," she snaps, sending a rage glare at the other woman. I think her name might be Laura or Laurie. Stephanie returns her attention to Ronan. "I'm close with everyone else. Even my stepmother."

"Well that's...nice." He takes a deliberate step back, away from her petting and the phallic cookie. "You ladies enjoy the cookie decorating." He makes a move toward the door.

"Aren't you forgetting something?" I call out.

"Huh?" His gaze shifts to me.

I hold up the small box I set aside for him. It contains two cupcakes. They're themed for tonight's bachelorette party. Although I decorated these especially for Ronan, as I always do.

"Oh, right."

He rushes over and tries to grab the box from my hands, but I maintain my protective hold on it, smiling serenely. "Don't you want to know what kind they are?"

"I'm sure I'll love them."

"Me, too, but you should sample one, don't you think?" I bat my lashes and smile wider. "These ladies have yet to try the cupcakes. I'm sure they want your seal of approval, don't you?"

A chorus of "Yes!" comes from the table, followed by some additional hoots, hollers, and taunts. You'd think we were at a strip club, not a freaking cupcake cocktail café.

Ronan narrows his eyes.

"You heard them. You don't want to disappoint the bride-to-be." I flip the lid open and his eyes flare and meet mine.

For the first time, Ronan is less than 100 percent composed. In fact, his cheeks have turned a lovely shade of pink. "You gotta be shitting me." He rubs the back of his neck.

"They look real, don't they?"

"Ooooh! What are they? Can we see?" Stephanie claps her hands together excitedly. I should probably hydrate this group before I send them next door.

"Why don't you show them, Ronan?" I hold my smile.

"No way."

I go for the cupcake on the left.

"Hell no." Ronan smacks the back of my hand and his eyes dart to the women. "I'm not eating that in front of them."

That little smack seems to reverberate through my entire body, pinging around like a marble in places that haven't had attention in a long time. Ironic considering the design on the cupcake I'm about to make him eat in front of these women.

"So this one, then?" I lift it from the box and turn it so it's facing the right way for him.

"I'm going to get you back for this." His tone is low and dark: equal parts threat and promise.

"Totally worth it." I nod to the cake perched in my open palm.

He grudgingly takes it.

The women have abandoned the table and their cookies to gather around the spectacle that Ronan has become. Because he's holding a vagina cupcake. The other option is, of course, the male anatomy. Both are convincing in their authenticity.

"Eat it, Ronan!" Stephanie shouts. The rest of the bachelorette party join in and chant his name.

His ears are red, his glare tells me he's so freaking pissed off, but he's also aware that these ladies are going to come over to his bar and drop stupid amounts of money on shots and girlie drinks as soon as they're done here. Customers are worth more than his pride in this moment. Also, Ronan has proven that he isn't the kind of man who backs down from a challenge, and for some reason I hate him a tiny bit less because of it. For now.

I covertly slip my hand in my pocket, searching for my phone as he peels the Bride-to-Be wrapper from the cake. Thankfully, Ronan is sufficiently distracted by Stephanie, who's snaked her arm around his waist and is screaming his name like she's the one about to get eaten.

I manage to pull up the camera app, switch it to video

mode, and hit Record before he fully unwraps the cake. He holds my gaze as he brings it to his mouth, opening wide. I lift the phone, making sure I catch him when he takes a robust, rather sensual bite.

And all the while his eyes tell me he wants to mash the cupcake in my face. But he doesn't. Instead he puts on a show. I'm hashtagging this cupcake porn. Because that's 100 percent what it is, literally and figuratively. Even the bite placement is purposeful, and so is his groan when the flavors hit his tongue. The sweetness of vanilla cake, the hint of cocoa in the thin layer of icing before the light buttercream registers and then there's the vanilla custard center, because come on, I'm nothing if not detail oriented.

He obviously doesn't expect the filling, which of course is the point. Custard dribbles down his chin, but he's so busy glaring at me while I record this epic moment that he doesn't notice.

I can't resist the opportunity. I bite my lip, fighting my own smile. "Oh! You're making a mess, Ronan. Here, let me help." I make sure the video is still rolling and I catch the dribble before it drips off his chin.

Before I can pull my hand away, he wraps his fingers around my wrist. There have been very few instances in which Ronan has made intentional, prolonged physical contact with me. The most body-to-body contact we've had to date was when he picked me up and removed me from behind his bar. After the fact, I can admit that he was right in that situation and

I was not. Did he really need to fireman-carry me out from behind the bar? Probably not. Have I thought about all that physical contact countless times since then? Not at all. Okay, maybe a few. Hundred times.

So when he yanks me forward by my wrist I stumble and my hips meet the counter. I have to remember to keep the phone trained on his face when he bites my finger at the first knuckle. And I have to swallow down the gasp when his tongue swirls around my finger, cleaning off the custard.

He releases my finger with a wet suctioned pop, drops my wrist and jams the rest of the cupcake in his mouth. The whole thing. I cut the video because he's killed the sexy, but I know I can edit it into something useable.

He chews quickly and swallows, swiping at his mouth with the back of his hand. "Post that and you'll regret it."

"I'll regret it or you will? That was cupcake porn gold, wasn't it, ladies?"

The women cheer and he jerks back, like he's suddenly aware there are other people here besides us.

He nabs the box, halfway to crushing it. "Just remember you pulled the pin, Alice." And with that he spins around, excuses himself, and leaves the café.

"Okay." The bride-to-be raises both of her hands like she's trying to stop traffic. "Please tell me you're sleeping with him. You have to be sleeping with him. I'm pretty sure I just came vicariously through you."

"I'm sorry." I splutter and smooth out my apron—totally a

nervous move. "I don't know what you're talking about. He's my rival, not my... boyfriend."

Stephanie grabs my arm, eyes wide and alarmed. "Fuck buddy? Please tell me you're boning him."

"Uhhh—"

"You will be soon if you're not already," the bride-to-be says.

"I don't even *like* him," I scoff.

She smiles. "You don't need to like him to ride him; you just need to want to use him for stress relief. That's how me and Tristan started out and now we're getting married. I see wedding bells in your future!"

I see a whole lot of retribution and Ronan doing whatever he can to get back at me, probably by making a crap-ton of noise, but I don't bother to tell these ladies that. They're the end of my night, and whatever trouble they have brewing isn't going to be mine to endure. It'll be Ronan's and I'm more than happy to let them wreak havoc on him.

Forty-five minutes later, my bachelorette party has defected next door and I've finished cleaning up. I consider stopping at The Knight Cap to see how things are going over there.

Off-key singing filters through the barrier of the wall separating our places. I decide I can drop in for five minutes to check how the girls are doing.

I reapply my lipstick, check my hair, and grab my purse. I'm almost out the door when I realize I'm still wearing my apron. I take it off—careful not to mess up my hair—and throw it in the washing machine, knowing I can toss it in the dryer in the morning when I come in to decorate the cupcakes for tomorrow. Then I lock up and head next door.

The place is packed with people, and I spot the bachelorette ladies on the stage, one of them belting out a tuneless "Wrecking Ball" by Miley Cyrus. Everyone is cheering, likely because of her backup dancers twerking their way around the stage. The ladies are significantly more intoxicated than they were when they left my place. The song finally comes to an end, which is a relief because the horrible singing gets worse the longer it goes on.

Ronan steps up and takes the microphone from the bride-to-be before she can start another song. "That was fantastic! A round of applause for Amanda. You definitely outdid yourself with that one!" The crowd bursts into applause and laughter. Thankfully the bride is way too intoxicated to know that she sounded like a dying goose on methamphetamines.

I turn to leave, satisfied that I've accomplished what I set out to—make Ronan's life a little more difficult—but people have moved in behind me, so I can't get to the door.

"Blaire!" Ronan's deep voice echoes through the speakers and I freeze. "I see you out there. Come on up! The cupcake queen from next door has graced us with her gorgeous presence. Who wants to hear her sing?"

The crowd erupts in a cheer.

"You heard them, Blaire. They want you to sing for them. Don't be shy!" A spotlight is suddenly on me, the glare blindingly bright. "Come on, ladies, go get Blaire and bring her up here for me."

Of course he commissions the drunk bachelorettes to help.

I don't blend in very well in my fifties-inspired dress—tonight it's pink and has a diamond ring theme—so it means that every single person is now staring at me.

The bachelorette crew grabs my arms and pulls me toward the stage. Ronan is grinning like the cat who ate the canary. He did promise to get me back for the vagina cupcake. And I totally posted the video in my stories as soon as he left. I figure it's great advertising for future bachelorette parties.

I don't bother to fight. If Ronan thinks dragging me onstage in front of a bunch of drunk college kids is going to embarrass me, he's got another thing coming.

When I reach the stage, he holds out his hand in faux-chivalry. I slip my palm into his, and warmth zings through my body at the contact. I climb the stairs and he tugs me against his side, smiling down at me, eyes twinkling with malicious mirth. "I'm so glad you stopped in to see what was happening here tonight, Blaire."

I wrap my fingers around his wrist and angle the microphone down. "I couldn't miss hearing my girls sing!"

His grin widens. "They were certainly a delight, weren't they?" He addresses the crowd, and they all clap and whistle.

Ronan is ridiculously charismatic. It doesn't matter that the bride and her wedding party sucked more than a Hoover on the highest setting; they love him and in turn they love the ladies' terrible performance.

"Well, now that I have you up here, what should I do with you?" Ronan's tongue peeks out and the right side of his mouth quirks up in a half-smirk. He tips the microphone toward me.

"What do you want to do with me?" I'd like to say my voice is purposely low and smoky, but honestly, the question and the way he's looking at me seems almost lascivious.

"Hmmm." He sucks his teeth. "Not so sure I should answer that honestly."

That gets a loud cheer from the crowd.

He gives them all a look and I roll my eyes. "Aren't I up here to sing?"

"Right. Yeah. What's your jam? How about 'Let's Get It On'?"

I scoff and take the microphone from him. "Mmm, I think we can come up with something better than that." I tap my lip. "Have you been up here yet, Ronan?"

"I'm running the show, not in it." He laughs, but his eyes glint with a warning look.

"Why can't you do both? Who wants to hear Ronan sing? What do you guys say, should we do a duet?"

The cheer is so loud it makes my ears ring.

"You heard them, they want us to do it together."

"There's only one microphone."

I lift a shoulder in a light shrug. "We can share, can't we?" I drop the mic and whisper. "You're not getting out of this."

He gives his head a slight shake, but his smile tells me he knows he's screwed himself with this. "What're we gonna sing?"

"Hmm." I pretend to think about it for a few seconds. "How about 'You're the One that I Want'?"

Ronan laughs. "I should've known you'd be a *Grease* fan." He motions to the deejay. "All right, you heard the lady. Let's do it."

What Ronan doesn't know is that I've probably watched the movie a thousand times. And I've seen the play at least twenty times. I also have the soundtrack and I listen to it in my car all the time. I don't even need the lyric feed. My love for *Grease* is a good part of the reason I wear the dresses I do.

When I adopt an obsession, I don't half ass it; I commit fully. Much like my obsession with Harry Potter and cupcakes. When I was a teenager, I used to love drama class. Even in college I would join the theater groups for fun. I didn't ever want it to be a job. Once I was the understudy for the role of Sandy, so I know the entire song by heart, actions included.

I smooth my hands over my skirt and hand the microphone back to him. I love that he has to start.

I have to hand it to Ronan. He really does try to hit the notes and he doesn't do a half bad job, but he has to keep looking at the screen. His gaze keeps darting back and forth. It makes it that much more satisfying when I cover his hand with mine, tip the microphone down and sing to him, telling him he's the one that I want.

It's obvious he's shocked, possibly because I don't need the lyric prompt, possibly because I'm not a half bad singer. He almost misses the cue to join me, but I nudge him and nod to the screen, forcing him to drag his eyes away from mine.

He tries to keep up. It's rather commendable, and I will say, what he lacks in vocal range he makes up for in hip shaking.

When the song ends, the crowd bursts into uncontrollable applause and shouts for an encore. I slip my hand into Ronan's, noting his damp palm, and we take a bow.

I hand him back the microphone and tug on the collar of his shirt, pulling him down. My lips brush the shell of his ear and his skin pebbles as I whisper, "Not quite how you thought it was going to go down, huh?"

@buttercreamandbooze:

You're the Cupcake I Want

chapter eight

SHOULD'VE BEEN MY WIN

Blaire

The next morning I'm still sort of floating on the high of last night's win. I have to say, I'm feeling pretty damn awesome right now. I continue riding that same fabulous wave all the way in to work. Everything is awesome. Nothing can ruin my fantastic mood, not even the fact that I haven't slept much.

I find a box sitting on the front step and carry it inside with me. I don't recognize the name of the company, but maybe Daphne ordered something for our next event as a surprise.

I pluck a pair of scissors from the jar next to the cash register, sliding it carefully along the seam.

Before I have a chance to open it, the back doors swing open and Paul wheels a cart of boxes down the hall. "Hey! You're here early!" He's smiling, but he looks tired.

The scissors clatter to the floor, narrowly missing my foot. "Geez! You scared the crap out of me. I expected you to be long gone by now."

"I had to shift around some deliveries because of the holiday." Paul has had to do that a lot more recently. Either dropping off cupcakes in the evening, or coming in extra early so he can get specialty ones done for me. A few times it's been down to the wire.

Paul agreed to help me through Thanksgiving, but after that he'll be done paying me back for the truck, and I'll have to either hire another baker or take on the job myself. Based on finances, it looks like it's probably going to be me taking on the extra workload, so my already limited sleep is going to suffer even more.

He maneuvers the cart of cupcakes behind the register so I can check them out. I flip the box on top open. They smell delicious—like pumpkin pie spice—and will be even more amazing once I add the cream cheese center filling and vanilla buttercream icing, topped with an adorable pumpkin candy. "These smell like heaven."

"Well, it's your recipe, so you can take the credit for that." He's still grinning. "You feeling like a rock star this morning?"

"Uh, not particularly, no." I lean against the counter, legs still shaky from the scare.

His smile fades and his face scrunches up. "I take it you haven't heard?"

"Heard what?" I drag my attention away from the cupcakes, imagining how perfect they're going to look when I'm done with them.

"There's a video of you."

"What kind of video?" A shot of panic hits me. I'm not sure why. It's not like I've ever made one of *those* kinds of video. And honestly, there are loads of videos of me posted on YouTube since I have a channel and I upload there all the time.

He arches a brow. "Wow, your face right now makes me want to ask a lot of questions, many of which I don't necessarily think I want the answer to."

I wave the comment away. "Stop being dramatic and cryptic and tell me what's going on."

"Someone posted your performance from last night." He tips his chin toward the wall connecting us to The Knight Cap.

"Oh, that. It wasn't a big deal." I pull a tray of cupcakes from the cart and begin arranging them carefully in the display case.

"Well, maybe not to you, but it's sure getting lots of attention."

"What kind of attention?"

Paul fishes his phone out of his pocket and opens YouTube. It appears the video was uploaded by Ronan's bartender Lars—apparently his name isn't Larry. Paul hands me the device.

"This can't be right. It's been viewed more than a million times?"

"He tagged that YouTuber Tori in the video and she shared it." He taps the screen right under the video, where Lars has captioned it "Best Bar in the Pacific Northwest Challenge"

#toritaylorbestof #TheKnightCap #BestBarPNW and about seven hundred more hashtags. The video has tons of likes.

"Damn it!" I grouse, scrolling through the comments. "I can't believe this."

"You sound great. I mean I always knew you could sing, but you really nailed that performance."

"I know I can sing."

Paul's eyebrows lift. "Humble much?"

I give him a look. "It's not ego talking. I was always in theater. I can sing. It's a fact, and now Ronan is getting the accolades for it." I hit Play on the video for additional self-torture.

Ronan and I appear on the screen, although only half of me because the focus is on Ronan, at least at the beginning since he's singing and the center of attention. He doesn't have a terrible voice, and he's annoyingly nice to look at. The camera really loves him and all his pretty man angles.

When it's my turn I nab the microphone from him and start singing. "Damn!" Lars turns the camera around and there's a closeup of his face and wide eyes. Like Ronan, he's also nice to look at. "Listen to that voice." He flips the camera around again, turns it sideways and pans back to me.

"How the hell am I going to beat him now?" I pass Paul his phone back before I do something like throw it against a wall. I don't have the funds to replace it. "He didn't even tag me or B&B in the comments! What a jerk."

"If Tori ends up coming to Seattle, you'll have a chance to

prove you're the better bar." Paul gives my shoulder a squeeze. I hate that his expression holds guilt as well. "I can try to help out for a little longer if you need me."

I wave the offer away. "We both know that won't work. Especially not with you moving an hour away. I can totally handle this." I motion to the naked cupcakes. I can definitely do all the baking, but I'm worried about how it's going to impact everything else. Running a business is a lot of work. Especially with all the paperwork and keeping track of inventory and ingredients. It's been nice to have the help while it lasted. "Anyway, let's check this out." The box is unusually light, so maybe it's sample napkins or something. The company we bought ours from routinely does that.

I fold back the flaps and a balloon with the word BOOM! floats out, heading for the ceiling. Paul and I give each other a quizzical look as a second balloon rises out of the box. Both of them pop at the same time and suddenly I find myself covered in a shower of hot pink glitter.

"Oh my God! The cupcakes!" I shriek and try to push Paul out of the way so I can save the open box from the glitter bomb, but it's too late. The cakes are already sparkling. I shout a bunch of nonsense profanity, because Paul's hard work and two dozen of my income source are now trash.

"What the hell is this stuff?" Paul raises his hand, about to run his fingers through his hair.

"That was a glitter bomb! You can't do that in here! You'll

make it worse!" I guide him to the back door, hoping to minimize the damage.

"A glitter bomb?" Paul asks as I help him shake the glitter out of his hair and brush it off his shoulders.

I give my own head a shake. My palms are sparkling. "Glitter is the herpes of crafting. It'll be everywhere for weeks! I'll never get rid of it."

"Who would send you one of those?"

"How the hell—" I stop mid-sentence and glance next door. "That sonofabitch. First he steals all the goddamn glory last night and now this?" There's only one person I can think of who would do something like this. Freaking Ronan.

I spend the rest of the day trying to clean up glitter between customers, but it's literally everywhere and anyone who comes into the shop is an immediate victim of a glitter attack. Thankfully I have a couple of short breaks between the lunch and afternoon rush, so I have time to de-glitter my café. Apart from a mangled pumpkin spice one and the glitter-covered ones that weren't for sale I manage to sell out of cupcakes.

I'll be closed on Thursday for Thanksgiving and will have a skeleton staff the day before and through the weekend so Callie can spend the holiday with her family. I would try to get out of my own family obligations, but I haven't been home to visit since I opened Buttercream and Booze, and my dad would be disappointed if I didn't come for dinner. As much as I don't love their interfering ways, or their general bossiness and insanity, I do love them.

Ronan stops in as I'm shutting down for the day, grinning like a fool. "Hey, super star! You get my awesome present this morning?"

I don't return the smile. "I sure did." I spin around and grab the box of ruined cupcakes from the shelf behind me and set it on the counter in front of him.

He tips his head to the side, and lifts his hand as if he's about to touch my face. I jerk back. "What're you doing?"

"You have some glitter on your cheek."

I throw my hands in the air. "I have glitter literally everywhere. It's even in my damn underwear!"

Ronan's smile turns into a grimace at my unnecessary overshare, and his face falls even further as I flip the box of cupcakes open. "Oh shit."

"Oh shit is right. Thank you so much for your kind, thoughtful gift."

"I figured you would've opened it in your office."

"Well I guess you figured wrong."

He chews on the corner of his plush bottom lip. "I'm so sorry, Blaire. I thought it would be funny."

I cross my arms. "Do you have any idea how impossible it is to clean up glitter? I'm going to be finding sparkly crap where the sun doesn't shine for weeks."

He fishes his wallet out of his back pocket and glances at the menu board where the price list is posted. He peels off four twenties.

"What are you doing?"

"Well you couldn't sell those today, could you?"

"Not covered in glitter, no."

"So I'm paying for them because even though they're bathed in glitter they smell fantastic and I bet you would've sold them if they hadn't been ruined."

"You really don't have to do that." But I could use the eighty bucks right now, which is sort of depressing. He obviously feels bad if he's willing to fork over the money I lost as a result of his prank.

"Yes I do. I honestly didn't mean to make such a mess of your day, or cost you potential revenue." He pushes the money toward me and picks up one of the glitter-covered cakes. He proceeds to shake it off, and then he tries to brush off the rest of the glitter, which means he ends up getting it all over his hands.

"You're not going to eat that, are you?"

He gives me a look. "And let it go to waste?"

"It's not even decorated." Wow, he must really feel bad.

"Sure it is, with glitter."

"Glitter isn't really digestible, or particularly safe to eat. Might be advisable to leave the top if you're going to give that a whirl."

He reluctantly pries the top off, then takes a huge bite and chews exaggeratedly. His expression is priceless and he makes a lot of noises, some of delight and some of surprise. "It's a little—"

"Gritty?"

He nods and raises his hand in front of his mouth. "But still delicious."

It's hard not to laugh. "I do have one left over that's mangled but isn't covered in glitter."

"Really?"

"You can have it on one condition."

"Sure. Anything."

"You help me de-glitter my counter space." It's clear that he really didn't mean to cause me problems today, but it doesn't mean I'm not going to make him suffer at least a little for it.

I hand him a damp cloth and he goes to work wiping down all the surfaces that still hold traces of glitter. The best part is that no matter how careful he tries to be, sparkles get stuck to his face. I guarantee he'll be glittering all night long, like a disco ball.

On Wednesday morning I've just arrived at B&B when Ronan comes busting out the back door. He looks frazzled and exhausted. His hair is also an unusual mess. It's actually quite sexy, to be honest. Like he rolled out of bed and came straight here. His clothes are even rumpled. "Hey. Hi. I'm so glad you're here."

This is a new greeting. "Um, it's nice to see you, too?"

"Can I ask you a huge favor? Please?"

"Ahhh. Now the friendliness makes more sense. What do you need?"

"I'm supposed to get a whole load of Thanksgiving supplies delivered this morning, but the guy is running late and I have to take my grandfather up to my brother's. I'm supposed to leave"—he checks his watch—"ten minutes ago. And Gramps hates being late for stuff and I have to drive four hours there and back. I tried to call Lars, but I doubt he'll get the message until it's way too late."

I hold up a hand. "I can sign for the order."

"It all needs to go in the fridge."

"I can make sure that happens."

"Really?"

"Really."

He drops a key to The Knight Cap in my hand and pulls me in for a shockingly tight hug. "Thank you so much, Blaire. I really owe you big time. I always enjoy seeing you, even when you're tearing me a new one. I gotta run. Thank you. A million times over." And he's off.

"You're welcome," I mutter and head back to B&B to start on the icing for today's cupcakes.

Forty-five minutes later the delivery truck shows up. I'm in the middle of a particularly tricky caramel filling and Paul is on his way out so he accepts the delivery—which I ask him to sign for—and makes sure it's safely in the fridge before he takes off.

@buttercreamandbooze:

If life gives you lemons, add tequila and salt.

chapter nine

NOT THE PAYBACK I WAS LOOKING FOR

Blaire

Even though B&B isn't open on Thanksgiving, I still head into the shop first thing in the morning. I need to frost the cupcakes for my family's dinner and all my supplies are there. Plus I want to drop off yesterday's unsold goods at the local soup kitchen, along with any other treats that won't be fresh by tomorrow. Usually one of their staff comes to pick them up, but they couldn't make it yesterday and I figured it was easier for me to do the dropping off on the way out of town.

I'm surprised to see Ronan in the back alley outside The Knight Cap. He usually isn't in until sometime after ten, and it's barely eight thirty. He's pacing as he talks on the phone, his tone clipped and annoyed. He's not wearing his usual plaid-and-jeans uniform, either. Today he's in a pair of gray sweats and a hoodie, his hair is a mess, again, and he has a serious five-o'clock shadow going on. He's wearing his glasses, like he rolled out of bed and came straight here. Amazingly, he still manages to look delicious.

"Well what the hell am I supposed to do now?" He spins around and stalks back into The Knight Cap.

Looks like it's his turn to be in a mood.

I'm about to go back inside, but a tired-looking Lars steps out and sags against the wall, cringing when Ronan's loud, angry voice filters through the gap in the door.

"What's going on?"

He startles and holds his finger to his lips. "I'm hiding."

"Why are you here this early?"

"Because I was supposed to help with food prep and get double pay today, but it looks like that's not happening."

Ronan comes busting out into the back alley again and the door nearly hits Lars in the face, but his reaction time is at least decent, because he manages to get out of the way before the steel connects with his nose.

"What the fuck am I going to do?" Ronan grabs his hair and kicks the giant metal trash bin.

I've never seen Ronan anything but calm. "Are you okay?" I ask, even though it's very obvious that he's definitely not okay.

"No!" He throws his hands in the air. "I'm not fucking okay!"

"Is there anything I can do to help?"

"Unless you can magically thaw twenty-five damn Cornish game hens in the next three hours, then no."

A sinking feeling hits me. I let Paul sign for the order

yesterday and then I got busy with customers. It was nonstop all day. "Oh my God. Is this my fault? Did they go in the freezer instead of the fridge?"

Ronan's brow furrows. "What? No. The freaking company I ordered from messed it up. I ordered fresh Cornish game hens and they brought me frozen ones and a bunch of cans of damn pie filling instead of pie."

"Oh no! I hope they're giving you your money back." I can't even imagine what it would do to my bank account if something like that happened to me.

"Yeah, but that's not going to help me tonight. Now all I have to serve for Thanksgiving is potatoes, stuffing, and freaking vegetables."

He paces the alley, hands still in his hair. I try not to ogle his tattoos, or the way his jogging pants do a great job of hugging his butt, but it's a challenge.

"What if we put them in a cold water bath?" I suggest.

"They're rock solid. It'll take at least six hours and then we'd still have to prep and cook them. I spent eleven damn hours in a car yesterday so I could be open on Thanksgiving and this is what I get. I should've checked last night." He scrubs his face with both hands. "Lars, you might as well go home. Enjoy the day off."

"We could do wings or something," he offers.

"It's Thanksgiving. People don't want wings. They want a proper dinner, and we don't have one. We don't even have a dessert to serve. There just really isn't a point."

"Sorry, Ronan. I know you had big plans for today."

He waves him off. "It's fine. It's not your fault."

"I guess I'll see you tomorrow?" Lars takes a step toward the door.

"Yeah. Thanks for coming in early. I know you'd rather be sleeping."

Lars leaves and Ronan slips his hands in his pockets and drops his head with a sigh.

I feel awful for him. Thanksgiving can be a good opportunity to make money, if you have the food to serve. "Do you need any help with anything?"

He rubs the back of his neck. "Nah. Guess I'm gonna sit on the couch and watch football today."

"Why don't you come over and I'll make you a boozy coffee." I incline my head toward B&B. It's really the least I can do.

He blows out a breath. "Yeah, sure. Why not? It's not like I have anything better to do."

I'd be offended, but I don't think it's a personal attack, more that he's upset about the sudden and unexpected crappy turn his day took.

I make us both special lattes, his spiked with booze, mine not since I have some baking to do. "I need to frost some cupcakes. If you're interested in hanging around, you can be my taste tester."

"Uh sure, yeah. I could do that."

I lead him to the kitchen and set him up with a stool.

I pull the naked cupcakes from the fridge so they have time to warm up, don a hairnet—hygiene before vanity—wash my hands and slip out of my heels and into a pair of flats before I get the rest of the ingredients out.

"Do you need any help?"

"Nope. You're good to just hang out and drink coffee. I'm sorry about the delivery. We had a busy day yesterday and I let Paul accept it. I didn't even check what it was."

"It wouldn't have mattered. I didn't tell you what was supposed to be delivered and I should've checked everything last night, but that drive was hell. There was an accident on the way back and it took seven hours instead of four, which is already long enough, you know? I just didn't plan this as well as I should have. Rookie mistake, I guess."

"You can always do a post-Thanksgiving dinner this week-end, can't you? Maybe on Saturday you can do a Cornish game hen special?" I tie my apron and set up the industrial mixer so I can work on the buttercream.

"That's what I'll have to do. They've already been in the fridge overnight. I'm hoping by tomorrow afternoon they'll be thawed and then the kitchen staff can prep and cook them."

"At the very least you'll be able to thaw them the rest of the way in a water bath, won't you?"

"Mmm. Yeah." He watches me measure ingredients, turn on the mixer and set the timer before I move to a smaller one to prepare the chocolate buttercream for the triple chocolate cupcakes. My dad put in a special request for those. He put in several special requests. Sometimes it's hard to understand why he just won't let me live my dream when it's so clear I know what I'm doing.

"I can't believe you're wearing a dress and working with chocolate."

"I do everything in a dress."

One of his eyebrows lifts.

"Almost everything," I amend. I don't know why my mind immediately goes to sex on account of his eyebrow raise. Possibly because Ronan's hair is sticking out all over the place like he's just been screwed? Or because he looks half–book nerd and half badass with the glasses, sweats, and full sleeves. Or because I haven't had it in forever.

I'll go with the last one.

I stick my head in the fridge and take far longer than necessary to retrieve the milk so he can't see my embarrassment.

"Do you ever wear pants?"

"Not often."

"What about when you're at home?"

"I still prefer dresses most of the time. I mean, of course I have things like leggings for when it gets cold, but this is how I'm most comfortable." I push up on my toes to try to reach the container of icing sugar. I don't know why Paul insists on putting it up this high all the time. Probably because he gets a chuckle out of it.

"Why?"

I look over my shoulder. "Why did you cover your arms in tattoos?"

"Because I want to wear my memories, see them every day and remember." It seems a lot like an unfinished sentence. He hops off his stool, plucks the canister from the shelf and hands it to me. "You still haven't answered my question. Why are you more comfortable in dresses than pants? You have killer calves, and the waist up is easy on the eyes. I gotta imagine whatever you're hiding under those skirts matches the rest of you."

I give him a sideways look. "Is that a compliment?"

"It's an observation, and if you'd like to take it as a compliment, feel free."

I laugh. "This is my style." There's actually a lot more to it than just being my style, but it's not really something I tend to share with people, let alone a rival bar owner who barely tolerates me and is probably humoring me. "Just like plaid shirts and black rimmed glasses and sleeve tattoos are yours."

"I'm going to say something, and I don't want you to take offense to it."

"Does that mean it's going to be offensive?"

Ronan chuckles. "I think it could be misconstrued as an insult when that's not how I intend it."

"Go ahead then." I check on the icing and start measuring out the ingredients for the chocolate buttercream.

"You give off this classy pinup girl vibe crossed with a fifties housewife, but you're an entrepreneur. It's sort of a contradiction, isn't it? And here you are, all dressed up at nine in the morning, making me coffee and whipping up buttercream icing."

"I made you coffee because you looked like you needed a break and a shot. And do you mean to say I don't look like I should be taken seriously because I'm not wearing a pantsuit?"

"That's not what I said."

"Sometimes it's good to be underestimated, don't you think?" I set another timer for seven minutes while I let the butter cream.

"I don't think it's about underestimating you. I mean, clearly you have vision and business savvy, but you don't come across as . . . threatening, I guess."

"Sort of goes hand in hand with being underestimated." I dip a spoon into the chocolate ganache and hand it to him, before I do the same for myself. My sample is much smaller than his. I wait until he's done groaning his way through the spoonful before I ask another question. "So tell me about The Knight Cap. Your grandfather owns it and you decided to come work with him? Or take it over?"

"He lost my grams a little over a year ago; they worked here together since they were teenagers, so doing it without her was . . . hard. That's what all the framed couple pictures are about on the wall opposite the booths. It's the story of their life together, which was spent at the bar for the most part."

I press my hand to my chest. "Did they meet there?"

"They did." He nods, his eyes suddenly far away. "The bar has been in our family for three generations. Gramps bartended and Grams was a waitress. Fell head over heels in love with each other. Caused a big ruckus since she was a few years younger than him and her parents were hoping she'd marry up, but no one and nothing could keep them apart." He smiles softly; it's full of fondness and sadness. "They even dated in secret for a while. Lots of backroom and closet stories, I'm sure. Not that Gramps would ever disrespect Grams by telling any of them."

I laugh and then sigh. "Did she get sick?"

"Uh no, she was healthy all the way to the end, thankfully. She had a heart attack and passed in her sleep." He flips his spoon absently between his fingers.

The timer on the vanilla buttercream goes off, and I slow down the speed so I can add the sugar and vanilla. "Your poor grandpa. Was he with her?"

"Yeah. It was rough there for a bit and running this place on his own was just too much, so things kind of slipped. I was working in finance and hating it, so Gramps gave me an opportunity I couldn't refuse."

"Which was to bring this place back to life?" I supply.

"Yeah. He said if I could run it successfully for a year he'd loan me the money to start up my own brewery, which is something I've always wanted to do, but banks aren't all that excited about giving you money for that kind of thing when you don't have the entrepreneurial experience behind you."

"Don't I know it. It took me three years before the bank would give me a freaking loan for this place."

"What'd you do before you set up shop here?"

"I had a cupcake truck."

"Seriously?" He looks like he wants to laugh.

"Don't knock it. I started out with tents at food festivals and then weekend market booths until eventually I had a pretty decent following. When I saved up enough I invested in a truck."

"And you did that on your own?"

"Paul helped, actually."

"What's the deal with you two?" He gives me a curious look.

"He's a friend, and he helped me get started. We worked together for almost five years."

"And that's all you've ever been? Friends?"

"Yup. We were good at being in business together, and even that had its limitations. But I learned a lot from him and he was a great mentor."

"He never tried for more?" Ronan presses.

"Nope. Selling cupcakes out of a truck puts you in seriously close quarters with another person. He's seen all my sides, the good, the bad, and terrifying. Besides, getting in bed with a coworker or colleague is a recipe for disaster. Pun completely intended."

He laughs and shakes his head. "Yeah, can't imagine it's a great idea for a lot of reasons, although my gramps would likely disagree."

"Those were different times, weren't they?"

"Less complicated in a lot of ways, and yet more at the same time." Ronan nods.

Twenty minutes later, I have batches of icing ready for decorating.

Ronan is practically drooling as he watches me put it in piping bags, so I get out a bunch of spoons and bowls and let him sample a bit of each as I decorate the cupcakes for dinner.

"I thought you weren't opening up today."

"I'm not." I pipe chocolate mocha buttercream on the triple chocolate cupcake. "These are for my family dinner." Although, half my family will probably make the sign of the cross at them. My mom and sisters are huge keto fans. The easy conversation shifts into that slightly awkward *what-now* limbo. "Do you usually spend Thanksgiving with your gramps?"

"Typically he was always here for Thanksgiving. Grams really loved the holiday and always wanted to make sure people who didn't have family to celebrate with could go somewhere and have a nice dinner, which is why I ordered all the Cornish game hens. It's been hard for Gramps to be here without her, though, so I told him I'd run things today. He went to my brother's place. He's staying there for a few days and won't be back until Sunday sometime. You're going to spend the day with your parents?"

"Yup. I haven't seen them since I opened this place, so I'm due for a visit." Before I can really consider what I'm saying I blurt, "You should come with me."

Ronan's eyebrows lift. "To your family Thanksgiving?"

"Yeah. Yes." I nod slightly more vigorously than necessary.

"You can't spend the holiday alone. My parents always make a huge production of it. You need to stuff yourself with turkey and beer. It'll be fun!" I'm not sure that *fun* is really the best description for my family events, but it's too late to take it back now.

"I don't know. I should probably plan for `the rest of the weekend," Ronan says slowly.

"You already have a plan, a post-Thanksgiving dinner. Come with me. No one should be alone during the holidays."

He grins. "You're sure?"

"Absolutely positive."

"Can I sample the cupcakes before we go?"

"Of course." The eye roll and the *duh* are implied in my tone.

"Okay. I'm in."

"Fabulous!"

What the hell have I just gotten myself into?

@buttercreamandbooze:

I'm just a cupcake, looking for my stud muffin.

♡ ✉ ✎   ☆

chapter ten

TURKEY TIME

Ronan

I'm not sure how to read Blaire's reaction to my saying yes.

If I'm completely honest, the cupcakes are the clincher. They're dangerously addictive. Like nicotine, or heroin, or cocaine—none of which has ever been an addiction of mine. Hence the reason I hastily agreed to spend an entire day with Blaire and her family when I know very little about her.

If nothing else, this should prove to be an entertaining day. Blaire is...a lot of personality. And I don't mean that in a bad way. I'm still trying to figure her out and I guess now I'll have the opportunity to do that.

I put a note on the front door of The Knight Cap apologizing for the closure today, and indicating we'll be open again tomorrow, which is when I notice a sign on the empty building across the street. "Is that new?" I ask Blaire. She's busy inspecting all the framed photos of my grandparents that line the wall opposite the booths. I'm sure they have new meaning for her now that she knows the story behind them.

"Hmm?" She drags her gaze away from a black-and-white photo of Gramps and Grams when they were young—younger than I am now.

I point across the street. "Looks like someone finally leased that place. I wonder what's opening there."

She crosses over to where I'm standing. "It's a big building. Wasn't it a law office before or something?"

"I think so, yeah?" It's changed hands a number of times over the years.

"So it's probably something similar, which will be good for both of us." She tips her chin up and looks at me. "More business professionals to cater to."

"Let's hope that's what it is, then." More patrons means The Knight Cap has even greater potential to do well.

"Should I follow you back to your place so you can change, and then we can head to my parents' place?"

I look down at my old white T-shirt and my sweats. "Probably a good idea. Not sure sweats are appropriate for much other than the gym and lazy days at home."

Blaire takes down my address so she can follow me to my place. It's not far from the pub. Making her wait in the car is rude, so I invite her up to my apartment.

It feels weird to have her in my personal space. Although, honestly, the only thing I do here lately is sleep.

"Wow. I don't think it gets more man cave than this," Blaire says as she takes in my loft apartment. It's not huge, but it's comfortable.

"It's just me." I'm not sure if I should be defensive about her assessment or not.

"I can see that." She runs her fingertips along the edge of the distressed wood table I rarely use. I'm not here enough to entertain, and eating dinner alone at a table meant for six is kind of depressing. Mostly I eat at the bar, or on rare occasions when I'm not in a rush, in front of the TV.

"Let me guess: Your place looks like a unicorn vomited a rainbow of happiness all over it?" Mostly I'm poking fun at her.

She laughs. "You would be guessing wrong."

"So you don't have eleven million throw cushions with inspirational phrases on them?" I toe off my shoes and toss them by the door.

"Ahh, just ten million or so, and only a few have cute unicorns farting inspirational phrases." The way she rolls her shoulder back and her narrow-eyed glare tells me everything I need to know.

I've totally hit a nerve. I don't know why I enjoy needling her as much as I do. Maybe because she's so prone to reacting. "I bet your place is decorated for the holiday. All sorts of cute pumpkin stuff everywhere, a papier-mâché turkey centerpiece that you made at some workshop on your dining room table."

Her cheeks flush pink. "I don't have a dining room table."

"But you have a papier-mâché turkey?"

"I had several construction paper ones when I was a child. I probably would have kept them for all eternity if my parents hadn't thrown out my box of homemade crafts when I was a teenager in the name of decluttering."

I file that little piece of information away, feeling like she's told me a secret she didn't intend to. "Pumpkin, then?" I press.

I can tell it irritates her that I can read her so easily, but all anyone has to do is step foot inside Buttercream and Booze to see how much she loves the holidays. "Ceramic, not papier-mâché."

"And you painted it yourself?"

"Maybe." She pokes me in the shoulder. "Enough with all the questions. It's an hour and a half drive; you'll have loads of time trapped in a car to make fun of me."

"Right. Yeah." I'm not sure what a long ride in a car together is going to be like. "I'll just change real quick. Can I get you something to drink while you wait?"

"I'm fine, thanks."

I leave her to wander around my apartment while I change. She doesn't seem the type to snoop, but you never know. Considering Blaire is wearing one of her dresses complete with festive holiday print, I decide a pair of black casual pants, dress shirt, and plaid tie are appropriate. I don't bother with contacts since my eyes already feel gritty from lack of sleep.

I find her in my living room, staring up at a collage of family photos. "Ready to roll?"

She turns her head slowly, her expression soft. "I'm so

sorry." She reaches up and adjusts the wooden picture frame, and suddenly her apology makes sense. That was the last family photo we took, and the phrase "In loving memory" is etched into the matte in silver letters.

It's never level, always listing to the right because the frame itself is unbalanced. I refuse to change it, though, because it was one of my first woodshop projects, and my dad and I worked on it together. It's old and cracked and a whole lot ugly, but it's a memory I can't let go of. I nod and swallow around the lump in my throat. "Oh, uh, thanks. It was a long time ago." But on days like this it feels like it was yesterday, not a decade ago, that they passed.

"How old were you when you lost them?" She presses her hand to her chest. "You don't have to answer that if it's not something you want to talk about."

"It's okay." I jam my hands in my pockets and clear my throat again as I step up beside her. "I was twenty."

She blows out a slow, tremulous breath, her smile sad. "That must have been so hard. It looks like you were close."

"We were a tight family. My brothers are both older, so they were more settled, with careers and partners. It shook us all up pretty good. I ended up living with my gramps and grams for a couple of years after they passed."

She nods, putting together the pieces of the puzzle, like why I took over The Knight Cap and why I kept all the pictures of him and Grams up.

"I'm sorry you're not with your family today."

"I'm used to celebrating after the fact." If my brother's place wasn't so far away I might have made the effort to drive out there again today. But after spending all day yesterday taking Gramps up there and coming back, I just don't have the energy. And sometimes the family stuff is harder on days like today, especially since my brothers are in committed relationships, and everyone gets on me for being alone. I force a smile and change the subject. "We should probably hit the road, huh?"

She gives her head a slight shake, as if she's been lost in her own thoughts. "Oh yes. Definitely." She squeezes my forearm gently. "Endless food awaits."

Blaire wasn't lying about her love of the movie *Grease*. The soundtrack is saved as a playlist. Apparently she's a huge fan of movie and musical soundtracks.

"Feel free to change it to whatever you like. I know this isn't everyone's cup of tea." She motions to the stereo system.

Blaire drives a midsized SUV that has a pretty prominent rattle in the engine. It also boasts a Buttercream and Booze magnetic sign on both the driver and passenger side doors. The engine rattle makes me wonder what kind of restaurant background she comes from and how much her family has struggled to make a living at it.

"You said your family is in the restaurant industry, right?" I ask, making small talk.

"Yup, they are." Blaire taps the steering wheel, like she's drumming to the beat of the song.

"So why don't you work with them? Why go out on your

own?" Clearly they're at least somewhat close if she's willing to drive an hour and a half for dinner.

"They're more steak and lobster, and that isn't where my passion lies," she replies. "They like to hobnob, and I like . . . not to."

There's clearly more to that story, but I don't know if I should push it too much since despite all our interactions— which have been mostly Blaire being pissed off at me for something—I'm not sure we're at a place where she feels comfortable sharing too much personal information. Although I'm attending Thanksgiving dinner with her family, in part because it was better than being alone, and also because I'm curious about Blaire. It's a bit of a strange situation all the way around. "Do you want to expand on that?"

She grips and releases the steering wheel, blowing out a breath. "My family is a little . . . odd."

Considering Blaire dresses like she's June Cleaver's pinup-worthy sister I can't say I'm all that surprised. "Aren't all families odd?"

"Mine more than most, I think. They're all very Type A and concerned about money and being the best. And of course I want to be the best, too, but on my own merit and not theirs. I could've worked my way up the ladder in one of their restaurants, but I love baking, and that was never going to fly with them, so I went out on my own instead." She signals right and takes the next exit off the freeway. "They're also kind of insane, and I spent the first twenty-five years of my life dealing with it on a daily basis. I figured I deserved some separation from that."

"That's fair. I love my brothers, but they drive me nuts on a good day. We worked for the same company for a while, but they ended up going out on their own and I don't know that I could ever really work for them." Which was part of the reason I went in a different direction. They wanted the three of us to go into business together and I already didn't love the job.

"Mmm. Family businesses can be tough. It would be a lot easier financially if I went in the direction they wanted me to. They'd love to have me as their pastry chef, designing intricate, elaborate creations that would get them written up by all the highbrow foodie bloggers. But that's not my style. I'd rather struggle to make ends meet for a while than give up my own dream."

"I can't imagine how intense it must be doing it all on your own." It makes me even more grateful for Gramps's support.

"The first couple of years are always hard, but I'm hoping in the end it'll pay off. Someday I'll be able to get more than five hours of sleep a night and my diet won't consist mostly of leftover cupcakes and almost-expired sandwiches."

"Because you don't have time to cook?"

She lifts a shoulder. "Everything I have is tied up in Buttercream and Booze so if the money's already spent on the food, then I might as well eat it rather than buy groceries that are going to rot in my fridge because I'm never home."

"Do you remember the last time you had a lazy Saturday?" I ask.

"Nope." Blaire raises her finger in the air. "Wait. I had the flu two years ago and had to take a Saturday off because of it."

"I don't think that counts as a lazy day." This conversation makes me highly aware of just how hard Blaire has to work to get where she is. It explains why she was so hostile the first time I met her.

Blaire turns down a country road and the distance between houses increases. The farther we get from the freeway, the antsier Blaire becomes. She stops asking questions and her answers grow shorter, more clipped. She starts to nibble on her bottom lip, eyes darting to me and away every so often.

"Having second thoughts?" I'm kind of joking, kind of not. We don't know each other all that well and while I find myself strangely attracted to her, I'm not sure if it's completely one-sided or not. I believe the invite was more her feeling bad for me, but there's also been more than one interaction that's included thinly veiled innuendo and what seems like flirting.

"No. Not really. I mean—" She cringes. "I should probably warn you; my family is a bit . . . unconventional."

"Unconventional how?" Maybe they're circus-performing restaurateurs.

Blaire slows the SUV and makes a careful right. She stops at the gated entrance. For the first time I notice the eight-foot wrought-iron fence that stretches out on both sides into the distance. It's surrounded by forest. Maybe they're part of a commune. Or a cult. I sincerely hope I make it out of this alive.

Blaire punches in a code and the gate opens slowly. She clutches the steering wheel until her knuckles turn white as we make our way down the narrow tree-lined driveway.

"Holy crap," I mutter when the house comes into view. Because it's not a house. It's a goddamn palace. A seriously eccentric, gaudy as hell, gothic and creepy palace. Okay, that's a bit of an exaggeration, but based on the vehicle Blaire drives, the knowledge that she had a freaking cupcake *truck*, and the cheap rent she must pay for Buttercream and Booze, I'm a little shocked. This doesn't really add up. "Your family lives here?" Maybe they're the help and we'll be eating in the servant quarters. Or we'll have to actually serve dinner before we get to eat it.

"Yup." Blaire nods stiffly.

No fewer than three Bentleys are parked in the driveway. There's also a black Ferrari and some obscure European sports car I can't identify. That's almost three million dollars in cars parked out front.

"Am I underdressed?" I feel like a tux would've been more appropriate.

She waves a nervous hand around in the air and smiles almost manically. "Oh no. You're perfect. It's really anything goes."

She parks her crappy SUV, leaving lots of space between it and one of the six-figure cars, and practically throws herself out of the vehicle. She pops the hatch and I help her carry the boxes of cupcakes up the massive staircase—I'm almost out of breath by the time we get to the top.

She shifts her hold on the boxes, which makes me nervous since she seems shaky and more high-strung than usual all of a sudden. I don't want any cupcake casualties. Although if they're ruined they can't be served and then I could bring them home and eat them all.

She punches in a code and the doors open on their own. Andddd…it only gets weirder. Two statues take up the space on either side of the massive entrance. They're naked butlers, and their butler trays are not held up by their hands. More naked statues function as the banisters on the winding staircase with a tacky gold inlay. It's like a Greek mythology museum, a medieval knight, and bad porn slammed into each other, and the result is this strange mash-up. Blaire places the boxes of cupcakes on one of the naked butlers' trays. She tips her head toward the ceiling and murmurs something I don't catch, then takes a deep breath. She smiles stiffly and gives my arm a squeeze. I'm not sure if it's meant to be reassuring for her or me. Or both.

"Hello! I'm here! And I brought a friend with me!" Blaire shouts, her voice echoing off the ceiling of the cavernous open foyer. A butler—*an actual fucking butler*, dressed in one of those suits with the long tails—appears out of thin air. "Miss Blaire, it's wonderful to have you home today."

"Buster, it's so lovely to see you."

Buster the butler. Classic. I wonder if it's his real name or if they changed it for the alliteration.

He lifts the lid and peeks inside one of the boxes resting on the naked butler statue tray. "Oh! All of my favorites, Miss Blaire. You've outdone yourself."

"One of those boxes is for you and the staff. You might want to hide it so the cupcakes don't all disappear before dinner." She takes the smaller box I'm still holding. "And these are for you to take home."

"You're too good to me." His smile is fond and warm.

She winks. "Not nearly good enough, considering what you put up with on a regular basis."

He laughs. "It's like living on the set of one of Margaret's soap operas." He nods to me. "Welcome to the Calloway house, Mr. . . . ."

"Oh, this is my friend, Ronan. All his birds were frozen so I brought him along for dinner." She pats my arm.

The weird phrasing doesn't seem to faze Buster. "Well, keep an eye on him in this house." He winks and strides off.

I'm about to ask her what that means, and why the hell she drives an old SUV when it appears her family has enough money to buy a medium-sized country, but she takes a deep breath and squares her shoulders. "I should mention that my parents are divorced but still friendly with each other."

"So they'll both be here?" I'm starting to wonder what I've gotten myself into.

"Yes, and they're both remarried—"

"Care Blaire! You finally made it! Cocktail hour started at

noon!" A woman crosses the expansive, marble foyer. Based on her features, she's most definitely Blaire's mother. Although Blaire is softer around the edges with Marilyn Monroe curves, and her mother looks more like an aging Twiggy. She's also wearing a short, tight and sparkly dress more appropriate for a nightclub. "Oh! I didn't know you were bringing a date! Lawrence, Blaire brought a date!" she calls over her shoulder.

"I'm sorry that you're trapped here with me now. I promise the booze and food will make it worth it," Blaire mutters before her mother pulls her into one of those loose, fake hugs and air kisses both of her cheeks.

Her mother grabs her by the shoulders. "You look tired. I think you're probably working too much. Have you gained weight? I have a great juice detox that will shed some of that baby fat like—" She snaps her fingers beside Blaire's ear, making her jump.

"Mom, I'm almost thirty. The baby fat is here to stay."

"It's all the carbs, honey."

"I like carbs more than I like food deprivation. Anyway, Mom, this is Ronan." She motions to me. "Ronan, this is my mother—"

"—Glinda. Like the good witch from *The Wizard of Oz*." Her hand shoots out. "Enchanted, I'm sure. And I'm sorry for my terrible manners, but we haven't seen our Care Blaire since the summer. So much catching up to do! How long have you two been dating?"

"He's a friend, Mom. We're not dating."

"Yet?" she asks, hopefully. "When was the last time you had a boyfriend, darling?"

"Not since Maddy stole the last one," Blaire replies.

"They were better suited for each other." Glinda gives her a patronizing look before she turns her attention back to me and looks me over as if I'm an accessory she's unsure of. "Where did you meet my Care Blaire?"

"I own the bar next door to Buttercream and Booze."

"Next door to what?" Glinda looks confused.

"My café," Blaire mumbles.

"Oh!" Glinda claps her bony hands. "So you're the rival! How fun that you're here."

I glance at Blaire, whose lips are pursed. "Thank you for that, Mom."

"I don't know if I'd call us rivals. I serve beer and wings, and Blaire serves the most delicious cupcakes in the universe." I'm not trying to suck up to her mother, but I am sort of sucking up to Blaire. Mostly because I have a feeling that her relationship with her family is complicated. Her mother has basically called her fat and chastised her on her dating habits. In front of me.

I wonder if Blaire invited me so I'd be a distraction of some kind. Or a shield.

"Hmm, she is quite adept with the buttercream and a spatula." She pinches Blaire's side. "As is evidenced by all the taste testing we must be doing."

A man who looks like Hugh Hefner from two decades ago appears in the foyer. He's wearing a velvet smoking jacket, burgundy silk pants, and black slippers. He's also holding an unlit cigar. "Blaire! We were wondering when you were going to arrive."

"Hi, Uncle Lawrence."

He glides across the room and does the same air-kiss thing as her mother did before he shakes my hand.

"We didn't realize Blaire was bringing a date."

"He's a friend, not a date," Blaire corrects.

"Well, you're introducing him to the family so that must mean you're interested in turning him into your date." He turns to Glinda. "Doesn't it, darling?"

"I would agree, but maybe Care Blaire would prefer to keep that little detail to herself in case Skylar gets an idea to steal him away."

"I guess that means my cousin made it back from San Francisco for dinner tonight." Blaire smiles tightly.

"You know how she hates missing family events," Lawrence says.

I can't tell if they're joking. Or what's going on, because Blaire's mom is now caressing Lawrence's arm in a way that seems overly friendly for someone who's either supposed to be her brother or her brother-in-law. This whole thing is hella confusing and eye-opening.

"I thought I heard your voice! How's my baby girl?" A balding, potbellied man wearing a white linen suit ambles into the room. He looks more like he's ready for bed than for a Thanksgiving dinner party.

"Hey, Dad!" A huge smile breaks across her face and she opens her arms, wrapping them around his expansive belly.

He kisses her on top of the head and his gaze shifts to me. "You brought a date?"

"She's telling everyone he's just a friend," Glinda supplies.

"Because she doesn't want Skylar to try to steal him," Lawrence adds.

"It doesn't have anything to do with Skylar." Blaire tries to defend herself, but is interrupted by yet another woman.

"Care Blaire! Please tell me you brought your cupcakes! Gran-Gran has been asking about them all afternoon!"

"Hi, Aunt Nora. I certainly did." And we go through another round of introductions.

I'm once again confused when Blaire's aunt moves in beside her dad and pats his belly. I can see the physical resemblance between Nora and Glinda, which I'm assuming means they're sisters. Either that or they are uncannily similar.

We're ushered through a massive sitting room, and into the kitchen where everyone dons an apron and returns to whatever station they were at before we arrived. It smells amazing, and the kitchen is insane. It looks like a very high-end restaurant kitchen merged with more gaudy glitz and glamour. Now I need to know what restaurants they actually own, because I'm thinking they must be pretty damn successful if this is their pad.

The sound of mixing, stirring, and chopping is accompanied

by orders being given, and in the middle of all of this they're also trying to carry on an actual conversation. It's impossible to follow.

Blaire opens a door and searches through the aprons hanging from a hook until she finds the one she wants. She hugs it to her chest before she pulls it over her head and reaches behind her to tie it.

"I can help with that." I step up and brush her hands out of the way.

She jumps at the contact. "Oh, thanks." She picks out a black apron and hands it to me, returning the favor. She slips her arm through mine, and tugs so I bend until her lips are at my ear. "I meant to tell you before you met them, but my mom is married to my uncle and my aunt is married to my dad."

I turn my head to see whether she's kidding, because that is some next-level fucked-up shit, but don't take into account how close our faces are, so the end of my nose brushes hers.

"Ah ha!" Someone shouts, startling the hell out of us. "I knew it! You were kissing! Ronan *is* your date."

Blaire drops my arm and takes one excessively large step away from me. "We weren't kissing. I was bringing him up to speed on the family dynamic."

Aunt Nora claps gleefully. "I saw it with my own eyes."

"Then you need new glasses," Blaire grumbles.

The accidental nose brush incites a ridiculous slew of questions, beginning with how long we've been secretly dating, how we met, and whether I've ever been incarcerated. In the very short time I've been here, I come to the conclusion that Blaire's family is entertaining, but definitely a whole bag of WTF with a side of *this reminds me of a bad reality show*.

Another woman who looks to be a couple of years younger than Blaire glides into the room, a well-dressed man lagging behind her. Everyone looks like they're ready to attend some kind of formal event, apart from her uncle in his Hugh Hefner getup and her dad in his pajama suit.

"Care Blaire! Yay!" She waves her arms in the air like the inflatable balloon guy while she shuffle-runs across the room in her extra high heels and throws her arms around Blaire. She's at least four inches taller and looks like her last good meal was probably five years ago. I don't understand how people who cook food that smells this delicious can be that thin. She does the same thing Blaire's mother did and holds her at arm's length. "This dress is so cute! Have you gained some weight?"

"At least thirty pounds," Blaire deadpans. "Madeline, this is my friend Ronan. Ronan, this is my younger, more attractive and thinner sister, Madeline."

"You can call me Maddy." She giggles, gives me a simpering look, bats her lashes, and holds out her hand.

I shake it, because it's rude not to, and bite my tongue, because all I want to do is defend Blaire and give her hell for not doing it herself when I know for a fact that she's got bigger balls than most men I know.

A tall, somewhat wiry guy slings his arm over Maddy's shoulder and extends his free hand. "I'm Matthew, Maddy's husband."

"Ronan."

He's still shaking my hand, but he's not looking at me. His eyes are on Blaire, and the way he's looking at her seems really inappropriate. "Ballsy move, bringing a date with Skylar on the rebound."

She rolls her eyes. "Skylar is always on the rebound."

Maddy chuckles and claps her hands together. "This is going to be so much fun!"

As if on cue, another very thin woman enters the kitchen, wearing a club-appropriate minidress and holding a half-empty martini glass. Her gaze hones in on Blaire and a slightly evil smile tips up the corner of her mouth.

"Care Blaire!" Her voice is high-pitched, like nails on a chalkboard. She saunters over, the sway of her hips highly exaggerated as she crosses the room. Instead of taking the most direct route to Blaire, which would be to go around Maddy, she slides her chest along Matthew's bicep, gives me a very blatant once-over, and then air kisses Blaire's cheeks. "Your dress is so cute! It makes your waist look so narrow!"

Sweet baby Jesus riding a skateboard down a freeway without a helmet, Blaire's family is a bunch of assholes.

"And your dress makes you look like you belong in the red light district," Blaire says through gritted teeth and a brittle smile.

"That's exactly where I got it!" She turns to me. "And who might your delicious friend be?"

Blaire introduces me tonelessly to Skylar, the cousin on the rebound everyone seems to think is going to try to steal me. Based on the way she presses her entire body against mine and kisses me on both cheeks, I'm inclined to believe it wasn't a joke.

The last person I'm introduced to is Blaire's Gran-Gran. I'm relieved when all she does is shake my hand and tell Blaire she's so happy she could make it for dinner and that they need to schedule a proper lunch date so she can whup Blaire's ass at gin rummy—those are her exact words.

I'm offered a drink and Blaire mutters that I should definitely take it, even though she declines the alcohol, citing that she'll have to drive home later.

"You two can always stay the night." Skylar dons an apron, grabs me by the arm, leads me over to the kitchen island, and pushes me onto one of the high-back stools. "Let's all get to know each other!" She picks up a knife and starts chopping carrots into thin discs without even looking at what she's doing.

"How's your little bakeshop doing, Blaire?" her uncle asks as he stirs some kind of sauce. Blaire is drinking ginger ale and whisking something in a bowl—at least two people suggested sparkling water or a diet variety of soda. I want to punch everyone in the room out, apart from Gran-Gran, who hasn't said anything mean. Yet.

"My little bakeshop is doing fine, thanks for asking."

I glance over at her—she's standing on my right, keeping an eye on Skylar, whose arm keeps bumping mine she's so freaking close.

"It's actually doing amazing," I interject.

I stretch my arm across the back of the stool and angle my body toward Blaire and away from Skylar. Whatever the reason I'm here—whether as a distraction for her crazy-ass family or because she honestly felt bad that my day was shot and I would be spending Thanksgiving alone—I decide I'm going to play the role of the boyfriend everyone thinks I am tonight, if for no other reason than to keep Skylar from humping my leg while her family watches.

"Awww, isn't that so lovely to hear." Her mother's tone is patronizing at best. "Well, you know that there's always a place for you back here if you get tired of the grueling hours. It must be hard to make a living on five-dollar cupcakes."

"People buy them by the dozen. You've all been by to see it, haven't you?" I ask, which gets me a swift elbow to the ribs.

"Oh no, Blaire made it seem like it wasn't a trip we needed to make with our busy schedules." Her mother smiles, but I can't quite read the emotion behind it. Indulgent? Hurt? Accusatory?

"Really, Blaire?" I can't bring myself to add Care in front of it. It's the worst fucking nickname in the history of the universe. It's condescending and it doesn't fit her at all. Alice, which is terrible in its own right considering the implications, is still a million times better. "I can't believe you haven't invited your family down for the full Buttercream and Booze experience."

"They're busy," she says through clenched teeth.

I should probably back off, but I'm pretty pissed off at how little regard her family seems to have for her and what she's accomplished, apparently all on her own. I also don't like that the strong, in your face, demanding, combative woman who I thoroughly enjoy riling up is just...taking their shit.

I reach out and pull Blaire into my side and make a show of pressing my lips to her temple. Neither of us expects the static-like shock that accompanies what should be a very innocent display of affection—were we actually dating. She grabs my thigh and I breathe "Sorry" in her ear.

Even though I'm not. And that becomes even more obvious when I say, "But not too busy to celebrate their daughter's accomplishments."

"Of course not," her father jumps in, sending a hard look my way. "We didn't want to push ourselves on Blaire. She has her own way of doing things and we don't want to step on her toes."

Gran-Gran Calloway, who reminds me of a younger Betty White during the *Golden Girls* era and is clearly senile, jumps into the conversation to ask when Blaire's due. I decide I need a break from the crazy before I tell someone off on Blaire's behalf.

"Sweetheart, can you show me where the bathroom is?"

"I can show you!" Skylar's knife clatters on the counter and she grabs my free arm.

I don't even look in Skylar's direction when I respond. "Thanks, but Blaire can take care of me." Yes, I mean for it to sound 100 percent suggestive.

I stand up and extend my hand. Blaire has no choice but to take it, unless she wants to make more of a scene. She leads me out of the kitchen, down a hallway, passing three doors before she finally stops. I push it open and take the opportunity for what it is by pulling her inside and closing her in with me.

The light isn't on, though, so we're submerged in darkness.

"What're you doing?" Her voice is all pitchy.

"What are *you* doing?" I slap around on the wall, trying to find a switch.

Half a second later we're both blinded by light. "Showing you where the bathroom is." Her gaze bounces all over the room.

As does mine, but for very different reasons. "What the hell is going on in here?" Everything is gold. The wallpaper, the vanity, the sink, even the toilet. The floor, however, is black marble and reflective.

"My family is eclectic," she replies, not defensively, but matter-of-factly.

"Is this real gold? Actually, don't answer that, I don't want to know." I motion toward the door. "Why am I here?"

"Because I invited you, which in hindsight may not have been the best idea, at least not without some preparation. I'm used to my family, so I forget how crazy they really are." I've never seen Blaire quite so fidgety.

I give her a look that tells her I think that's utter bullshit.

She throws her hands in the air. "Okay, I didn't forget that they were crazy, but I felt bad that you didn't have plans for Thanksgiving and no one should be alone on the holidays, so it was kind of a kneejerk reaction to invite you along. It wasn't until we were on the way here that I really considered what it would be like for you, and me, frankly."

"Right, okay. So what's the deal with Skylar?"

"She's harmless."

"She's a sexual harassment lawsuit waiting to happen."

"She's actually a total professional at work. She just enjoys getting under my skin and putting on a show."

I point a finger at her. "Your job tonight is to keep her away from me."

"I can try, but she's persistent."

"And what the hell is with you letting your family treat you like garbage?"

"They don't treat me like garbage."

And there's the defensiveness I've been waiting for. "Your *little bakeshop*? When you get tired of the grueling hours you can work for the family? And they haven't even come out to see your place." I don't know why I'm so pissed off about this. Maybe because I know how hard she works? I'm always fighting to keep up. I'm lucky that college kids are willing to pay money for things like throwing axes.

"It's better they don't interfere. Otherwise I'll have to start serving hundred-dollar kobe beef cupcakes."

I make a face because that sounds disgusting. Although she did make a Guinness and bacon cupcake that nearly killed me, it was that good, and I really expected to hate it. "Since when do you let other people dictate your actions?"

"I don't; that's the point."

"But they should see how hard you work."

Blaire sighs. "Look, Ronan, your irritation on my behalf is endearing, but you don't know what you're saying. You've spent less than half an hour with them and we're already locked in a bathroom together and you have a million questions. Which I will answer. Later. On the drive home. But for now I need you to trust me when I say I do not want my family visiting B&B because it will inevitably mean they will try to take over. They are well-meaning but insane."

I stare at her for several long seconds, digesting, accepting. "You are spilling the beans on the drive home."

"There probably won't be much to spill by the time we leave, but sure." She shrugs and turns to open the door.

I stop her from leaving by pressing my palm against it. "Hold up."

She sighs and her shoulders curl forward. "Can't it wait?"

"What's the deal with Matthew?"

She doesn't turn around, but her head drops and she seems to deflate even further. "We used to date."

"Excuse me?"

"We dated. It didn't work out. He married my sister. Oh, and I think Skylar slept with him, too, before they started dating, but then she's done that a few times with various boyfriends, so sometimes it's hard to keep track."

"Wait. What? Skylar slept with your ex-boyfriend before your sister stole him from you?" I feel like my head is going to explode from this information.

"Yeah. Can I go now, please, before we get accused of grabbing a pre-dinner quickie in the bathroom?"

I lift my hand from the door, and she slips out without another word.

Blaire's offhand mention of a quickie is apparently an appealing idea to my man parts, so it takes me a minute to calm down before I'm able to relieve myself.

As I wait I decide two things: I'm not drinking any more alcohol tonight and I'm going to play up being Blaire's boyfriend for the rest of our time here. It's not like her family is going to see me again. I might as well leave them with one hell of a lasting impression.

@the_knightcap:

I prefer my KALE with a silent K.

chapter eleven

THIS ISN'T THE GAME
I WAS PLAYING

Blaire

Hindsight. It's a bitch. I should have warned Ronan about my family and how insane they are. But at the same time, he's been messing with me since day one, and a little payback never hurt anyone.

However, I'm not excited about the prospect of Skylar mauling Ronan all night, as she likes to do with other people's significant others. Between her and Maddy, I've lost at least four dateable prospects.

I realize it doesn't say much about the guys I went out with, but Skylar will fuck a long john if she's desperate enough. As for Maddy and Matthew, they belong together. They're both vain, shallow, and entirely too wrapped up in taking staged photos with celebrities and enjoying the perks of the family wealth.

Despite all this, my family generally has good intentions. It's just their execution is quite lacking. Also, the fact that my mother and her sister swapped husbands is just plain weird.

So, yeah. Thanksgiving dinner is turning out to be a bit of a clusterfuck. Dinner should be served shortly and we can leave right after dessert. I'm still standing in the hallway outside the bathroom. I don't know that Ronan and I should return to the kitchen together, but I'm not certain he'll be able to find his way back on his own. There's also a significant chance that Skylar will be hiding around the corner, ready to pounce on him, so I wait.

Thankfully, dinner is ready to be served when we return and there's too much commotion and passing of dishes for anyone to comment on our brief disappearance.

Ronan stays glued to my side, palm resting against the small of my back as we make our way to the dining room. Skylar has obviously been in here, tinkering with the seating arrangements because originally Ronan isn't even sitting next to me, but he switches the name cards around and pulls my chair out.

Maddy makes a joke about being careful, since we like to play musical chairs in this family. I want to sink into the floor and disappear. And they wonder why I never bring dates over to meet the family. Dinner is a decadent affair, as usual. It's family style instead of plated, but every dish looks like a work of art. The turkey is a deep-fried masterpiece.

My mother, aunt, cousin, and sister are all on some keto bullshit or other so they refuse all carbs or anything that might contain sugar but load up on fried brussels sprouts and whatever other keto-friendly stuff they've prepared.

There are even cauliflower "mashed potatoes" loaded with cream and butter and lord knows what else. Skylar goes on about how all she had today was her detox tea so she could enjoy her dinner.

My dad, however, samples everything, dissecting the delicacy of the flavors. And beside me, Ronan quietly groans his food lust. "This is unbelievable," he mumbles through a mouthful of turkey.

"Don't forget to save room for dessert." It's sort of tongue in cheek since half the people at the table balk at dessert. Or there will be some kind of carb- and flavor-free option that tastes like sadness and cardboard.

Every single member of my family has their phone beside their plate and keeps checking messages between bites. "The manager at the LA location of Decadence wants to meet about the New Year menu. Maddy and I are flying out in the morning to hit up the one in San Diego. Do you want me to stop there, too?" Matthew asks my dad.

"That would be great. If you have time, you might want to make the trip to Vegas while you're out that way. Nora and I are heading to New York, and Glinda and Lawrence, you're taking the Midwest locations, is that correct?"

"What about me?" Skylar asks.

"We need you here to keep an eye on things."

"Or I could go to Vegas with Matthew and Maddy. Why do they get to go to all the fun places and I have to hang out here?"

"We can discuss it after dinner, sweetheart," Lawrence says with a practiced smile.

My parents shift the discussion to which big stars are hiring them for catering over the holidays—it's always a particularly busy time for them—and it's like name-dropping central.

"You've met Daxton Hughes? That teen actor who became an entertainment lawyer?" Ronan dabs at his mouth before he continues. "My ex in high school used to be in love with him."

"I have a crush on him now," my mother replies with a grin.

"He hit on me," Skylar adds.

"No, honey, you hit on him. It was me he was hitting on." Gran-Gran Calloway winks in my direction.

The rest of dinner is spent listening to Gran-Gran tell stories about all the famous people she's met over her lifetime.

Buster brings in the cupcakes I made on a special platter, and of course my mom, aunt, cousin, and sister all have their special keto-friendly dessert brought out. It looks like some kind of chocolate thing served with three berries and a mint leaf, which are on the approved carb list, I guess.

"You're not going to have one of Blaire's cupcakes?" Ronan looks dumbfounded. I'd like to say it's an innocent question, but based on his expression and his tone, it's not.

I don't know why he's so annoyed on my behalf, but I can't say I don't appreciate it.

"Too many carbs and far too much sugar. Sugar is more addictive than cocaine, you know," Skylar says haughtily.

"You would know," I mutter.

"Well, at least I can't end up with a deviated septum or psychosis on account of my sugar consumption," Ronan replies and then asks Buster for one of each cupcake flavor.

Ronan proceeds to inhale all of them while making noises that sound a lot like the ones I'd hear were he naked and I was riding him. And now that image is in my head.

I start to wonder if maybe the ink on his arms spans his back, and possibly his chest as well. In my mind, I decorate the rest of his right arm in more, pretty flowers and the left side in an expansive landscape.

His exuberance seems to compel my mother to fold. She peels the wrapper off, wipes her hands on her napkin and daintily uses her fork to take the tiniest bite. Her eyes go wide, and she blinks several times. "Oh, this is heavenly. Lawrence, did you try this one? You really must."

My aunt also folds and offers to share a cupcake with my dad, who has polished off three already, based on the stack of discarded wrappers.

Skylar is watching Ronan devour cupcakes like it's porn. And honestly, so am I.

When he's finished the last cupcake, he sucks the icing off his fingers—loudly—and turns his gaze on me. His eyes are half-mast, making it look like he's recently had an orgasm. The effects of a sugar rush, the crash soon to follow.

His brows rise. "Everything okay?"

I can't even imagine what my expression must be. "Did you enjoy those?"

He grins. "Immensely. The only cupcake I enjoyed more was the one you made me eat in front of those women at the bachelorette party."

I can feel the heat rising in my cheeks and his grin widens. I will never forget how he looked biting into the vagina cake. Or the way the custard center dribbled down his chin. We're still staring at each other, possibly both lost in that memory.

The stare-off ends when my mother asks what kind of cupcakes they are, and of course she and my father decide to guess the ingredients, arguing about the merits of cooked versus uncooked buttercream.

While this takes place, Skylar keeps edging closer to Ronan, which means he keeps edging closer to me. At this point, his arm is draped over the back of my chair, and he's halfway into my lap. It's kind of funny and also highly distracting because every once in a while his fingers graze the back of my neck and I have to fight off a shiver.

I'm still nibbling my way through my own cupcake, savoring instead of devouring. Despite the fact that Maddy and Skylar refused to try one, there are none left. I'm pretty sure my dad ate half a dozen.

"If you don't hurry up and finish that, I'm stealing it," Ronan whispers, warm breath fanning across my cheek.

"Try it and I'll stab you with my fork." I slide another small bite between my lips and *mmm* my delight.

I can feel his eyes on me. He's so close, if I turn my head

there's a good chance we'll be brushing noses again. "You've got icing on your lip."

I lick them self-consciously and lean away so I can turn my head and make eye contact—the kind that should signal him to back off. "All gone?"

"Nope. Still there."

I raise my napkin with the intent of wiping my face, because there's nothing more embarrassing than having icing on my face, but he covers my hand with his. "I'll get it for you."

"Really, I can do it myself." Now I'm embarrassed because my entire family is watching and Ronan seems oblivious to all the attention. Or maybe this is on purpose.

"Really, I got it." He's right in my personal space, his grin full of villainous mirth. Which I finally understand when he licks the corner of my mouth.

A hot feeling shoots down my spine to settle between my legs. He freezes, his eyes wide, likely with the same shock I'm currently experiencing because *Ronan just licked my face*. I don't understand why he looks so horrified since he's the one who licked me and not the other way around.

"What the hell, Ronan?" I swat his chest and wipe his saliva from the corner of my mouth.

He recovers, expression returning to that same mirthful deviousness. "Hold on. I didn't get it all." He leans in again and I put my hands on his chest, trying to keep him at bay. I honestly have no idea what his plan is, or why he's being so damn flirty.

He backs off as quickly as he tried to attack me, his grin ridiculously wide as he pops what's left of my cupcake into his mouth.

"You jerk!"

"Oh my gosh, you two are so freaking cute. Aren't they the cutest?" Maddy claps excitedly, reminding me that we are not alone. In fact, my entire family is watching this display with rapt interest.

Except Skylar. Her arms are crossed over her chest and she's pouting. "You should probably get a room," she says.

"Maybe you two need another bathroom quickie." Maddy's smirking. Of course she was just waiting for the opportunity to draw attention to our disappearance right before dinner.

Skylar looks scandalized. "Ew! You did not."

Ronan wipes his mouth with his napkin and swallows the rest of my cupcake. "I prefer to take my time and savor the experience when it comes to anything that has to do with Blaire, apart from her cupcakes." He takes my hand in his.

I try to yank mine free, but he tightens his grip and brings it to his lips, biting my knuckle with another one of his mischievous grins.

"Well, I think it's great that these two lovebirds can't keep their hands or tongue to themselves, even at the dinner table. That's the kind of passion every couple should have." Gran-Gran slaps the table. "I need a glass of brandy. Let's retire to the sitting room."

I take the out while I can. "We should probably think about

heading home, actually." This time Ronan lets me yank my hand free from his grasp. I push my chair back, looking to put some space between us.

"You're not staying the night?" My father's disappointment is obvious.

"We both have to be up early for work tomorrow." It's not a lie. Also, the charade with Ronan has gone on long enough. I'm not sleeping in the same room as him to keep up false pretenses. Besides, I don't trust Skylar not to pick the lock and try to hump him in the middle of the night.

"That's too bad. Next time you'll have to plan to stay," my mom says.

I doubt I'll be able to do that anytime soon, but I don't bother to argue. We spend another ten minutes debating whether we really need to leave. Ronan yawns. I can't tell if it's real or forced, but I use it to our advantage.

"Looks like someone is crashing from all the buttercream."

The entire family walks Ronan and me to the door. Then it's a round of awkward hugs and lots of people whispering in my ear about how they hope I bring him back at Christmas. Ronan uses me as a shield to avoid a hug from Skylar. Quite literally. He moves to stand behind me, his forearm coming to rest against my collarbones, fingers curling around my shoulder. The entire front of his body is pressed up against the back of mine. I find myself sort of melting into him as Skylar does some kind of weird dance move like she's trying to find a way between us.

He rests his chin on my opposite shoulder and extends his hand. "It was a pleasure to meet you, Skylawn."

"Skylar." She gives it a dead-fish shake, pouting the entire time.

"Right, my bad." He brushes the shell of my ear with the tip of his nose. "Time to go home, *Care Blaire*. Dessert round two is calling my name."

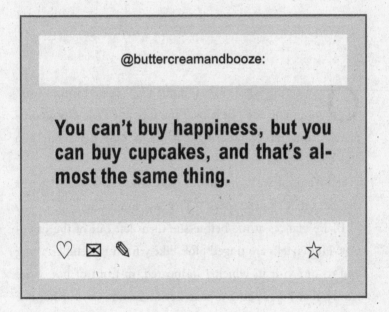

@buttercreamandbooze:

You can't buy happiness, but you can buy cupcakes, and that's almost the same thing.

chapter twelve

THE REVEALING RIDE HOME

Ronan

Okay, so the whole sexual innuendo, "dessert round two" comment was a little over the top, but I felt it was completely justified considering Blaire's cousin needs an ego check.

It isn't until we're in Blaire's SUV and we've made it past the gates that I finally speak. "That was interesting."

Blaire glances at me before she turns left out of the driveway. Her cheeks are tinged pink, likely from the embarrassing end to our visit in which I insinuated, in front of her entire family, that I was going to take her home and devour her like one of her cupcakes. "Sorry I didn't adequately prepare you for the experience."

"I don't think anything could have adequately prepared me for that."

"They're well-meaning but crazy." She tucks a few wayward strands of hair behind her ear.

"You can say that again. How the hell did your parents end up swapping partners?" I wonder how many people Blaire's had to explain this to and whether it ever gets easier.

Blaire blows out a breath. "Uh, I don't really know what precipitated it, but my whole family has always been really close, traveling together to get new restaurants up and running. Skylar, Maddy, and I were pretty much raised as sisters, and whoever wasn't on the road looked after us. The parental roles were basically interchangeable."

She grips the steering wheel tightly. "When I was a sophomore in high school, Mom, Dad, Aunt Nora, and Uncle Lawrence sat us kids down and explained that things were going to change." She shakes her head, maybe remembering how it all went down. "It was the weirdest conversation I've ever been involved in. At least until Maddy and Matthew told me they'd started dating."

The whole Maddy and Matthew situation is its own crazy nightmare, I'm sure. I'd have to come back to that, though. "You were in high school when it happened?"

She nods once. "Yup."

"That must've been rough."

"Uh, well, not much changed to be honest. I mean, there were obvious things, like my mom and dad stopped sleeping in the same bedroom, but the actual family dynamic stayed pretty much the same. Outside the house it was a whole different story, though."

"Can I ask how, or do you not want to talk about it?

Because honestly, I can totally understand if you don't want to, but I can't lie and tell you I'm not curious."

"It's like a bad daytime talk show episode."

I can't tell if she's embarrassed or what, so I give her an out. "We can change the subject."

"It's fine. It was a long time ago. I'm mostly over it. I'm pretty removed from the situation at this point. I love my family, but the whole situation is weird and kind of squicky, you know?" She grimaces. "Actually, you probably don't know, which is a really good thing. Anyway, my parents thought the best plan would be to have everyone move into the house together, less disruption for us kids, and my aunt and uncle were always over anyway. So they pooled their resources and built that tacky monstrosity and we all moved in there. My mom and my uncle took a wing, and my dad and my aunt took a wing, and us girls were just supposed to deal with it."

"Is that how it worked out?" Having two families mesh together like an incestuous Brady Bunch doesn't seem like something teenage girls would just be able to roll with.

She lifts a shoulder in what I assume is meant to be a careless shrug. "Yes and no. Was it awkward? Definitely. We went to this really exclusive, expensive private school where everyone was super gossipy, and my parents own some insanely successful restaurants all over the world, so . . ."

"It did not go unnoticed." I can't even imagine how awful it would be to have your family's messed-up drama become public knowledge.

"Nope. Teens aren't very forgiving when your parents and your aunt and uncle switch partners. I think their lack of convention made me crave normalcy. I became obsessed with family shows, especially *Leave It to Beaver*. I loved everything about shows with stereotypical family units who were solidly average."

"I can see how that would be appealing." I take in her appearance, from the perfectly styled hair and makeup to the full-skirted dress and cute heels. "I'm assuming it also inspired your fashion sense."

"Kind of, yeah. The whole thing sort of came out around Halloween and I was already in my *Leave It to Beaver* phase, and I was in the play *Grease*, so I started wearing the dresses and never really stopped. It was easier to have people whispering about my weird fashion choices than it was to have them talk about how my parents were probably swingers."

"People said that to you?"

"There was speculation, and honestly, I wouldn't be surprised to learn that it was true, however I'm happy to be blissfully ignorant on that front for the rest of my damn life."

Everything I've learned about Blaire tonight shifts my perception of her. She's even stronger than I realized, not taking the easy road where everything could've been handed to her on a silver platter.

She sighs. "Anyway, I love them, really I do, but there's just too much crazy. I know my dad would've tried to find a way to let me pursue my passion for baking if I'd really pushed for it, but I needed the separation and I didn't want to have to compromise. Besides, Maddy and Matthew are up to their elbows in the family biz, and I would really like to steer clear of that whole situation. Not to mention the Skylar situation."

She's opened the door to the topic, so I'm happy to walk right through it. Also, she's right: This is totally like a horrible Jerry Springer episode. "You mentioned you and Matthew dated before?"

Blaire grips the steering wheel tightly and nods once. "He was sort of a rebound. I knew he wasn't the right one, but he seemed like a decent in-between. I guess that sounds bad. I'd gotten out of a particularly toxic relationship and Matthew came along. He was safe and . . . very even."

"Sounds boring."

She laughs, which is good because this conversation has been a whole lot of heavy. "He was *painfully* boring. *Is*, not past tense. I've never met a more monochromatic human being in my life, apart from Maddy anyway. They are perfect for each other. All they want to do is work for the family because of all the perks and their ability to take selfies with famous people and travel all over America, while depriving themselves of carbs so they can be Insta-pretty."

"Doesn't sound like your type at all." I don't know what her type is, but boring and vapid sounds like the opposite of what she'd go for.

"He wasn't. Like I said, he was a rebound. He was uncomplicated and he seemed to like me. I went out of town for a convention and by the time I came back, well, he and Maddy had hit it off."

"How freaking long was the convention?"

She gives me a sidelong glance. "Five days."

"She stole your boyfriend in five days?" Her family really is a bunch of jerks.

"*Stole* sounds harsh. Matthew and I were not destined for white picket fences, two-point-two children, and a purebred poodle. Besides, we'd only been seeing each other for a couple of months."

"That's still shitty."

"What was shitty was when they ambushed me the second I got home and sat me down together to ask for my blessing to date."

"And you obviously gave it." I want to be angry that she folded, but clearly Matthew is a douche and so is Maddy, so it's better they ended up together. Or at least that's my assumption.

"Seemed pointless not to when it was obvious they planned to date regardless. I also got to be a bridesmaid at their wedding. On the upside, I'm well aware that Matthew is painfully average in every way." She motions toward her crotch, as if it needed further explanation.

I don't want to think about Blaire with that asshole. I don't want to think about Blaire with anyone, which I realize should raise some serious red flags. However, I'm inclined to ignore those at the moment.

I decide to leave that information alone. For now it's enough to know he's barely adequate and vapid. "And what's the deal with Skylar?"

"She's always been a hot mess. She was young when the swap happened, so I honestly think it messed her up more than the rest of us. She doesn't have any kind of moral compass at all, or direction, or independent thoughts. I actually sometimes wonder if she's my half sister and not just my cousin."

"That's a mind fuck, right there."

"My whole family is a mind fuck. And like I said, I love them and I know they love me even if they suck at showing it. I just want a normal life where I can do what I love without my family trying to railroad me and make all the decisions for me."

"You're incredible. You know that, right?"

"My family doesn't think so."

"No offense, but your family is fucked."

She laughs. "This is very true. I knew I would fall short if I tried to work with them."

"Fall short how? You're amazingly talented."

She chews her bottom lip for a moment. "I don't share the same values as they do. They're all about appearances and who they know, and that's never really mattered to me. Our goals just don't align. I want to do what I love, not necessarily what's going to make me the most money. And maybe that's naïve, or shortsighted or whatever, but it's how I feel. So I avoided the potential disappointment by going in a completely different direction and now here I am, eking out a living, but doing it on my own."

"They won't help you?"

"My dad has tried to loan me money half a dozen times. He's constantly offering to transfer funds into my account, but if I take their money, I also have to take their advice, and that is not something I want. Like when I wanted to buy the cupcake truck, my dad was there with a big old check, but it came with all kinds of stipulations, so I thanked him and told him I wanted to do it on my own and that's what I did—well, with Paul's help, anyway."

This explains why Blaire is all about doing things her own way. "Do they get how hard you're working?"

She shrugs. "Maybe? I'm not looking for their approval, or a pat on the back, though. I stopped doing that a long time ago when I realized their view of success and mine were so different."

"My brothers are a lot like that. It's always been about how much money they can make and how fast they can make it. For a while I was the same way, but it was making me miserable. No matter how hard I worked, my heart wasn't really in it, so when they wanted to go out on their own, I had to reevaluate my own goals."

"That makes sense." She smiles and glances at me before focusing on the road again. "It seems like you really love the bar."

"I do. It's not going to make me rich, but it makes me a

hell of a lot happier than working in finance ever did. And eventually I want to open a small brewery, so this is a great stepping stone." It's definitely something we have in common, loving what we do.

"A brewery? Really?"

"Yeah. It's a passion project, but it'll take time to make it happen."

"Hmm, what about your brothers? Do they love what they do or do they love the money?"

"Both, I think, and they're good at it. Finance is a natural fit for them, but it really never was for me."

"So are you kind of a black sheep like me?"

"You're not a black sheep. You're an outlier, Blaire. My parents were always about doing what made us happy, as long as it wasn't rotting our brains with garbage TV and hours of video gaming. But I guess in some ways I'm the black sheep. Both of my brothers have significant others and lucrative careers. They kind of fit the conventional stereotype of success: big house, nice cars, gorgeous wife or girlfriend—and my oldest brother, Daniel, is going to be a dad this year, so they're on their way to the two kids and a dog scenario."

"So you're going to be an uncle. That's exciting! I'm not sure if Maddy and Matthew will have kids or not, since Maddy is terrified of stretch marks."

I laugh, but realize she's serious. "That's kind of..."

"Sad and self-centered?" Blaire supplies. "Honestly, I don't think Maddy would be all that involved in raising her kids.

She's more the kind of person who would Insta-pose them and make it look like her family is picture perfect and then hand them over to the nanny to deal with the feedings and dirty diapers while she gets a facial." She grimaces. "God, I'm making her sound horrible. She's really not. We just had an atypical upbringing, and our parents made some less than perfect choices when it came to smoothing over the fallout of the partner swap, like overindulging us."

"You're not overindulged."

"I'm a different person than she is, though."

I have to agree with that.

She waves a hand around in the air. "Anyway, enough about that. Tell me more about you and your grandpa. You seem like you're really close."

"Mmm, yeah, we always have been, even before my parents passed. My first job was bussing tables at The Knight Cap as a teenager, and then later I became a bartender there. Plus, I ended up living with him and Grams during my last two years of college after my parents passed, and that brought us closer. We're a lot alike. Same core values, same work ethic."

"He sounds like a good guy." Her voice has that soft edge, somewhere between empathy and envy.

"He is. Thinks you're quite the looker." I cringe, wishing I'd kept that detail to myself.

But it gets another chuckle out of her, which I like. We talk about our childhoods, all our time spent in family restaurants—it sounds like her experiences were a lot different than mine and I love the way her face lights up and her eyes go all dreamy when she talks about the patisseries in France and how they solidified her love of all things sweet.

The rest of the drive passes quickly, and soon she's stopping in front of my building. I consider inviting her up for a drink. It sends a message I'm not entirely opposed to, but it could add a layer of complication. Especially since we work side by side and today is the first time we've spent more than five minutes in each other's presence without arguing. So I decide against it and just go with: "Thanks for the entertaining evening. I had fun."

She graces me with one of her gorgeous smiles. "Me, too. Thanks for coming along, and for not being all weird about my crazy family."

"They made this the most exciting Thanksgiving ever. Nothing will top it."

She widens her eyes and whispers. "You should see what Christmas is like with them." Her gaze darts to my mouth, but she looks away just as quickly. "Anyway, see you tomorrow."

"See you tomorrow." I get out of the car. "Drive safe, Blaire."

"I will." She waits for me to let myself into my building before she pulls away, her SUV clunking down the street.

Under those layers of pretty fabric, full skirts, and perfectly coiffed hair is one hell of a dynamic woman. Yeah, it was probably a good idea *not* to invite her up. Otherwise I might have wanted to make good on that comment I made about a second helping of dessert in the form of a Blaire cupcake.

@the_knightcap:

Alcohol: Because no great story ever started with a salad.

chapter thirteen

DICK AND BOBBY INVASION

Blaire

Despite my rather short sleep, I'm in a surprisingly good mood this morning. Maybe because I had fun at a family event for once in my life, and even though Skylar was her flirty, obvious self, Ronan didn't so much as give her a second glance. It was a refreshing change from past events when I brought a date and Skylar basically tried to hump him in front of me. Despite the boyfriend thieving and how inappropriate she is, I do love her. We went through a lot together as teens, so as much as I can't stand the crap she pulls, I'm aware that she's more messed up than the rest of us.

I would be lying if I said I didn't like all the attention he threw my way, either. I'm sure he did it to play up the whole fake-date situation, but still. He's a good-looking guy who smells nice. Who wouldn't want a hot man to lick icing off their mouth in front of their boyfriend-stealing sister and cousin?

I check my reflection in the rearview mirror before I get out of my SUV and cross the parking lot. The Knight Cap is still locked up, but it's barely after eight in the morning, and usually no one is there before nine thirty. Although with Ronan needing to deal with the frozen bird situation, I'm sure he'll be in early.

Daphne is visiting her parents, and Paul is with his family and after next week I'm on my own with the cupcakes. Callie offered to come in later, so it's just me this morning.

I pare down the menu to specials in celebration of the holiday. My diehards who have to work like me pop in for coffees, scones, the festive turkey, brie, and cranberry wraps I ordered in, and cupcakes. Most of the cupcake orders have already gone out for the weekend, apart from a few stragglers, so it's a quiet day.

Ronan pops his head in to say hello just before eleven, but I'm with a customer, so he doesn't stick around. By six it's a ghost town, which is to be expected, and I close early.

I pack the daily leftovers and make up a box of cupcakes for Ronan. My stomach does a twist and leap as I check my reflection in the mirror. I look tired, but otherwise I'm presentable, so I head over to The Knight Cap to deliver the cupcakes. Maybe I'll stay for a drink tonight.

I glance at the building across the street, the one that's been empty since we both opened shop. Brown paper still covers the windows, but there's a new sign plastered across the front that wasn't there yesterday. In huge gaudy red letters is the very familiar logo for Dick and Bobby's, a chain of restaurants that boasts massive TVs and broadcasts every major sporting event in existence, even that not-real sport where people ride those hobby-horse things. Plus they televise all the MMA fights. And they have pool tables and all sorts of games. It's the grown-up version of Chuck E. Cheese with booze, horrible greasy food, and sports. I'd like to believe it's not going to be an issue since B&B caters to a slightly more sophisticated crowd, but we really don't need new competition around here.

I open the door to The Knight Cap. It's pretty quiet, only a handful of tables occupied. There are a few older men sitting at the bar, nursing pints and watching the football game.

Ronan glances at the door when it chimes, signaling my arrival. A fluttery feeling in my stomach makes me pause as images and sensations from last night flash through my head: the way he pulled me into his side, how I seemed to fit quite nicely under his arm, how it felt to have his fingers brushing along the back of my neck when we were seated at the dinner table. A warm shiver runs down my spine as I remember the shock of him licking me close to the corner of my mouth.

It's so silly. He was just playing the part of my date, mostly because he couldn't believe that my cousin was actually hitting on him in front of the entire family. Still, he's smiling, and that's a whole lot different from his usual "oh, you again" scowl.

He wipes his hands on a bar towel. "Hey, Alice, how's Wonderland?" He winks, though, so I know he's playing around.

"Wonderland was empty and I was bored, so I thought I'd stop by." I set the box on the bar top. "Have you seen what's going on across the street?"

He wipes down a pint glass before he shelves it, tattooed forearms flexing enticingly. I drag my eyes up to his face, which is also nice to look at. He's wearing his glasses today, and I've decided they're sexy. He looks like an intellectual lumberjack. A badass one. The plaid is definitely growing on me and so is the man wearing the plaid.

"Earth to Blaire? You sure you're not still in Wonderland?"

"Huh?"

"You said something was going on across the street." He arches a brow. "Have you been sampling the martinis this afternoon?"

"Oh! Right! No. I haven't." I crook a finger at him. "Come with me, I want to show you something."

He looks pointedly at his customers and I roll my eyes.

"It'll only take a minute and it's better if I show you, rather than tell. Besides, Lars can watch the bar, can't you?"

Lars winks at me. "Anything for you."

"Thank you." I wink back and give Ronan my attention again. "Why can't you be so accommodating?"

"I can be accommodating. When the situation warrants it, and don't encourage this one. His ego is already big enough. He doesn't need you flirting with him to inflate it even more."

Ronan whips him on the back of the arm with the towel

as he rounds the bar and saunters toward me, apparently in no hurry.

As soon as he's close enough I slip my arm through his, noting how nice and firm his bicep is. I have the urge to trace the outline of the delicate, colorful blooms decorating his forearm. I notice, for the first time, that there's a woman's face set in the middle of them. I realize it's the same woman in the picture on Ronan's living room wall: his mother. And now I understand what he meant about wanting to see his memories and remember.

I pull him toward the door, yank it open and step out onto the sidewalk. It's cold and dreary, so I press myself closer, using him as a barrier against the wind and rain. "Look." I point across the street at the ugly sign.

"Oh shit," he mutters and looks down at me, eyes wide. "Is this a joke? This has to be a joke. That place was a damn law office three months ago." I still have my arm threaded through his, so when he moves toward the edge of the sidewalk he takes me with him.

He checks for traffic before he drags me across the street. To be fair, I could let go of his arm, but I don't really want to. He smells good—like beer, cologne, and laundry detergent. It's a nice combination.

I snuggle in closer, trying to claim some of his body heat as I read the notice taped to the inside of the window beside the Dick and Bobby's sign.

"Damn it, they're supposed to open in a month. How is that even possible? They have to gut this entire place."

"It's a chain, though, right? They have loads of money. It wouldn't take much for them to be able to afford to renovate."

"Why aren't you upset about this?" Ronan snaps.

I shrug, trying to understand why he's so panicked. "It's a huge, impersonal big box place. Loud, awful, and the food is terrible."

"Newsflash, Blaire, college kids don't have discerning palates. This is like an indoor play place for grown-ups, with food and beer and gross coolers that only college students can stomach."

"And I should be upset that they're going to serve disgusting coolers, gross beer, and bad food?" My teeth start to chatter because it's cold and even though I'm wearing my jacket, my legs are bare and there's a breeze up my skirt.

"It's all cheap. Cheap and shitty, but still cheap and do you know what college kids love?" He doesn't give me a chance to answer. "Cheap shit, Blaire. They love cheap shit. When are we busiest? When we have some kind of event and a promotion. Five-dollar pints draw college kids, three-dollar garbage draft is going to kill my business."

"I think you're getting your knickers in a knot over nothing, but I'm willing to listen as long as we can talk about how their awful beer is going to ruin your business *inside* your place of business before my legs turn into popsicles."

His gaze moves over my bare legs, all the way back up to my face and more specifically my mouth. My teeth bang against each other, which explains why that's where his focus is. "Yeah. Of course. You must be freezing."

I hold my fingers apart a fraction of an inch. "Just a bit."

We rush back across the street. "Take a seat and I'll get you something to warm you up."

"Sure. Okay." I climb up on one of the barstools close to the draft taps. I rub my arms and blow warm air into my clasped hands. It's really starting to feel like winter is on its way now. I should've put on tights today, but I was in a rush having slept in later than usual this morning.

Ronan brings me a steaming mug with THE KNIGHT CAP logo on it. It's topped with whipped cream and chocolate drizzle. I grin and flip up the lid on the box of treats I brought over. The cupcakes are still Thanksgiving themed, but these I made special. They're turkey butts that read EAT ME!

He smirks and plucks one from the box. "These don't have some kind of chocolate filling in them, do they?"

"I guess you'll have to eat it to find out."

He shrugs and peels off the wrapper, taking a big bite. "So fucking delicious," he groans. Once he's polished off a cupcake he leans on the bar. "So D&B are going to be a problem for both of us."

I sip my spiked hot chocolate. "Explain why you think that. Buttercream and Booze has a fun vibe, we serve specialty drinks, gourmet cupcakes. You serve local craft beers and great pub fare. Sure, you have the staples, like fries and wings, but you also have a great variety of other options to appeal to a more upscale customer. We also both have cool entertainment, which the people around here love."

"I agree with all of those things, but do you know what D&B has that we don't?"

"Bad ambiance and a tacky name?"

"Yes and yes, but also money for marketing. Lots of it."

He waits for that to sink in. It doesn't take long. I pull my phone out of my purse and bring up their social media. They have a massive following and they've just announced their new location coming soon on its own social media profile. I click on it and of course they already have double the followers I do. Neither of us has the kind of money they do to throw at TV and billboard ads. "And no matter how crappy a bar they are, that money equals visibility we don't have, plus a recognizable name."

"Exactly." Ronan raps on the bar with his knuckles.

"You really think they're going to be a threat?" For the first time since I saw that horrible sign, I'm struck with a niggle of worry.

"I honestly don't see how they can't be. Chain restaurants are notorious for killing off small businesses. They're huge competition. I don't know about you, but I have reno costs I still need to recoup and losing business to that nightmare is going to make it that much more of a struggle."

I chew on my bottom lip. "I'm barely scraping by," I admit.

He seems surprised by that revelation. "It's that bad? Your place is always hopping."

"I got a really good deal on rent, which is basically the only reason I can afford the storefront, and Paul paid off the cupcake truck in actual cupcakes. At the end of next week I'm going to be on my own with cupcake production. Honestly, any loss of business is going to be bad for my bottom line." And my bank account.

Ronan taps his bottom lip with his index finger. "You know what we need to do?"

"Find a new storefront that isn't across the street from Dick and Bobby's?" Not that I could even hope to afford it. Also, this location is prime, which is obviously what the owners of D&B realized.

"It really is an awful name for a restaurant." He gives his head a shake. "Anyway, we need to get as many loyal customers as we can before that place opens."

"Agreed."

"We should host combined events to get even more people to come out. Have big simultaneous promotions."

I stare at him from over the rim of my delicious alcohol-laced coffee.

"You have to admit it's a good idea." He plucks another cupcake from the box.

"What about the Best Bar competition?"

"We can still compete against each other for best bar thing, but this is a way bigger threat, and more important because it has the potential to flush both of our businesses down the toilet." He bites into the chocolate cupcake.

"So you want us to work together?"

He nods. "Yeah, what do you say?"

"Okay. We can do it, but it's an even split on events and promotions. And we have to promote each other equally on our social media."

"That's a good idea." He wipes his hand on his pants and holds it out. "Deal?"

I slip mine into his. "Deal."

There are far worse people I could get into bed with—proverbially speaking, of course.

@buttercreamandbooze:

Making the world a better place, one cupcake at a time.

chapter fourteen

COORDINATION NATION

Blaire

Over the next few days, Ronan and I work out a calendar of events leading up to the Christmas holidays. I'm a visual person so I color coordinate everything, and send it to him via email, but I also print a copy and have it blown up in color so we can post it in our respective shops. On top of that, I have daily social media posts prepared.

It's Thursday and tonight I have trivia night followed by Ronan's karaoke. The timing is great, since the quarterfinals for Best Bar are going to be announced next week, narrowing it down to the top twenty-five bars. I'm pretty excited about it, because now that we're working together, I don't have to worry about him starting early and stealing my business, although he stopped doing that a while ago. Plus we both have specials, and if they move from one bar to the other they get an additional coupon to use for a future event, which means more incentive to keep coming back.

I have a plan, but to orchestrate it I need to acquire some pertinent information about Ronan and free up a couple of hours this afternoon. I could get the information by asking him, but I kind of want it to be a fun surprise. It's nine in the morning, and Ronan usually isn't in until closer to ten, so I step out into the back alley. As I expected, the back door of The Knight Cap is propped open with a wedge.

I peek inside but don't make my presence known. Instead I sneak down the hall. It's a bit of a feat, considering I'm wearing heels and have to go extra-high on my tippy toes so they don't click on the floor.

I pass the bar to get to Ronan's office. I scan the area, spotting Lars and one of the female servers close talking. They're too wrapped up in each other to notice me, so I make it past them undetected and slip into Ronan's office. It still hasn't been updated like the rest of the place, but it smells like his cologne. The same old dilapidated chair with a full-blown butt groove and picked-apart armrests sits in front of the ancient, pitted desk.

Originally, I found this office rather disgusting, but now, knowing what I do about this place it's sweet that Ronan hasn't changed a thing about it.

In the corner is a coat rack. I smile when I spot what I'm looking for—two plaid shirts hanging from the hooks. I nab one and check the size. It's an extra large, as I suspected, considering his broad shoulders, not to mention how thick his biceps are. I bring the shirt to my nose and inhale. It holds the faint scent of laundry detergent, his cologne, and the pervasive odor of fried food that comes from working in a bar. I always smell like vanilla, butter, icing sugar, and sometimes coffee. I decide it's a good idea to take the shirt with me, because sizing can vary depending on the store, so it will be good to bring it along for comparison's sake.

I turn around, still holding the shirt up to my nose, humming contentedly. And slam right into a chest, which happens to be wrapped in exactly the same plaid shirt I'm huffing.

"Oh!" My gasp is muffled by the fabric.

I tip my head up and meet Ronan's inquisitive, amused gaze. "Are you sniffing my shirt?"

"I was checking to see if it was clean." It's only sort of a lie. Okay, it's a complete lie and I can feel my face turning red.

"Right. Okay." He nods once, eyes narrowed. "And where exactly are you going with my shirt?"

"I uh, I need to borrow it."

He crosses his arms over his chest. "For what?"

"It's supposed to be for a surprise, which you're currently ruining." And now I'm snappy to go along with my embarrassment.

He smiles, eyes moving over my face slowly, lingering on my lip, which I'm currently biting. "Am I going to get my shirt back?"

"Yes."

"In one piece?"

"Of course."

"Okay." He steps aside. "You can borrow it, then."

I smile brightly, trying to mask my mortification as I brush past him. "Great."

"Blaire."

"Hmm?" I pause and glance over my shoulder. He's right behind me.

He dips down, nose brushing the shell of my ear. He makes a low sound in the back of his throat, a purr, and murmurs, "I like the way you smell, too."

"Good to know." I leave feeling slightly less embarrassed and a whole lot turned on.

Two hours later I return from my shopping trip. I've been getting my dresses from the same store for years. I always hit their sample and sale rack—even before I had to scrimp and save every penny—so I get my dresses for around forty dollars each, often 25 percent of the full price. It means I have a closet full of dresses that I've amassed over the past decade and a half, and because they're very much fashioned after the fifties, they never really go out of style.

The lunch rush is in full swing, so I leave my purchases in my office and dive back into work. It isn't until after two that we finally have a lull in the constant stream of customers. Not that I'm going to complain.

I pop back over to The Knight Cap to somewhat reluctantly

return Ronan's borrowed shirt. I resist the urge to get in a couple more sniffs because I'll be able to sniff the real thing shortly.

I find Ronan sitting in the last seat at the end of the bar with his laptop propped open, reviewing spreadsheets. Like my place, his is quieter this time of day—between lunch and dinner. Several tables are occupied with groups of college students studying over afternoon pints and local business people grabbing a bite while they work.

"Hey! Do you have a minute?" I have to fight with my body not to get all bouncy because I'm excited.

Ronan glances up from the laptop, a wry grin pulling up the corner of his mouth. "Sure. What's up?"

"Can we go to your office? I have something to show you." I'm holding a huge bag behind my back, most of which is hidden by my skirt.

"Why can't you show me here?" He tries to peek around me, where my hands are clasped behind my back.

"No peeking!" I shrug, trying to remain nonchalant. "And because I don't want anyone else to see yet."

He closes his laptop, tucks it under his arm and slides off the stool. He motions toward the hall leading to his office. "Ladies first."

I practically bounce down the hall, giddy with excitement. I hang his shirt on the rack, set the bag on his executive chair and spin to face him. He's standing in the doorway, leaning against the jamb, arms crossed over his chest, expression halfway between curious and amused.

I pull him inside and close the door, trapping us together in the small, crowded room that smells like him, paper, and more faintly of food.

I pull the garment bag out of the shopping bag and lay it over the back of the chair. "So I had this idea." I turn away from him, unzip the garment bag and pull out the dress I picked out for tonight's event.

"And you need my opinion on a dress?" He seems confused.

I give him a look. "No, silly. I don't need your opinion. Although you're welcome to give it if you'd like." I pull out the plaid shirt that matches the color scheme of the dress—blue with yellow neon accents, also on sale—spin around to face him and hold them both up. "Ta-da!"

Ronan's eyes shift back and forth between the shirt—in his size—and the dress. "I don't get it."

I roll my eyes. "You're such a dude. Look at the colors."

"What about them?"

"They match."

He blinks.

Obviously he requires more of an explanation aside from the visual, which I thought made it pretty clear. "It's for when we do combined events, so we match." I motion between us.

"So we match?" he repeats.

I expected him to be more excited about this, which is maybe naïve of me. He's a guy who lives in jeans and the same kind of plaid shirt every day of the week. It's possible it's his forever uniform and he even wears it when he's at home. Or sweats, which I've only ever seen him in a couple of times. I lose a little of my zeal at his lack of reaction. "Or maybe not. Are the colors too much? It was just a thought. I can return the shirts."

"You got me more than one?" He moves into my personal space and peeks inside the garment bag. It's stuffed pretty full with my dresses and the shirts I'm now probably going to have to return.

"It's not a big deal. I thought it might be fun, but it's okay if that's not something you're interested in. I should've talked to you about it first." I try to brush his hand aside so I can tuck the shirt and dress back in the bag. I'm so embarrassed right now, and deflated to be quite honest.

He covers my hand with his. "I think it's a great idea, Blaire."

"You're just saying that," I mutter.

"No, I'm not. I honestly think it's a good idea. An amazing one. I just didn't get it at first, but it totally makes sense for us to match when we're doing these shared events and it was really thoughtful of you to go out and get all this stuff as a surprise."

"You're sure you think it's a good idea?" I can't tell if he's just trying to save my bruised ego or what.

"I swear, I think it's fantastic." He gives me the Boy Scout salute. "It sure isn't anything I would've thought of."

"Really?"

"Really." He nods.

"Great!" I beam up at him and get lost in his smile. Our eyes lock and hold for several long seconds, warmth blossoming in my stomach and radiating through my limbs. I give my head a shake. "Let me show you the rest of them, and you can try them on and make sure they fit properly. I used the shirt I borrowed to cross reference the size because sometimes they don't all fit the same. There's this great store a few blocks away and they have a crazy selection of plaid shirts. I stumbled across it online and thought it would work out really well." I'm excited-rambling now, but with Ronan on board I can see in my mind exactly how well this will work, and Daphne is going to love it. "If you're game for it we can take some fun pictures to post on social media being all matchy-matchy. I think it'll look great and really help unify the collaborated event."

"I like the sound of all of this."

"Really?"

"Yeah. I think it's super smart."

"Can I ask you something?"

"Sure." Ronan starts unbuttoning his shirt.

"Why do you always wear plaid?"

"The same reason you always wear dresses, I guess."

"You're obsessed with *Leave It to Beaver*–style shows?"

He laughs, but his expression sobers quickly and he focuses on the task of flicking open buttons. "After my parents passed, I had to go through the house and clean it out. My dad had all of these plaid shirts. It was his thing, I guess. I couldn't really conceive of getting rid of them, so I started wearing them and never really stopped."

"So it became your thing, too." Another way to stay connected to a person he loved and lost.

"Exactly." He gives me a wry smile as he shrugs out of his button-down. He's wearing a white undershirt beneath his usual red and black plaid. The fabric is thin and stretched tight, conforming to the contours and planes of muscle. "It wasn't long after that I started on the body art."

I allow my gaze to soak in the designs decorating his exposed arms. Based on the slightly sheer quality of the shirt, I discover that Ronan's artwork extends to his chest. Muted colors seep through and I wonder if I'll ever have the chance to see all of it. "How many tattoos do you have?" I finally manage to drag my eyes back up to his face—it's not a hardship.

"Quite a few."

Maybe how many is the wrong question. "Are they just from the waist up?"

A slight grin appears. "Most of them, yeah."

He reaches around me and grabs the first shirt with the navy and neon yellow plaid print and shrugs into it. It fits perfectly.

"I can throw that one in the wash right now so it's ready for the event tonight."

"You don't need to do that. I can wear it as is."

"I don't mind, and it'll feel nicer if it's been washed and not so stiff. I'll add which shirt to wear and when on the calendar to make it easy for you."

"I don't want to put that all on you. We could do it together."

"Sure. Okay. We can check out calendars later and figure out what works best?"

"That'd be great."

"Hey, Ronan, a couple of the girls need you to sign off so they can cash out." Lars peeks his head in the office. "Oh, hey, Blaire, I didn't realize you were here." He gives me a once-over. "You look pretty, but then you always do."

"Save the flirting for someone you actually have a chance with, Lars," Ronan says tonelessly.

I chuckle. "I should go. I'll see you both later tonight."

"Looking forward to it, Blaire," Lars calls after me as I walk down the hall toward the back exit carrying the garment bag of dresses and shirts.

I wave at them both over my shoulder and head back to B&B in a buoyant mood.

My matchy-matchy plan turns out to be a great one. We look adorable in our coordinated outfits, and they make for fantastic social media posts. The first few collaborative events go over really well. Both of our businesses see an increase in revenue, and the more we work together the busier we get. Meanwhile, we're holding our own in the Best Bar competition, although Ronan's a few spots above me.

We each end up having to hire another bartender so we can keep up with the new demands on our promotional nights. As the holidays approach, I suggest that we collaborate on a New Year's event and Ronan agrees.

It's much more involved and means planning sessions take place outside of business hours, not in our respective bars where interruptions abound. Which is how I end up at Ronan's apartment on a Sunday night after hours. Well, my hours, not his. He left work early so I wouldn't end up completely bleary-eyed in the morning.

"Do you mind if I change real quick so I don't smell like stale beer and wing sauce?" Ronan asks once we're in his apartment.

"Not at all."

"Great. Just make yourself comfortable. I'll be back in a minute." He motions to the living room with the oversized dark leather furniture. The whole place is rustic with warm tones, like an open-concept cottage transplanted into an apartment building in the city. The floors are dark, rough-hewn hardwood and although I'm wearing tights, I shiver as the cold hits the soles of my feet and travels up my spine.

I cross over to the pictures hung on the walls, taking them in with new eyes now that I know more about the history of the bar and Ronan's relationship with his grandfather. It makes me sad that he lost his parents at such a young age.

As whacked out as my family may be, I'm lucky to have them. They love me in their own weird way. There are a few more photos of an older Ronan with his grandfather and grandmother. I don't know if it's just me, but his smile doesn't seem quite as bright. Maybe they were taken not long after he lost his parents.

Ronan returns a minute later wearing a pair of loose jogging pants and a T-shirt. He's changed from contacts to glasses. His hair is less than perfect, as if he rushed to change. The shirt pulls tight across his chest and hugs his biceps. I can't complain about the view.

He holds up a pair of wool socks—the kind with a cream and red band at the top. "The floors are kind of cold in here. I thought you might want these."

He meets me halfway across the living room to pass them over. Without my heels on he's quite a bit taller than me, so I have to tip my head back to look up at him. "Thanks, my feet are perpetually cold. I'm pretty much in slippers between October and April."

"Or heels." He inclines his head toward the kitchen. "Come have a seat and I'll make us a drink before we get down to business."

I hoist myself up on a stool and pull on the warm wool socks. They're so big they almost reach my knees. Ronan roots around in the fridge and returns with four bottles, which he lines up in front of me. "Do you like craft beer?"

"Depends on the beer, but I'm always game to try something new." I pick up the one closest to me and read the handwritten label. "Rhubarb ale?"

"I have a few new flavors I've been trying out and I need a guinea pig. I can pour us each a flight and you can sample a few?"

"Sounds good. Can I help with anything?"

"Nope. I've got it covered."

While Ronan pours us beers, I take the opportunity to inspect his body art more closely. From my vantage point, I have a great view of the woman's portrait surrounded by blooming roses. I reach out and trace the contour of her face.

Ronan's in the middle of pouring a beer, and I startle him with the unexpected contact, so some of it sloshes onto the counter.

"Oh! Sorry. That's my fault; let me clean that up." I hop off the stool and grab the closest rag.

"That's okay, I got it." His fingers wrap around my wrist and that warm, buttery feeling coasts through my veins. I'm sure my face is red. You'd think with the amount of time we spend together that I'd have gotten over my fascination with his art and the way his touch seems to affect me, but if anything it's gotten worse, not better. Or maybe more intense is a more accurate way to explain it? I don't know, but I'm definitely attracted to him.

Acting on that would not be a good idea. Too complicated. What if he's bad in bed and we still have to cohost all of these events? Or worse, what if he thinks I'm bad in bed? And why am I suddenly thinking about sleeping with him just because he's making innocuous physical contact?

"Blaire, I got it. No big deal," he repeats, and I realize I've been staring at his hand wrapped around my wrist, lost in my own head. I hope it wasn't for long.

"Really, I startled you. I can clean it up."

"Blaire." This time his tone makes me look up.

"Just let me help," I press.

"You're not holding a dishrag." He's sort of smirking, but his cheeks are pink.

"What?" I glance back down to the cloth in my hand.

"Just give it to me, please." He tries to pry it from my fingers, but his sudden desperation to take it away makes me want to hold on tighter.

"Just let go," I tell him.

"No. *You* let go."

Are we really having a kindergarten-style fight over this? He spins me around so my back is against his chest and bars his free arm around me, but I'm wiggly and for once it's him who seems to be embarrassed. And suddenly I realize why.

Instead of a dishcloth, I'm holding a pair of boxer briefs with a cartoon Santa holding a beer on them. "Oh my God! Why the hell do you have boxers on your counter! Are they dirty?"

Ronan lets me go and raises both hands in the air. "They're fresh from the laundry, I swear. They fell out of my laundry basket and I found them on the floor and tossed them on the counter this morning on the way out the door. I know I live alone and I'm a dude, but I don't normally keep my underwear on the counter."

This time it's Ronan who's red-faced instead of the other way around. I decide I should savor the experience since I have no idea when it's going to happen again. I hold them up and frown at the way the peen pouch holds its shape. "What's going on here?" I poke at the pouch.

He makes a noise that sounds half like he's choking and also a groan. "Don't do that."

"Why not? You said they're clean. Are you lying?"

"I'm not lying," he croaks.

I know he's telling the truth because the fresh smell of his laundry detergent prevails as I wave around his festive underwear. This is more fun than it should be. I peek inside. These aren't like regular underwear at all. "Are these for sports or something? Like they have a built-in jockstrap?"

He tries to grab them from me but I spin out of reach, putting the island between us as a barrier. He pokes at his cheek with his tongue. "They offer support." He uses his hand to demonstrate, but in the air, not by cupping his actual junk.

"Like a bra for your balls?" I make the same cupping motion in front of my chest. His underwear dangle from my pinkie.

"Yeah, sort of like a bra for my balls."

"So it lifts and separates?"

"Same basic principle." He closes his eyes for a few seconds, exhaling a long slow breath before he opens them again. "Can we stop talking about this now?"

"You're the one who leaves underwear on your counter. I don't think it's unreasonable for me to be curious about them."

He swallows thickly. "Is your curiosity sated?"

"Partially. I might have more questions later. Why? Is this conversation making you uncomfortable?"

He blinks a couple of times before his eyebrows rise. "We're talking about my balls and your tits, Blaire."

"And?" I play dumb, because this whole conversation is making me think about cupping his junk, so I have to assume it's making him think about the same thing and possibly him acting as a human bra for my boobs.

"Well, Blaire, you're fondling my underwear, we're discussing cupping balls, you're drawing attention to your chest, and men are visual creatures. So as you're talking I'm imagining every single one of those things. And I'm wearing gray sweatpants and I'm commando now."

"Seriously?" I push up on my tiptoes and try to get a look at his crotch, which is a silly thing to do because it's not like I can see if he's commando through his sweats.

He points a finger at me. "You stay right where you are."

"Why?"

"Do you really need to ask?"

I shrug and give him a look that tells him I do, in fact, need to ask.

He plants his fists on the counter and huffs a laugh. He keeps his head bowed but lifts his gaze. "This conversation is *stimulating*."

"Oh." I glance down and back up a few times. "*Oh!* Are you *aroused*?"

All he does is glare at me.

"I see." I nod primly and place his boxer briefs on the counter. I carefully smooth them out, bite my lip, and push them in his direction. "You know." I wrinkle my nose. "I think I'm just going to excuse myself to the bathroom for a minute. It's down the hall, isn't it?" I motion in the direction he went when he changed into gray sweats.

"First door on the left," he grinds out.

"I'll give you a minute to . . . calm down, then," I whisper. Yes, it's sultry and on purpose.

"Much appreciated, Blaire."

I wait until I'm halfway down the hall before I allow myself to smile. It's nice to know I'm not the only one affected.

When I return from the bathroom—I take an extra long time and wish I'd thought to bring my purse along so I can fix my makeup—the underwear is no longer sitting on the counter, and Ronan has relocated to the couch.

In addition to the flights of beer, he's set out bowls of chips, nuts, and popcorn. I grab my laptop and clipboard and join him.

I leave a cushion of space between us and adjust my dress so I can tuck my legs under all the fabric. If I'd been thinking, I would have lost the crinoline. It makes the skirt extra poofy—and hides my thighs and butt, which Maddy and Skylar had a habit of smacking anytime I wore jeans because, unlike them, I actually have a butt. Crinolines, while great for keeping the booty under wraps, are not necessarily the most comfortable thing to sit around in.

I battle the fabric down and use a throw pillow—there's only one and it looks like it might have been cross-stitched by a grandmother—to keep it from poofing up again.

"I'd offer you a pair of jogging pants, but I think you'd swim in mine."

"It's fine. I'm used to it."

"You don't look all that comfortable."

He gives me the raised eyebrow and I stare at him for a few more seconds before I finally give in, stand up, pull the crinoline down and step out of it. It holds its shape for a few long seconds, resembling a pretty fabric volcano before it sinks into a puddle on the floor.

"Happy now?" I sit back down and tuck my legs back under the skirt again.

"As long as you're happy and comfortable, I'm happy and comfortable. You wear that thing every day?"

"It's comfy, for the most part."

"I'll take your word for it." He motions to the spread. "Help yourself, but let me give you a rundown of the beers and what goes best with which snack." He describes each craft brew: pumpkin, orange, rhubarb, and a hopped mango ale and tells me which snack to pair it with. I take a sip after each description, then follow it with a nibble of the accompanying snack so I can experience the way the flavors complement one another. "Where did these beers come from? They're all delicious." I go back to the rhubarb ale, because I favor the hint of sweetness and the tart, gentle tang that follows the initial bitterness of the hops.

"I made them."

"What? When would you have time for that?"

"Gramps let me set up a brew in his garage. It's just small

batches, but I think it'll be enough to have some decent options for New Year's. What do you think?"

I set my beer down and clap my hands excitedly, and then grab his. "Oh my God! What about a craft beer and champagne theme! We can have specialty cupcakes based on the beer flavors and champagne. You can host the dinner and I'll handle dessert. Do you think we can apply to have a gated outdoor space so people can go back and forth between our places as long as there's security? Or is that too much? It might be too much."

"I think it's a great idea, and it's sort of exactly what I was already thinking."

"I'll shut down B&B at ten and move the party over to The Knight Cap. We can have a cupcake table and appetizers and all the delicious craft beer. This is going to be fantastic."

We spend the next hour sipping beers, eating snacks, and planning our New Year's co-celebration. I start to get tired— beer hits me a lot faster than vodka for some reason—and when Ronan excuses himself to the bathroom, I stretch out and close my eyes for a few seconds.

I blink and try to roll over, but my face hits...a wall? No wait. Walls aren't soft, and they aren't made of...leather? I blink a couple of times, but close my eyes right away because the morning sun is streaming through the windows, blinding me. It's enough time for me to come to the conclusion that I'm not in my own apartment.

Panic takes over for a few disorienting seconds until the

familiar smell of Ronan's cologne registers. I blink again, still trying to adjust to the light beyond my eyelids.

I can't believe I fell asleep. Well, that's not true; I've been burning the candle at both ends, working long hours, basically seven days a week, since the beginning of the summer. That I passed out on Ronan's couch isn't much of a surprise. That he didn't wake me up and send me home sort of is.

Or maybe he tried and failed. That would be both embarrassing and not entirely impossible given the above facts.

I note the soft pillow tucked under my head—not the cross-stitched one I was hugging last night. I'm also covered in a blanket that smells like Ronan. On the table beside me is a glass of water.

The food and drinks from last night have been cleared away and sit on the counter across the room. I must have passed out so hard. I check the time. It's barely after seven, but I have to stop at home to change at the very least and manage my makeup situation, so there's no way I'm going to make it in before eight thirty. I'm glad I had the foresight to prepare most of the cupcakes for today last night, otherwise we'd be in real short supply this morning.

I throw off the covers, consider leaving them in a heap, but decide that's super rude, so I fold everything—half-assed folding, but still—and look around the floor for my crinoline.

I spot all my stuff—purse, laptop, clipboard, and crinoline—on the club chair across from the couch. I can sincerely appreciate Ronan's tidiness.

Once my mess is straightened up, I find a piece of paper,

scribble an apology and a thank you, and gather up my things, shoving the crinoline in my purse because carrying it is awkward.

Of course my attempt to make a stealthy exit is thwarted when my purse knocks into a wooden sculpture of a beaver and it clatters to the floor. I carefully put it back, glad it wasn't glass, and tiptoe to the door, careful not to bang into anything else. I realize I'm still wearing Ronan's socks, so I have to take those off before I can slip my feet into my shoes. This also requires me to set down all the things I'm carrying because the socks are clinging to my tights.

"Morning." The gravelly voice gives me pause.

"I'm so sorry I fell asleep on you." I turn to give him an apologetic smile to go with the verbal one, but I'm pretty sure all I'm capable of is drooling. "Oh." I'm excessively breathy as I murmur, "Good morning to me."

Ronan is standing about ten feet away, wearing the same gray sweats as last night. Except he's gloriously shirtless, all his artwork and his lovely, defined muscles on display. There's a lot of both to appreciate.

I'd like to say I make an attempt to conceal my gawking, but I don't. I scan his torso, drinking in the ink that covers the left side of his chest and merges with the ink running down his arm. I also admire the delicious V of muscle that disappears under the waistband of his sweats.

Eventually I make it up to his face. Even the smirk he's wearing is adorably delicious. A five o'clock shadow covers his jaw and sleep lines cut across his face. His hair sticks up all over the place. *This is a sight I wouldn't mind waking up to more often.*

"Blaire?" His right brow arches.

Damn it, he's asked me a question and I've been too busy thinking about how it's too bad he doesn't sleep completely naked to be bothered to pay attention. "I'm sorry if I woke you. I knocked a beaver over." I thumb over my shoulder. "But I didn't break it or anything. And I'm sorry I fell asleep on you. I know I'm impossible to wake up."

He runs a hand through his hair, making more of it stand on end. "I would've moved you to the spare bedroom, but you were out like a light and I figured you probably needed the rest. I hope you slept okay."

"Like the dead, actually. I should go, though." God, this is awkward.

Ronan gives me a lopsided grin. "You don't want to stay and make me breakfast?"

It's my turn for my eyebrows to climb my forehead. "I need to shower and change before work." Plus Daphne said she was going to stop by this morning with a few things she thought might be helpful for the New Year's celebration and she seemed particularly excited. No matter how many times I tell her I can manage, she always makes herself available on the nights with special events.

"It's only just seven, and I'm kidding about you making me breakfast, Blaire. But *I* could make *you* breakfast."

"Oh, you don't need to do that. I've already overstayed my welcome."

"If that was true, I would've stayed in bed and let you leave. You can let Callie open up, can't you? I won't make you late. I can whip up a mean breakfast sandwich." His tone is light and playful, but his expression is earnest.

Warmth courses through my veins and pools in my stomach. "I guess I could stay for breakfast. I need to call Callie, though."

"Great. I'll put on a pot of coffee while you do that." His warm fingertips graze the back of my hand as he passes. I don't think it's an accident.

After I call Callie, who's happy to open up for me, I message Daphne about coming in a little late this morning.

Her response is immediate:

Daphne: Are you sick?

Blaire: No. Late night planning with Ronan. I'll explain when I see you.

Daphne: Please tell me he has a big 🍆 and you rode it all night long.

I ignore her text.

Blaire: See you in a couple hours.

"Everything okay? You still good to stay for breakfast?" Ronan asks.

"Yup. All set. What can I do to help?"

He hands me a mug. "You can get this ready to be filled with coffee. I'm going to throw on a shirt, and then I'll start breakfast."

"Okay." I can't remember the last time a guy made me breakfast. Especially not after an accidental sleepover, which did not include sex. I think I kind of like it.

He pads across the living room and I get a look at his back, also covered in art. He's a living, breathing canvas. One I'd love to explore every inch of. And not just with my eyes.

@buttercreamandbooze:

You're the icing to my cupcake.

chapter fifteen

MISS MISTLETOE

Blaire

Look at the traction this post is getting!" Daphne shoves her phone in my face and waves it around, making it impossible to focus on the image.

I grab it from her, so I can see what she's so excited about. I frown, not because it's a bad image, but because I have no idea who took it or why it has so many comments or likes. It's a picture of Ronan and me, his arm slung over my shoulder and mine wrapped around his waist. We're smiling at each other, and while it's on his feed, it was taken in my shop. Based on what's happening in the background and my outfit, it was taken a couple of days ago when we had a post-Christmas, pre–New Year's collaborative event—which is what most of our events are at this point.

And it's turned out to be incredibly positive in terms of the Best Bar competition. We both made it through to the quarterfinals, although The Knight Cap managed to secure spot number twelve, while B&B ranked as number fifteen. I think it has a lot to do with our duets during karaoke nights, not that I'll say it out loud.

I read the caption. I'm aware that Ronan leaves that stuff to Lars and one of his servers, who sometimes pass things by me or Daphne, so they can manage what to post and when. This is clearly not a pre-approved post, but people seem to love it. Because they've dubbed us The Knight Cakes and have given us a hashtag.

"Who approved this hashtag? It's terrible."

"Really? I think it's cute." Daphne gives me her innocent look, which isn't innocent at all.

"Blonan is not a cute hashtag. It's too close to blowjob. Was this your idea? Who took this picture?"

"I had nothing to do with the hashtag. Your followers came up with it, and they're loving it. Everyone ships you two."

I roll my eyes. "We're not dating, we're collaborating."

"*Yet*. You're not dating *yet*."

We've had this conversation several times over the past three weeks—ever since the night I fell asleep on Ronan's couch. "Am I attracted to him? Yes. Is it a good idea to get involved with him? No."

"Says who?"

"Says anyone who knows what it's like to date someone you're working with. It's a recipe for disaster. See Raphael for details." She can't argue with that logic, considering the way that entire situation blew up in my face.

Although, if that hadn't happened I might not be here, working for myself. I may barely be making ends meet, and I may also be very much in need of a month-long nap, but at least I'm doing what I love.

"Raphael was a douche canoe, and it's not the same situation at all. You were not his equal, you were his student and he took advantage of a position of power. And then he seriously screwed you over because he likes to stick his dick in everything that moves. Including Baked Alaska."

I shudder at that image. "It's still not advisable. We're competing against each other for Best Bar *and* we're working together to keep our businesses afloat so those fuckers don't push us out." I motion across the street to the yet-to-open massive adult indoor arcade and bar.

Their grand opening is New Year's Eve, of course. Which is why Ronan and I have been spending an inordinate amount of time together planning our own New Year's bash.

We've gone over all the fine details relentlessly. I have not, however, been back to his place since the night I fell asleep on his couch. Has there been a suggestion that we might want to work at his place? Maybe, but since B&B closes earlier than The Knight Cap, it makes sense for us to plan at my shop. At least that's been my rationale, and he hasn't really pushed it.

Not to mention, that morning when I went into work late one of Tori Taylor's people, who happens to be local, stopped in before I arrived. I missed my chance to make a good impression—or any impression at all, really.

And of course that same person ended up at Ronan's, because he's in the competition, too—only Ronan made it to the bar in time. I might find him attractive, but I don't want to lose out on any other opportunities, should they arise.

It doesn't mean we're not flirting, or that I don't find myself staring at his mouth, wondering how his lips would feel on mine.

It just means I've been circumventing the potential for further complications and excessive distractions. Until this Best Bar competition is over and done with and we see what the impact of this whole Dick and Bobby's grand opening has on our respective bottom lines, I don't think it's a great idea to jump into his bed. Or jump him in general.

I do think about it frequently when I'm in the shower, and in my own bed. And everywhere, really.

"Earth to Blaire." Daphne snaps her fingers in my face. At the same time her camera goes off.

I jerk back. "What?"

"You were totally thinking about boning Ronan just now, weren't you?"

"I was not!"

"You definitely were. Look at the expression on your face!" She holds up her phone so I can see the picture she took.

I'm biting my lip and touching my throat, lost in a daydream. About riding Ronan. I push her phone away. "Whatever. Thinking about it and doing it aren't the same thing."

Daphne wiggles her eyebrows. "I give you max two weeks before you fold."

Fortunately, Callie arrives for her shift, ending that conversation.

During the lead-up to New Year's Eve I average about four hours of sleep a night, and it sure as hell isn't the restful kind. On the upside, the cohosted events with Ronan have been keeping me from digging further into my line of credit. It's a little less terrifying to pay the bills when I know I'm not turning my overdraft into a black hole every time or adding to my debt.

New Year's planning means lots of expenses, but ticket sales for the event have been incredible and we sold out completely last week, which helps offset all the costs.

On New Year's Eve, I'm up before six in the morning even though I went to bed at two. Ronan and I sat at his bar and went over the plan for tonight, double and triple checking that we have everything we need. Our cohosted New Year's party has been getting a lot of attention and rumor has it Tori Taylor is planning to come our way soon as the semifinal round closes in.

When I arrive at B&B, I notice that Ronan's truck is already there, which seems a lot early for him. Imagine my surprise when I walk into my shop and find Ronan behind the bar, making cappuccinos. "What're you doing here?"

He glances at me, eyes moving over me in that familiar way that makes a shiver run down my spine and heat pool south of the navel. "Good morning to you, too."

"Sorry. It's just a surprise to see you here at this hour." Ronan usually doesn't roll in until nine thirty or ten. "Oh God, nothing happened next door? We don't have another wrong delivery, do we?"

Ronan wipes his hands on his apron—he's wearing one with the B&B logo; actually, it's mine because it has the cupcake with the crown decoration—and wraps his hands around my arms. "Take a deep breath, Blaire. You look like you're on the verge of panic, and there is absolutely nothing to be worried about."

Over the past few weeks I've grown accustomed to Ronan's touch. The way he casually slings his arm over my shoulder. The frequent occasions where he picks me up and moves me out of the way when I'm ranting about something and he wants to multitask. And although I'm accustomed to it, I'm definitely not immune. I clear my throat before I speak; otherwise I'm liable to sound all breathy. "It's barely eight in the morning. How are you here and did you even sleep last night?" His hands slide down my arms and I fight a shiver.

He shrugs, looking sheepish. "I got a few hours. I plan to sleep all day tomorrow. I borrowed Daphne's key. I figured you might need some help this morning since you likely went to bed around the same time as me."

"Oh, well that's incredibly sweet of you. I'm going to

sleep all the sleeps tomorrow, too. It's going to be magic." I fight a yawn.

His eyes widen comically. "Oh no! Don't do that! They're contagious." We both cup our hands over our mouths and yawn at the same time. My eyes water. Lord, I'm going to be exhausted tomorrow.

A loud clank and hiss comes from behind him and we both startle.

"What the heck?" I grab on to his arm and hide behind him as he spins around.

I peek over his shoulder and get a glimpse of the cappuccino maker, which is currently steaming in places it shouldn't be.

"Oh shit, that doesn't look right." His expression reflects his horror.

"That's because it's not." I move around him, pulling the plug before it blows.

Ronan helps me clean up the mess. It turns out one of the seals has broken, so we're down a freaking cappuccino maker. I call around frantically, looking to see if someone can come in and fix it today. While we can usually get by with one machine, it's going to be busy tonight.

I manage to find someone who can come in this afternoon, but of course it's going to cost me a freaking arm and a leg. Ronan apologizes profusely, obviously feeling bad about it. I assure him it wasn't his fault, and that it's just crap timing.

The morning flies by; people working half-days stop in to grab a quick bite, orders are picked up for events, and by the time two rolls around we're almost completely sold out, which is great because it means little in the way of cleanup before we set up for tonight.

The cappuccino maker is fixed, thankfully, before three in the afternoon, and a test run indicates that it's back in working order.

By three thirty B&B is ready for the evening, tables set up to display tiers of dessert cupcakes, glittery decorations everywhere, a perfect complement to the beer and champagne theme. Everything is gold and black and sparkly and beautiful.

I stand in the middle of the shop with my hands on my hips. "I think it looks perfect. What do you think?"

"Definitely perfect." Ronan is still wearing a Buttercream and Booze apron, but his focus isn't on the decorations.

"You're not even looking." I motion to the shop.

"I don't need to. I helped put them up, so I already know how they look."

"But it's everything put together. That's what makes it perfect."

"And you're the cherry on top. Or maybe you should be one of those little Eat Me candies instead. Those are delicious. You got any lying around?"

"You realize that made no sense at all, right?"

"Sure it did. This place looks perfect and not just because the decorations are on point, but because you're in the middle of it, looking radiant and proud as hell, as you should be. Now where are those Eat Me candies?"

"There aren't any Eat Me candies."

"Well, that's a disappointment. I guess I'll have to settle for a leftover cupcake." He plucks one from a box—that's all there is left—peels off the wrapper and devours it in two bites, groaning his enjoyment.

When he's done, we head over to The Knight Cap and enlist the help of his staff to decorate. Much to Ronan's dismay, I hang mistletoe above the bar and over the tables.

"Aren't we a little late for this?"

"It's never too late for mistletoe."

"Like people don't already have an excuse to make out on New Year's; now you're adding this?" He motions to the pretty sprig tied with a red, gold, and black plaid ribbon hanging from one of the lights above the bar—which I'm standing on top of, while wearing a pair of the steel-toed boots reserved for the axe throwers.

On account of tonight's festivities and the very high likelihood that many if not most of the patrons will be "super wasted," as Lars put it, the axes have all been locked away. Standing tables have been set up and stools line the walls so there's more room for mingling and dancing.

"Oh, come on, don't be a Scrooge. These should have been up all month!"

"I'm just saying, Lars doesn't need an excuse to make out with the customers."

"Maybe some poor shy girl who would never in a million years have the guts to kiss the guy she's interested in will find herself under this mistletoe and end up kissed by her very own Prince Charming."

"More likely a bleary-eyed, horny, drunk guy, but I get that you're throwing off your wonderland vibes tonight and prefer to live in a land of fairy tales and make-believe where college guys aren't a bunch of dirtbags."

"Were you a dirtbag?" I ask. Ronan is flirty, but not in a slimy way.

"Not as a general rule, no."

I move down the bar to the next hanging light so I can wrap the glittery garland around it, affixing yet another sprig of mistletoe. "So that means you occasionally *were* a dirtbag." It's more statement than question.

"I'm not perfect, and I was once a drunk, horny twenty-something. Try not to judge me too harshly."

I move on to the next light. "How old were you when you started with the body art?"

Ronan hands me another set of ribbons. "When I was eighteen, but it wasn't until after I lost my parents that I started on the sleeves. Why?"

"I bet the college girls loved you, all tatted up and badass." I tap my lip. "And I'm sure that hasn't changed at all."

He barks out a laugh. "Lars is more the college girl catnip."

I glance at Lars and shrug. "I mean, he's a cute kid, and I'm sure there are plenty of college girls who would fall all over themselves to get his attention, but he's got the grace of an elephant trying to be a ballerina when he's hitting on women. I mean, he told *me* he'd love to take a ride on the cougar express."

Ronan's jaw drops. "He said *what*?"

"It was a joke." At least I'm going to pretend it was.

"Like hell it was. When did he say that? Was it recently? It better not have been recently." If looks could kill, Lars would be the ashy remains of a cremated corpse.

I prop a fist on my hip. "I think it was actually meant as a backward compliment."

"He was trying to get into your pants, like he tries to do with every single female he encounters that he isn't related to. Or under your skirt, since I've never seen you in a pair of pants. Ever." His gaze moves over my legs. I'm wearing a pair of sparkly tights.

"So really you're saying he'll screw anything with a pulse, no matter what she looks like?"

"He's not very discerning."

"Well, thanks." That's a blow my ego certainly doesn't need from the guy I'm crushing on. "I know I'm not a model-esque, highly fashionable beauty queen, but I'm not an ogre, either!"

"I didn't mean that you're unattractive—"

"No, just that Lars will bone anyone with a vagina, so don't be flattered that he hit on me. I get it." I've reached the end of the bar and crouch so the jump down isn't as far. The last thing I need tonight is to roll an ankle. I'm super tired and stressed about the event tonight, and for whatever reason the whole Lars thing gets my back up.

"Let me help you down." Ronan holds out a hand.

I swat it away. "I don't need help."

"Are you serious right now? Why are you suddenly all pissy?"

"I'm not pissy," I say rather pissily.

"Really?"

"Move out of the way so I can get down." Now I'm snippy to go with the pissy. And because I'm extra overtired, and maybe a little too hopped up on caffeine, I'm also very close to irrational tears. I better not be getting my period on top of everything else.

"Or you could just let me help you."

"I told you, I'm fine." I put a hand on the edge of the bar so I can hop the three and a half feet to the floor.

But before I can make a move Ronan steps closer and wraps his hands around my waist. I don't expect him to lift me off the bar, so I tip forward. Grabbing his shoulder, I slide down the front of his body. His very firm, hard, muscular body.

Ronan has a lot of ridges and planes and angles. But as my hips glide down his abs I'm suddenly aware of a very significant, prominent lump as I make the trip past his fly.

He's still holding on to my waist, and I'm still clutching his shoulders. I attempt to step back, but his grip tightens. I tip my chin up and blink up at him.

His expression is mostly flat as he dips his head down until his mouth is at my ear. "I would appreciate it if you didn't call me out right now, Blaire, but as I'm sure you can feel, the head below the belt, which happens to respond to messages from my brain, does *not* find you unattractive. In fact, based on my inability to control said head, I would say that's evidence that we find you rather appealing and both of us would prefer it if Lars would keep his commentary to himself and his damn eyeballs off you."

He backs up enough that his face comes into focus. His expression is far from remote now; it's full of heat. The same kind of heat pooling in my belly. I'd like to say something cheeky about the fact that he's referring to his penis as if it's an independent thinker, but my mouth has gone dry.

I manage to whisper, "Noted."

"Great. I'm going to take a minute to get a handle on things." He cringes. "Not an actual handle. I'm just going to think about unappealing things. I'll be back."

He lets go of me and I drop my arms. I watch him walk away, stiffly.

Lars appears beside me. "Where's Ronan going?"

"He's taking a minute to collect himself." I don't mean to go with such blatant honesty.

Lars smirks and jerks his chin up. "I bet he is. Dude's been staring at your legs for the past half hour like he's watching a damn striptease. You two just need to hook up and get it over with. The sexual tension is making *me* all edgy and shit." He slings his towel over his shoulder and saunters back to the bar where he's skewering fruit for cocktails.

I glance up at the mistletoe hanging from the lights and consider how it might come in handy later.

By four thirty in the afternoon we're completely set up, the food is prepped, tables are decorated, and menus are laid out. Now it's just a matter of changing, freshening my makeup, and mainlining about four gallons of coffee.

The evening doesn't go off without a hitch; there are glitches. B&B runs out of the top-shelf vodka, but Ronan is there to save the day with his own stock. Thankfully we've agreed to split costs and revenue, so it's not a big deal. One of the servers slips on a French fry and loses an entire tray of cupcakes, but overall it's an incredible success. And while there's a line outside of Dick and Bobby's celebrating their grand opening, we're at max capacity and end up having to turn people away, which is unfortunate but also a good thing.

The adrenaline pumping through my veins means I'm probably going to crash hard when the bar finally closes, but for the time being I'm enjoying the success of the event.

As midnight approaches, I find myself behind the bar with Ronan, mixing drinks. His fireworks-patterned tie is thrown over his shoulder so it doesn't soak up anything spilled on the bartop. Despite the extra staff, they can't seem to keep up with the demands and the lineup to get to the bar is three deep as people order champagne cocktails to toast the New Year.

I lost my heels hours ago in exchange for the steel-toe boots required behind the bar, which means I've also lost three inches of height, and I have to stretch to reach the bottles on the high shelves.

Ronan reaches over me and grabs the bottle I need, then bends so his mouth is at my ear, shouting over the music so I can hear him. "Tell me what you need, and I'll get it for you." His lips brush the shell as he speaks, sending a warm shiver down my spine.

I nod because I've been shouting most of the night and my voice is pretty much gone. The front of my fireworks-and-champagne-glasses dress is damp from leaning over the bar, and I smell like champagne and beer, but I couldn't be happier.

We work together, passing bottles and garnishes without having to speak because we each seem to know what the other needs. He reaches around behind me, our bodies touching constantly as we pour and serve, pour and serve.

Then the countdown begins, and there's a tiny pause in the mayhem behind the bar as the crowd raise their drinks in the air, shouting and laughing their way into the New Year.

"Here, take this." Ronan wraps my hand around a shot glass and clinks his own against it.

"What is it?"

"Just drink it," he shouts.

We raise our glasses to our lips and I knock back the shot. Shouts of "Happy New Year!" rise to almost unbearable levels as it burns its way down my throat.

"Happy New Year!" Lars screams and gives us a double hug and then points to the light above us. "Look up." And then he's off down the bar, yelling "*Happy New Year!*" at the top of his lungs.

Ronan and I look up at the same time and realize that we happen to be standing directly under one of the sprigs of mistletoe. Our gazes meet, and I can see the resolve in his eyes. I'm sure the few shots we've done behind the bar tonight are fully responsible for what happens next.

Ronan slips one hand around my waist and pulls me against him. He tips his head to the side fractionally: a silent question. I respond by sliding my hands over his chest to lock them behind his neck, tugging gently as I tip my chin up.

His other hand curves around my nape as he dips down and his warm, minty breath mingles with mine. "Happy New Year, Blaire."

"Happy New Year, Ronan."

A shock of energy lights me up like a neon sign, zinging through my veins as our lips meet for the first time. It's a full-body tingle, starting at my scalp, working its way down my body. Heat funnels straight between my thighs and my toes curl.

We tip our heads in opposite directions, lips parting, tongues sliding against each other. He groans and I moan as we open wider, tongues stroking deeper. I grip the back of his neck and the hand on my waist drifts lower. Cupping my left butt cheek, Ronan pulls me tighter against him. I feel him hard against my stomach, and I press my hips closer.

I'm pretty sure the kiss would have lasted forever—or until

we got naked—except the sudden hoots, hollers, and shrill whistles remind us that we're not even remotely alone.

We break apart and I worry for a second that maybe this wasn't the best idea. Realistically it's not a good plan to get involved with my competition/neighbor, but that was one hell of a kiss.

Ronan blinks a couple of times and blows out a breath. "I don't think we're in Wonderland anymore, Alice."

I laugh, glad he's broken the tension.

"You're coming back to my place after we close tonight, right?"

I cock a brow.

"Or we can go to yours if that's better. Or closer," he adds.

"Are you saying you want more of this?" I motion to my lips.

The music has started again and there are patrons clamoring for drinks, but Ronan holds a finger up in their direction and leans in close so his lips are at my ear again. "I want all of this. Repeatedly. And while my office has a door that locks, I'm not sure I'll give my best performance in there."

"Mmm. Good point. Your place it is."

@buttercreamandbooze:

When stressed and in doubt, CUP-CAKE it out.

chapter sixteen

RINGING IN THE NEW YEAR

Ronan

It's after three in the morning by the time we get an Uber back to my place. I usher Blaire inside, lock the door, and turn around.

She's standing in the middle of my front hallway, still wearing the steel-toed boots I forced on her because there was no way I was risking her twisting an ankle behind the bar, which was where I wanted her. Right beside me all night long. Not on the floor where she'd get hit on relentlessly by drunk assholes.

It might sound chivalrous. It's not—my motives were purely self-serving.

She clasps her hands in front of her, looking demure and sexy in her fireworks dress with black and plaid accents. We matched, of course. Her teeth sink into her bottom lip. I kissed her lipstick off hours ago and she didn't bother to reapply, mostly because there was no time.

"Do you want something to drink?" My voice is rough like sandpaper.

Her brow furrows for a moment, as if she finds the question confusing. "Do you?"

I take a few steps in her direction. "Not particularly, no, but I figured I should be hospitable and offer rather than just attack you with my mouth and hands." *And parts below the waist.*

"Hmm." She taps her lip, a playful smile on those luscious lips of hers. "Water for hydration purposes might be a good idea, but that can probably wait until after you attack me with your mouth and hands." Her eyes move down my chest in a slow, hot sweep. "And other parts, hopefully."

We are so on the same page. And then we're on each other.

Blaire loops her arms over my shoulders and links her hands behind my neck, pulling my mouth to hers. I grip her waist and walk her backward through the short entryway, careful not to bump into the side table on the right. The bedroom seems too far away, so I swipe a hand blindly across the kitchen counter, knocking a few things out of the way before I lift her up and deposit her on top.

The kiss slows for all of two beats, and then we're right back at it, full force, teeth clashing, tongues battling, moaning into each other's mouths. Blaire tugs my shirt free from my pants, then starts on the buttons while I search the back of her dress for a zipper. All I find is smooth fabric.

She breaks the kiss long enough to say, "Hidden zipper."

I pull back, because that makes no sense. "What?"

"It's hidden." She abandons my shirt and pushes on my chest, forcing me back. I'm about to protest, but she reaches under her skirt and MacGyvers her poofy under-skirt thing off, tossing it on the floor. Then she grabs the front of my shirt and yanks me between her legs again.

I start feeling up and down her spine, in search of this hidden zipper. I finally find one, but it's tiny and I keep losing my grip on it.

"How do you get the zipper down?" I mumble around her tongue.

"Don't worry about it, all the important parts are easily accessible." She hikes the skirt of her dress higher, trying to shift the fabric out of the way.

I pull back so I can see her in the dimly lit kitchen. The lamp on the other side of the living room is weak, and the hall light leading to my bedroom is on a dimmer switch, set to low.

"I would like the full experience here, not just access to what's between your thighs." I motion to her crotch. "I mean, I definitely want that, but I plan to explore every last inch of you in the process."

I have every intention of devouring her, but I'd like to do that while also savoring the experience. I take my time unzipping the dress—actually, the tiny zipper tab is a pain in my ass, so half the slowing down is forced because it's a struggle and I'm determined to be the one to undress her, on my own, without her help.

I finally manage the zipper situation, but there's a freaking hook thing, too, which means more struggles on my end.

She chuckles against my lips, sucking on the bottom one. I finally unclasp it, but instead of removing the dress I delay my own gratification and hers. It's like unwrapping the best, belated birthday present.

I pull the bodice down, freeing her arms to reveal her bra. I let out a low, appreciative whistle. Under the dress with the gold and black plaid accents she's wearing a black bra with red and gold plaid accents. I'm willing to bet the panties match, because this is Blaire we're talking about and her wardrobe is always meticulously planned. I lift her skirt so I can take a peek. Yup, they totally match, which begs the question, "Were you planning to seduce me tonight?"

Her brow furrows. "What? No, of course not. Why would you think that?"

"Because..." I run my hands up her thighs, warm and soft, bunching up the skirt, exposing more skin as I do. I savor the feel of her under my hands, the way her breath stutters when I skim the edge of her panties with my fingertips. "This bra and panty set looks like it was picked out with me in mind."

"I wanted to coordinate it with my dress."

"Which you bought so we'd match." I slip my hands out from under her skirt, much to her dismay, so I can cup her full breasts in my palms and run my thumbs over her nipples through the fabric.

She arches and sucks in a breath. "I like things that match."

"So that means you did inadvertently buy these for me."

"If you need to stroke your own ego over my choice of bra and panties, go for it."

"Do you have matching sets for all of your dresses?" I slip my pinkie under the satin.

"Some, not all."

"Hmm." And now it's become my mission to unwrap her like a present as often as she'll allow so I can see what kind of lingerie she's wearing underneath. For that to happen, I need to guarantee that she's going to want a repeat of tonight. Which means bringing my A-game.

We get back to making out, her half-dressed, me still fully clothed. I loosen my tie with one hand while she tackles the remaining buttons on my shirt. They join the other clothes on the floor and I break the kiss long enough to get my undershirt off.

I'm ready to dive back in, but Blaire's palms connect with my chest, preventing our lips from meeting. She drags her nails from my pecs down to my abs. "So sexy," she murmurs on a soft sigh. She lifts her gaze. "You know, I never thought tattoos were hot before you, but now..." She traces the outline of the tree that decorates my side and disappears into the waistband of my pants. "So much yum."

I laugh and then groan when she goes lower and cups me through my pants.

"I was so disappointed when you put on a shirt the morning after I accidentally fell asleep on your couch."

"I was kind of disappointed that you fell asleep and didn't end up in my bed with me."

"Really?" She slips my belt through the loops and starts to unbuckle it.

"I went to the bathroom so I could brush my teeth and freshen up. I was thinking maybe I'd make a move, but when I came back you were out like a light."

"I had no idea." She pops the button.

"I've been flirting with you since day one."

"I was too busy being aggravated that you were my competition and you were so hot, and composed, and I was always too flustered to notice that you were flirting. Plus, it's your job to flirt." She drags the zipper down slowly.

"I'm friendly with customers, but I flirt with *you*. There's a difference."

"Hmm. You'll have to explain that difference later, so I'm in the know." She slips her index finger under the waistband of my boxer briefs and pulls them away from my skin, peeking inside. I doubt she can see much since the lights are low and it's dark in my underwear.

"What're you doing?"

"I want to see what I'm dealing with."

"You can touch him, he doesn't bite."

"Him?" She peeks up, her expression amused. "Does he have a name?"

I scoff. "Of course not." I call him The Sword of Destiny in my head, though.

"I don't believe you." She reaches inside and skims the length.

I groan and prop one fist on the counter, the other still cupping her breast. I have plans to take that bra off eventually, but I'm kind of in love with it and also distracted by the fact that her hand is in my pants.

She wraps her fingers around me, giving me a tentative squeeze before she frees me from my boxers. Her bottom lip is between her teeth and she peers down, exhaling what sounds like a relieved breath along with the words. "Thank God."

"Thank God, what?"

Her gaze flips back up to mine, and I have a feeling she didn't mean to say that out loud. Her cheeks might be turning pink, but the lighting makes it hard to tell.

"I just wasn't sure where the tattoos started and ended."

I bark out a laugh. "That's a hard pass area for me. There isn't much going on below the waist."

Blaire raises a brow and gives my erection a squeeze. "I'd beg to differ."

"I mean tattoo wise."

"Ah yes, well, I guess I'll be able to confirm that soon enough."

She pulls my mouth back to hers and I continue to tease her nipple while she strokes me. It's probably an awkward angle for her hand, considering I'm standing between her thighs, but I'm not all that interested in stopping her and she doesn't seem to mind.

When the sensation gets to be too much for me to handle— meaning when I'm worried I'm going to blow in her hand— I start kissing my way down her neck.

Reaching around behind her, I flick the clasp of her bra open. It slides down her arms and lands on the counter, then drops to the floor with the rest of our clothes. I kiss my way across her collarbone and down over the swell until I can cover a nipple with my mouth.

Blaire moans, and she loses her grip on my erection. It's not a bad thing, considering I'm already close to an edge I don't want to be near when we've hardly even started with the foreplay.

Her fingers slide into my hair, the other hand moving to grip my shoulder. I use her distraction to my advantage and tuck myself back into my pants so I can focus on making her feel good. If I can make her come before the sex—if we get to that, I'm not making assumptions but I'm hoping—then it'll take some of the pressure off.

I ease my palm up her thigh, moving inward. Her legs are parted to accommodate me, so when I reach the apex I brush my knuckles over the satin.

"Oh yes, please." She spreads her legs wider.

This is what I want, for all that uptight Instagram perfection to fall away. I want her uninhibited and unworried about anything but how she feels. I keep sweeping my knuckles back and forth, barely skimming the damp fabric. "Do you like that, Blaire?"

"Mmm, it's nice." She wriggles her butt.

I slip a single finger under the elastic and I'm met with hot, wet skin.

"Oh, that's so much nicer." Her eyes flutter closed as I stroke her center, easing a finger inside.

She props herself on her arms and she bites her lip, moaning softly when I add a second finger. Her head rolls on her shoulders and her lids flutter open, gaze dropping to where my forearm disappears under her skirt. "God, that is so hot," she groans, and her fingertips graze my inked arm.

"It is, isn't it?" I agree. "You look like a good girl who got caught up with a bad boy." She looks like she fell right out of the fifties with her perfect hair and retro dresses, which makes her current position, with the top hanging at her waist and my hand under the bunched-up skirt, seem that much more illicit. And those steel-toed boots paired with her thigh-high stockings are the icing on the sexy cupcake.

She drags her skirt up higher, exposing my hidden forearm and wrist, all the way up to where her panties are pushed to the side and I'm buried inside her.

I curl the fingers of my free hand around the back of her neck, thumb stroking along the edge of her jaw. "You like watching what I'm doing to you, Blaire?"

She fists the fabric and moans again. "Yes."

"You gonna be a good girl and come all over my hand?" I pump faster, taking cues from the way her breath catches.

"Oh God," she groans and tries to close her legs, but her knees hit my hips. And then her orgasm hits—she contracts around my fingers, hips swiveling as she rides my hand.

"You are so damn sexy," I assure her.

Before the orgasm wanes, I withdraw my fingers. She makes a plaintive sound, probably unimpressed that I stopped mid-orgasm, but I'm planning to make up for that. I yank her panties down. They get caught up on her boots, but I manage to get them off without shredding them. I grip her by the hip and drag her to the edge of the counter as I drop to my knees.

"What—"

The rest of her question dissolves into a gasp when I lick up her center.

She falls back on one elbow, the other hand sliding into my hair and gripping tight.

"Mmm, just like one of those cream-filled cupcakes you made me eat in front of that bachelorette party." I cover her sex with my mouth. "But tastes even better."

That gets a moan out of her, slightly embarrassed, but also totally turned on based on the way she rolls her hips and rides my tongue back to another orgasm.

As soon as I rise up, she grabs the nape of my neck with one hand and fuses her mouth to mine. She mumbles something completely unintelligible, mostly because she's sucking on my tongue. She frantically searches for the waistband of my underwear with the other one and jams her hand down the front, freeing me from my boxers.

She breaks the kiss. "You have condoms, right?"

I pull my wallet from my back pocket, flip it open, and slap it on the counter so I can retrieve the condom that's been in there since before August.

As soon as it's in my hand, Blaire nabs it and squints at the date before she tears it open. Her tongue peeks out as she rolls it down my length and uses her foot—the boots are still on, and I'm still wearing my pants—to pull me closer.

"Hold on. Raise your arms."

She frowns but complies, maybe because the orgasms have made her less argumentative, or possibly she's just as ready as I am for sex, even after two orgasms. I grab the bottom of her dress and lift it over her head. It messes up her perfect hair a little, but all that does is make her sexier.

And totally naked.

"You're a vision, Blaire." Anticipation makes my erection kick in my fist, but I force myself to slow it down for a beat. I drag the head of my condom-covered length along her sex. "You ready for me?"

"So damn ready." She bites her lip.

"You want slow and soft or fast and hard?" I line myself up and meet her hot, needy gaze.

She gives me a saucy grin. "Surprise me."

I chuckle. "Such a good bad girl." I grab her hips to steady her as I push inside.

She scrambles to lock her hands around the back of my neck. When I'm sure she's latched on good and tight I pull back out, almost all the way before I thrust again. Her jaw goes slack and her eyes roll up on a deep groan.

"Okay?" I ask, before I do it again.

"Yes. Please don't stop."

I shift her so she's right at the edge of the counter and pump into her, taking my cues from her moans and her pleas not to stop. As it turns out, Blaire seems to be a fan of hard and fast.

It doesn't take long before I'm warning her I'm about to come. I can always improve endurance on round two. She pries one hand from my neck and dips her fingers between her thighs. "Hold on, I'm so close."

I'm teetering on the edge, barely hanging on. "Listen to you, wanting more when you've come twice already."

"I know, I know, but it's so good. Please, Ronan."

"Better work fast," I warn.

I try to think of something, anything to stop the inevitable, but Blaire's lip is caught between her teeth, pressing in hard, and her fingers are moving at a furious pace between her legs, as if she's trying to light a damn fire.

I thrust one last time before the orgasm rockets down my spine, and I explode. That sensation is magnified a thousand-fold when Blaire contracts around me.

My legs threaten to give out, so I lean against the counter, letting it take some of my weight while I regain the ability to function. Blaire runs her fingers through my hair.

Eventually I lift my head and kiss a path up her shoulder to her mouth.

"Hey."

"Hey." She nibbles my bottom lip. "So that was fun."

I laugh, which makes her gasp and clench and my chuckle

turns into a groan as I slowly ease out. I remove the condom, tie it off and toss it in the garbage by the sink. "You're gonna stay the night, right?"

She blows out a breath. "Well, I mean, it's probably a good idea since I've been pretty greedy and I think we probably need to even out the orgasm totals so I'm not winning by such a wide margin."

@the_knightcap:

The hangover only lasts a day, but the memories last a lifetime.

chapter seventeen

AFTER THE ORGASMS

Blaire

I wake up to Ronan wrapped around me, although it's the sound of a phone ringing that drags me out of the delicious sleep haze. Based on the tone, it's not mine.

"Ronan?"

He grunts and shifts his hips.

I'm not entirely convinced he's awake.

His tattooed arm is wrapped around me, his forearm across my chest, his hand tucked under my shoulder, fingers curling around the back. I think we've been spooning the entire night.

While I can certainly believe last night happened because the attraction is strong with this one, what I didn't expect, and maybe should have, was exactly what kind of lover Ronan would be. Demanding, intense, giving, and insanely attentive.

We stumbled into his bed at four in the morning, and I

would have gone to sleep wearing those steel-toed boots if he hadn't been lucid enough to take them off for me. I did not have a chance to make good on my promise to even out our orgasms because we promptly passed out.

I crane my neck to check the clock on the nightstand. It's already one in the afternoon. That's not a huge surprise, given the ridiculous time we went to bed or the fact that we've both been running on a massive sleep deficit.

Regardless, sleeping the entire day away seems like a waste, since I have so few free ones. I wiggle around in Ronan's arm and he mutters something about being impatient and greedy and nuzzles into my neck.

His phone goes off again, and then again a minute later. Someone is clearly trying to get hold of him.

"Ronan, your phone keeps going off."

"I'm not awake." His raspy sleep voice does tingly things to my body, specifically in the area between my thighs.

"Then how come you're talking to me?"

"I'm not. You're dreaming."

I laugh and he rubs up against me.

"I can go get your phone for you so you don't have to leave this bed," I offer.

"No."

I try another tactic. "I need to use the bathroom, and when I come back I can help even out the lopsided orgasm tally from last night."

He releases me from his hold, rolls onto his back, and throws the covers off, giving me a great view of how excited he is about that prospect. "We'll be right here waiting for you."

Muscles ache that I didn't even know existed. And my tailbone is sore, probably from the counter sex. I use the bathroom first, then go in search of his phone. I find it on the edge of the kitchen counter; it looks as if we very nearly knocked it onto the floor last night. It starts ringing again on my way back to the bedroom.

"Six missed calls in the past twenty minutes. I think you should probably answer before we get sidetracked with extracurriculars." I toss the phone on the bed beside him.

He eyes it like it's a poisonous spider. He's ridiculously appealing, lying in bed, hair sleep-messed, pillow lines on his cheek, body art on display. I want to spend some time exploring all the designs and learning what each one means. After morning sex. Or afternoon sex, as it were. I climb back into bed and snuggle into his warm body. He slips his arm under me and pulls me closer. His lips find my temple as he glances at his phone.

"Oh shit, it's after one?" Ronan brings the device to his ear. "Hey, brother, I know I'm late. I'm sorry. It was a busy night and I slept in." He's silent for a few seconds. "I just woke up. Give me an hour and start without me if you need to, but save me a few of the cinnamon raisin ones, please. No, fuck off. And I'm bringing a friend." He ends the call and tosses his phone on the nightstand.

"What's going on?"

"We have to go to Gramps's place in a bit."

"We?"

"Yeah, you're coming with. It's a family tradition that we get together on New Year's Day. I was supposed to be there at noon, but forgot to set my alarm. I'm not letting you out of my sight for the rest of the day. But first, orgasms."

Half an hour later we have a very quick shower since our antics have put us even further behind. I'm forced to put my dress from last night back on. Not ideal, but then I didn't expect to ring in the New Year in Ronan's bed.

We have to Uber to the bar to get Ronan's truck before we can do anything else. "We'll stop at your place on the way so you don't have to wear last night's dress again."

"That'd be great." I slide into the passenger seat.

Since we're already running late, later than before, I rush up and decide to forgo the dress today, and throw on a pair of jeans and a sweater. I don't often wear jeans, but I do own a few cute pairs. I also pull my hair up into a ponytail. I'm mostly makeup free, but I give my lashes a quick swipe with the mascara brush and throw on a coat of lip gloss. I shrug into my winter coat and rush back down to Ronan, who's busy scrolling through his phone.

I slide back into the passenger seat and buckle up. His eyes move over my legs and up my thighs. From mid-thigh up, they're covered by my coat. "Is this okay? I don't need to be more formal, do I?"

"No. You look great. Jeans are perfect." He puts the truck into gear. "I've just never seen you in a pair before."

His gaze lingers on my legs before he shifts his focus to the road.

"So who's all going to be there?"

"My brothers, their significant others, and Lars may or may not come. Depends on what he got up to after the bar closed." Lars had a lot of attention last night. And I'm pretty sure three girls took advantage of the mistletoe hanging over the bar, and that was only what I saw when I wasn't too busy serving drinks. "Daniel is the oldest. He's thirty-seven, and a big-time financial advisor. His wife, Celia, is a teacher."

"Is she the pregnant one?"

Ronan nods. "Yup. And she's kind of at that weird in-between stage where she just looks like she's put on weight but there isn't enough of a bump that you can be sure she's pregnant, so she's taken to wearing shirts that advertise the fact that she hasn't eaten too many Christmas cookies, and my brother is ridiculous about it. So fucking proud that his sperm managed to hit the mark."

I chuckle at that. "Aw, that's kind of cute, though, isn't it?"

"Kind of, I guess. Mostly it makes me want to gag. You'll see what I mean."

"I literally cannot imagine Maddy or Skylar having children. God forbid they don't get a full night's sleep or have to change a messy diaper." I'd ask Ronan how he feels about kids, but I don't feel like that's a great conversation post first-sexy-times sleepover. "Okay, so Daniel is the oldest and he's married to Celia, who's a teacher and is pregnant. And your other brother, is he married, too?"

"Engaged, actually. Aiden and Leslie have been together for eight years, and living together for six, so the wedding is pretty much a formality. They were going to elope in Vegas, but she's an only child and her mom would have been devastated if she didn't have a real ceremony, so they decided a destination wedding was the best option."

"Oh, that's fun."

"We'll see. She's also in finance, and so is half of her family, so most dinner conversations revolve around the state of the stock market when they're all together."

"That sounds..."

"Boring?"

"Normal?" I offer.

"Boringly normal. Anyway, with Celia there we'll at least have some balance and I'm sure they'll ask you all sorts of questions and try to get you to let them manage your financial portfolio."

"I don't have much of a financial portfolio to speak of, so I'm not sure I'd be worth managing."

"Buttercream and Booze is doing amazingly well, though."

"Oh yes, definitely. But I'm putting pretty much everything I have into it right now, so there's not much extra to play around with. For now, anyway." I'm hopeful things keep going the way they are, but with Dick and Bobby's across the street we're bound to see a dip, at least while it's shiny and new. Hopefully it will all balance out after the initial excitement is over.

Ronan taps the steering wheel. "I really think it's commendable that you're doing it all on your own."

"It makes the reward of success that much greater, you know?"

"Yeah. I can see that, especially for someone like you." We pass over the freeway, heading away from Pioneer Square and the downtown area into the more residential neighborhoods.

"Someone like me?"

"You come from this family who could easily push you around, but you managed to stand your ground and prove to them that you can make your own mark. And they don't even really know." Ronan makes a right down a quiet residential street with older homes that have been well maintained.

"Their version of success and mine aren't the same. I don't want creepy statues with hard-ons all over my house. Or so much space that I could literally get lost on the way to my bedroom and never find my way back. I just want to do what I love and be surrounded by the people I care about."

"I feel exactly the same way." He gives my hand a squeeze, then pulls into the driveway of a quaint, brick, two-story house.

When we reach the front door, I have a moment of panic. "Oh no! I'm showing up empty-handed. Maybe we should stop somewhere and grab a bottle of wine? There has to be a convenience store open somewhere that sells wine, right?"

"Don't worry about it, Blaire. There's going to be more food and booze than an army can consume. And even if we found an open store, all they're going to have is cheap wine that tastes like tomorrow's headache. Trust me when I say it's okay that we're coming empty-handed. Plus I dropped stuff off a few days ago for this occasion, and my brew shed is out back, so we're all set."

He doesn't knock on the door, just lets himself in, ushering me ahead of him. I'm greeted by the most delicious combination of scents. I breathe in cinnamon and cloves along with hints of citrus and cranberry. But more pungent is the aroma of something fried and sweet. "Oh, wow, what is that smell?"

"New Year's cookies, but they're more like donuts and they're the perfect cure for a post–New Year's Eve hangover."

"I'm not hungover, though."

"Well, we're about to start drinking again, so these should help prevent one." He helps me out of my coat and groans. "Ah hell, Blaire."

"What? Is everything okay?" I'm about to spin around to see what's going on, but he grabs me by the hips.

He pulls me back into him, dropping his head so his lips are at my ear. "These jeans are going to kill me. Now I have a perfect visual of all those curves you keep hidden under those skirts. It's going to be a long, uncomfortable afternoon for me."

I grin. Unlike Maddy and Skylar, I have curves. I learned very early on to embrace those curves and love the hell out of them.

One Halloween—around the time the parent swap

happened—I dressed as June Cleaver. And surprisingly, I felt the most comfortable in my skin. Maybe because my conventional family unit had been obliterated. Maybe because I liked the idea of an uncomplicated life. Of pot roasts, family dinners, and parents who worked normal jobs.

While I might not fit the entire June Cleaver mold, considering I have my own business, it's the style I adopted so I could hold on to that comforting idea of family values and morals. Plus I love dresses, but I don't mind sliding into a pair of jeans once in a while, possibly more often if this is the kind of reaction I get.

"I thought I heard the door. Oh, Miss Cupcake! When Ronan said he was bringing a friend I didn't realize it would be you." Ronan's grandfather ambles slowly toward us. "What a pleasant surprise." He grins, and his eyes almost disappear under his bushy brows. I would guess he's somewhere around eighty. He's a few inches shorter than Ronan, although I'm sure he was closer to the same height in his younger years, before his shoulders rounded.

"Hi, Mr. Knight. I hope it's not an imposition." I've met Ronan's grandfather a couple of times in passing, and we've exchanged hellos and an introduction, but I've always been busy during the day and he's never been around by the end of the evening.

"Not at all, dearie. And you can call me Henry; no mister anything is necessary, or Gramps works if yer comfortable with that." He winks and clasps my hand between his gnarled fingers. "I wondered when my grandson would finally find his balls and ask ya out on a date."

"Really, Gramps?" I can practically feel Ronan's embarrassment.

"What? She's been all you can talk about for months, riles you right up and puts a smile on yer face. It was bound to happen when ya got yer head outta yer ass."

"Okay, Gramps, you're killin' my game."

"Is that Ronan?" Another man appears in an adjacent doorway. Based on his facial features, he's definitely one of Ronan's brothers. He's shorter than Ronan, but just as broad and athletic, with the same hair and eye coloring, except he has a little gray flirting at the temples. "'Bout time you got here!" He pulls his brother into a hug, and they exchange firm back pats. He lowers his voice, keeping Ronan close. "Celia's still got freaking morning sickness, so she can't help with shit. And Leslie thinks every single cookie needs to be uniform in shape, so we've only managed one damn batch. All I want to do is drink scotch and eat cookies. Help a brother out."

"I'm on it, don't worry." Ronan pulls me into his side. "And I brought reinforcements. Daniel, this is Blaire, and she can bake every single person here under the table."

"Hi, Blaire." He extends his hand. His palms are soft, like the most strenuous thing he does is swing a golf club. "Ronan didn't mention having a girlfriend at Christmas."

"Oh, I'm not his girlfriend." I glance at Ronan.

His gaze meets mine and he shrugs with a questioning expression. "Well, I mean..."

"Am I your girlfriend?" It's an actual question, because riding his metaphorical bologna pony doesn't necessarily mean we're a thing.

"I brought you to a family function, so that generally means I wouldn't have a problem introducing you as my girlfriend."

Daniel snorts, and Gramps's smile widens.

"I invited you to a family function when you and I were barely civil to each other." I'm not sure why I feel the need to bring this up, because all it's doing is making this awkward situation even more awkward, since Daniel and Gramps are ping-ponging between us, watching this go down with something like gleeful amusement.

"Yeah, but we had a connection right from the start. And you invited me because you felt guilty, so it wasn't an actual date. And come to think of it, I was a shield more than anything." Ronan's grinning, like he finds this entire thing entertaining as well.

My cheeks heat at his instant-connection reference since he's correct, even though I was determined not to find him sexy, at least when he was being inflexible and breaking my unicorn glasses. "You weren't a shield. It was a spur-of-the-moment invitation, and yes I felt some guilt, but that wasn't the sole impetus for asking you to come along. I mean, look at you." I motion to his casual attire, which consists of a long-sleeved shirt, pushed up to expose half of his forearms, and his dark wash jeans. "You're not exactly hard on the eyes. And while you were certainly a convenient distraction from my family's lunacy, it wasn't the dominant motivating factor."

Ronan cocks a brow. "I see how it is. You just wanted to objectify me."

I shrug. "Didn't hurt to have someone nice to look at while the insanity ensued."

Daniel claps Ronan on the shoulder. "You've finally met your match. This is so great. Just don't get hitched before Aiden and Leslie, or she's never going to let him live it down, and it'll be the rest of us who suffer."

Ronan gives him a *what the hell* look. "Thanks for making this introduction not awkward at all, Dan."

"I'm here for you, bro. Now please get your ass in the kitchen so I can eat some damn donuts."

"Watch yer language in front of Blaire," Gramps warns. He's been quietly standing off to the side, hands clasped in front of him, rocking back on his heels. Until the profanity anyway. Now his expression is adorably stern.

"It's fine, Henry." I put a comforting hand on his arm and wink. "I'm a big girl; I've heard all the bad words."

He pats my hand. "Oh, I'm sure you have. And they're not donuts, they're New Year's cookies. Dottie could nae stand it when the boys called them donuts. Drove her batty. Rest her soul." He makes the sign of the cross and blinks a few times, eyes shadowed in sadness for a moment before they clear. "Come, dear, let's get you a drink."

A full bar is set up, and I opt for one of Ronan's beers, because they're delicious and if I sip it slowly I won't have to worry about getting tipsy too fast.

We find Leslie and Aiden in the kitchen. This time Ronan introduces me as his girlfriend, and I don't dispute him. Aiden pulls Ronan in for a hug. "Thank God you're here, man. Save me, please."

Leslie looks frazzled and like she would rather be doing anything other than standing in front of a pot of boiling oil.

The kitchen probably hasn't been renovated since sometime in the nineties if I had to guess based on the cabinets. There's a new stainless steel stove, fridge, and dishwasher, though. I'm assuming either Ronan or his brothers were responsible for the updates to bring his grandfather into the twenty-first century, at least from an appliance standpoint.

I survey the counter, the giant bowl of dough, the variety of adds-ins in the form of cinnamon and sugarcoated apple chunks, chopped dried fruit, and raisins. "Oh! It's *oliebollen*!"

"Huh?" Everyone in the kitchen turns to look at me.

"*Oliebollen*. Mennonite New Year's cookies. They're the same thing. I loved these as a kid!" I motion to the spread.

"You know what these are?" Leslie asks. She sounds somewhere between hopeful and desperate.

"I haven't had them since I was a teenager, but definitely. My grandmother was Mennonite."

"Seriously?" Ronan's shock is actually reasonable.

"Non-practicing. She passed when I was fourteen, but up until then we had *oliebollen* every New Year's. They just bring back so many great memories." Before my family let all their crazy hang out. I realize I'm getting misty, which is embarrassing in front of a bunch of people I've just met who are related to my new boyfriend.

Thankfully, Leslie seems oblivious. "Do you know how to make them?"

"Blaire runs Buttercream and Booze, the place next to The Knight Cap."

"This is Alice in Wonderland?" Aiden's eyes dart between the two of us. "I mean. Damn."

"You've mentioned me before?" I arch a brow, waiting to see how he's going to try to get out of this.

"Mentioned you before? Dude was obsessed at the end of the summer, pretty much every single time I got on the phone with him he was moaning about how good your cupcakes were."

"Aiden," Ronan snaps.

"What?"

"You're a dick."

"Yeah. I know. I have zero social skills; just ask Leslie." He thumbs over his shoulder at his fiancée.

"He's right," Leslie chimes in. "But his brain is big and full of numbers, and I find that hopelessly sexy, so I decided to keep him." She passes her apron to me. "Please help us. All I want to do is eat donuts. I've been saving myself for these so all I've had today is a yogurt cup with blueberries and the ones I've made so far aren't all that great." She pokes at the overdone balls.

"They look super for your first time!" I lie. "Give me twenty minutes, and I'll have a fresh batch for you."

"You don't have to do that. I'm fully prepared to make cookies," Ronan interjects.

"Or we could do it together." I pull the apron over my head.

He grins. "Okay. Sure."

"Sheesh, I feel like I'm watching foreplay. Come on, babe. Let's leave them alone." Aiden claps Ronan on the shoulder. "Make sure you wash your hands if you put your fingers in places you're not supposed to."

"Aiden! Enough, or she'll never come back!" Leslie swats him on the butt with a dishtowel.

"Get your head out of the gutter. I meant places like his *nose*. All the pheromones must be getting to you. Should we go upstairs for a few minutes and check on that light bulb that needs to be changed?"

"What—" Her confusion turns into an eye roll. "Celia is napping upstairs, but nice try."

He ushers her out of the kitchen, leaving the two of us alone. I split the dough into several bowls so I can add the cinnamon apples, dried fruit mix, and the raisins to some. While I work on the add-ins, Ronan puts on a seventies-era apron and starts dropping balls of dough into the pot of boiling oil.

"Sorry about the razzing from my brothers. And the

girlfriend designation. That probably should've been a conversation prior to me opening my big mouth."

I shrug, not wanting to give him a hard time about it. "It's cute."

He cringes. "Cute?"

"Okay, maybe *cute* is the wrong word, considering you've turned a really horrible green color. How about sweet? I think it's sweet that you introduced me as your girlfriend. I like you, Ronan, a lot. And as your girlfriend, I can say I'm definitely interested in repeating the events of last night on a very regular basis."

He pulls me into him. "I can certainly accommodate that request. Once we're finished stuffing our faces with donuts." He gives me a quick peck, and then we get back to work.

Half an hour later, we have three bowls piled high with *oliebollen*. We have honey, sugar, powdered sugar, cinnamon sugar, and a delicious maple butter for dipping.

Celia comes down from her nap as we're getting settled at the dining room table. Ronan introduces me, and she promptly bursts into tears, blubbering about how she's so glad Ronan is finally settling down and how they've always wanted him to find someone.

Once she's no longer sobbing all over Daniel's shirt, he tucks her into the table and flits around, making sure she's comfortable. Then he loads up a plate for her, careful to make sure the maple dipped ones don't touch the cinnamon sugar.

"Sorry about that," Ronan mutters as we fill our plates.

"I think it's sweet that your family cares so much about you. It's nice to see." So much nicer than my boyfriend-stealing sister and my attempted-boyfriend-thieving cousin.

No one talks about which famous person they ran into last week, or the newest keto diet, or which plastic surgeon botched up what surgery. As predicted, the stock market comes up a couple of times, but Ronan is quick to shut down the hard sales pitch Daniel lobs my way.

They regale me with stories about Ronan and his science experiments as a teen. Apparently the desire to brew started early. Pre-legal drinking age early. By sixteen he'd made his first batch of moonshine.

He shrugs. "Booze was expensive and hard to get ahold of. I found a way around it."

After we stuff ourselves silly, we retire to the living room. Just like the rest of this house, it's a time warp back to the nineties. The carpet is an awful rose color, the furniture is boxy and worn, and the curtains boast a garish, retro floral pattern. It's horrible and homey and wonderful.

"I just need to help Daniel with something. You'll be okay for a few?" Ronan asks.

"Of course, you go right ahead."

He kisses me on the cheek and I cross over to the fireplace so I can check out the pictures on the mantel. A sixtieth wedding anniversary photo sits in the middle, Henry and the late Dottie dressed up as though they were ready to party. As I take in the background I realize they're in The Knight Cap.

"That was my Dottie." Henry picks up the framed photo, his smile fond but also sad.

"You look like you belonged together."

"Aye. We did. Met when we were just kids. I was eighteen and a fool. She smiled at me and I was a goner."

"Just like that, huh?"

"Sometimes you just know." His thumb smooths along the edge of the frame.

"I believe that. I love the wall of photos in The Knight Cap. It's like watching the progress of your love through still shots."

"Every year I made sure to put a picture on that wall so we could walk by and see our good times together. I know in this day people don't really make photo albums, but we always had one going."

"Will you show me?"

Henry's face lights up. "I'd be happy to." He ambles over to a bookshelf lined with photo albums. It's five shelves high, and there have to be at least ten albums on each shelf. He taps his lip. "Where to start. Ah!" He lifts an album from the shelf and motions for me to take a seat on the couch.

Setting the album between us, he flips to the first page. Old, yellowed, black and white images with captions and dates line each page.

The very first image is of a young woman, a teenager based on the softness of her features and the innocence of her smile.

"That's the first picture I ever took of Dottie." He taps the image. "Our parents were against us dating. I was a few years older and she was serving tables at the time, but love doesn't care about approval. We kept it a secret."

"Eventually they must have realized you were made for each other, though."

"Aye. Got married in that bar the day she turned eighteen, and then there was nothing anyone could do to keep us apart." He winks. "And grandbabies have a way of making people come around no matter what. We did every little thing together. She was my entire world for more than sixty years."

"I can see that." I flip to the next page and find more pictures of a teenage Dottie in various stages of laughter.

He clears his throat. "She had a heart condition. Born with it, and there wasn't a thing we could do to fix it. Despite that she loved damn hard, and you couldn't stop her from doing things she wanted to because she always said life was too short to be afraid of the end."

"Sounds like a smart woman."

"She was damn smart. Would've been some Wall Street working woman if she'd been born a few decades later. She's the one who kept The Knight Cap going all those years. She made me promise if something happened to her that I'd stick around to make sure our boy Ronan got himself settled."

"There's that big heart you're talking about."

"Aye. She loved that boy like he was her own, 'specially after Jim and Cindy's accident. Broke all of our hearts, but

Ronan's the most, I think. He's a lot like me, needs a partner even if he's done his damnedest to avoid it since we lost his parents." He shakes his head, like he's breaking himself out of a sad spell. "Anyway, the moment I heard about you giving him hell I thought: There she is, the reason he's back here with me. She's the woman who's going to settle his restless soul."

"Restless soul? He seems pretty settled here."

"Now he is," Gramps agrees. "But when he was younger he had a hard time staying in one place. He was always on the move. Even when he was in college, he took on a million things. Except for when he had a girlfriend."

"Did he have a lot of girlfriends?"

Gramps gives me a sly look. "That I met? No. But you better believe Ronan was serious when he brought a lady to a family event like this one."

"So you've met a few girlfriends then?" Ronan hasn't even mentioned an ex, although I'm sure there must have been some along the way.

"Only one, other than you."

"What happened?" I wave the question away. "You don't need to answer that. It's personal and I'm just curious."

"It's okay." He pats my hand. "Ronan isn't likely to talk about it, but it might help you understand him better. After his parents passed, he transferred colleges between his sophomore and junior year. I think his heart was already too broken, and he didn't want to risk it getting any more mangled than it was, so he found a way to end things without causing either of them too much heartache."

"That couldn't have been easy for either of them."

"It wasn't, but he put all of his energy into school and working at the bar. He went on dates, but it never got serious, which was hard to watch, because Ronan has a big heart, and he needs someone who's going to take care of it." He winks and squeezes my hand. "Someone like you."

We don't leave Ronan's grandfather's until late in the afternoon.

"That was so much fun." I buckle myself in. "Your family is so . . . normal."

"I don't know if I'd exactly call us normal, but I'm glad you enjoyed yourself."

"I had a fantastic time. Your brothers are great, and I can see why you and Henry are so close. He really loves you, you know."

Ronan nods. "Yeah. I'm pretty lucky to have him."

"That bar is so special to him. He has so many fantastic memories all caught up in that place, it's a wonder he let you renovate."

"Well, it helps that I made the suggestions a few years back and Grams had been on board. Gramps had a harder time with the possible changes because of how much of his heart is tied up in the place."

"I can see how that would be difficult. What do think is going to happen to The Knight Cap once you start your brewery?" It's heartbreaking to think of that legacy coming to an end.

"I don't know. I'm hopeful Lars will take more of an interest in the management side of things, but he's young yet, so we'll see." He taps the steering wheel, his expression hard to read, but it softens quickly. "We should stop and grab your SUV, shouldn't we?"

"Oh yes! That's a good idea, then I don't have to worry about how I'm getting to work in the morning."

He pulls into the lot behind the building and parks beside my SUV, tapping the wheel restlessly. "It's still early, did you want to come back to my place?"

"Or you could come back to mine?" My apartment isn't as nice as Ronan's, but it's cute and homey and a few minutes closer so getting up and out in the morning won't be as much of a challenge.

"I could definitely do that." His gaze moves over me in a slow sweep. "I haven't quite had my fill of you yet, today."

"I feel exactly the same way." I lean over and kiss him on the cheek. "See you back at my place, then."

@buttercreamandbooze:

Have your cupcake and eat it, too.

chapter eighteen

PURSE STRINGS

Blaire

"Wow, you're in a good mood," Daphne observes the next morning. "It's almost like you've got the post-laid afterglow going on."

I stop writing the daily special on the chalkboard to look at her.

Her eyes go wide. "Holy hell! You *did* get laid!"

I slap her arm. "I don't think the people outside heard you!"

She rushes toward the front door. I'm not sure if she's kidding or actually planning to scream it down the street, but I chase after her and slide my body in front of the door before she can open it and shout my private information to the world.

She rolls her eyes. "I wasn't really going to tell the entire neighborhood, you loon. What the hell happened?" She grabs me by the shoulders. "Oh my God, you slept with Ronan, didn't you?"

Judging by her expression, I don't need to respond with words.

"You did! How did that happen?"

"Well, Daphne, when a man and a woman get naked—"

She waves her hand in the air to stop me. "Don't be sarcastic. I mean, I guess it was bound to happen because you two have turned bickering into foreplay, but what happened to make it finally happen?"

"Mistletoe."

"Mistletoe?"

"He kissed me under the mistletoe at midnight on New Year's."

Her face falls. "That's actually romantic."

"Why do you look so disappointed?"

"Because I assumed you two would get into an argument and end up hate fucking each other or something. But that just sounds sweet."

"If it makes you feel better, he's a bit of a dirty talker."

Her expression is a mix of surprise and glee. "He is not!"

"Oh, he very much is."

"So the sex was stellar? He's got it going on?" She motions to her crotch.

"Oh yeah, he totally has it going on, and the sex was mind-blowing. He actually stayed over last night." I can feel my face heating up, partially at the memories of what happened between the sheets, and on top of them, and in the shower.

"Whoa, wait, so this isn't a one-time thing?"

I'm not sure what to make of her shock. "Uh, no, not a one-time thing."

She props her hip against the counter, concern furrowing her brow. "Is that really a good idea? I mean, sure, scratch the itch, but now you're what? Sleeping with the enemy on the regular?"

"He's not the enemy."

"Aren't you the one who said he's your competition? You're both in the semifinals for Best Bar, and he's got a lead on you." She makes a hand motion below the waist. "You don't want to let the D distract you when you're in the home stretch."

She makes a good point, one I'm not all that interested in admitting, if I'm going to be perfectly honest with myself. It's been a very, very long time since I've had great sex, and while she's right about not losing sight of my goals, I feel like I can balance having my cupcake and eating it, too.

I motion across the street to the gaudy, ugly glowing D&B sign. "We have bigger competition to worry about now."

Daphne raises a hand. "I know. I just don't want you to get taken for a ride." She rolls her eyes when I arch a brow. "You know what I mean. I don't want you to get taken advantage of. He's a smooth mother-fudger and damn pretty and you're gorgeous and definitely beddable. I want to make sure he's not using you to get what he wants aside from orgasms. There were orgasms, right?"

"Several." I smirk. "I don't think he's using me. I mean, he introduced me to his family yesterday."

"Seriously?"

"Yup. We went over for New Year's cookies at his grandpa's place and I met his brothers and their wives. Guys don't usually do the family-intro thing when their plan is a hump and dump."

"This is true." Daphne leans against the counter. "So this is a real thing?"

I shrug. "I think so. He introduced me as his girlfriend."

"Oh, wow. You must've been amazing in the sack." She rounds the cupcake display case. "You need to tell me all about it over coffee. I need details."

I fully expect there to be a bit of a lull in business after New Year's, especially with Dick and Bobby's opening across the street. January can be a slow month for businesses, everyone tightening their purse strings thanks to big credit card bills post-holiday spend.

What I don't expect is for B&B to be a virtual ghost town apart from when Ronan and I have our joint events. I was barely scraping by before, and now I'm veering into dangerous territory, dipping into my overdraft more and more often to make ends meet.

Even the attention we managed to garner from our New Year's party on social media doesn't buffer the impact of D&B opening up across the street. The great press from Tori Taylor and the fact that both The Knight Cap and B&B have made it into the top ten Best Bars doesn't seem to be helping me keep my head above water.

I'm terrified, because Tori Taylor is planning her trip to Seattle this month and now more than ever, I need business to pick up.

To combat the slowdown, Ronan and I coordinate more joint events with deals and promotions to help entice the college kids to come to us rather than Dick and Bobby's. I try not to let my desperation show, or to let Ronan know how bad things are getting. I know he's feeling the pinch, too, but I don't think it's nearly as dire for him as it is for me since The Knight Cap is long established and he only has to recover the renovation costs.

It's a Thursday morning and tonight I have a trivia night, followed by karaoke over at Ronan's bar. Our duets have become a thing over the past few months, and we've started allowing patrons to request songs. I figure it's a smart co-event with Tori coming to town because it always generates tons of posts and lots of interaction on social media before and after.

It's only nine in the morning when Ronan drops by, far earlier than usual for him, even on an event night. "Hey, you got a minute? I need to show you something next door."

"Sure, everything okay?"

"Oh yeah, I just want you to check something out."

I leave Callie in charge and follow Ronan next door to The Knight Cap.

He ushers me down the hall to his office. "In here."

I step inside, expecting there to be some kind of surprise, but it looks like the same old in-need-of-updating office. "Okay. What do I need to check out?"

I turn around and he takes my face between his hands, tips my head back, and slants his mouth over mine. I gasp in surprise but sink into the kiss.

His hand eases down my side and curves around my butt, over my dress, and he pulls me closer, grinding his erection against my stomach.

I fight a moan, not wanting anyone to know there are non-business-related things going on behind Ronan's office door. His other hand leaves my cheek and his ancient and very squeaky rolling chair bangs into the wall. A few seconds later he picks me up and deposits me on the desk.

"What're you doing?"

"Reenacting the fantasy I've had since New Year's." His left hand slides under my dress, up my thigh.

I have to press my knees together so they don't automatically part for him. "Someone will hear."

"They won't."

"I can't be that quiet and you can't *not* say dirty things." I'd like to say I can bite my tongue, or his shirt, or something, but whatever his plan is, there is no way in hell he's going to be able to keep his mouth shut and neither will I.

He gives me a knowing, satisfied grin. "We're alone. There's no one else here."

"No one?"

"No one. I came in early on purpose." He slides his other hand under my skirt and up my thigh.

"So you planned this?"

"Only after waking up for the seventh day in a row from the same damn dream."

"Which was what?" I lift my butt, allowing him to drag my panties down. I help by removing my crinoline.

"A repeat of New Year's, except on my desk." He tosses my panties and crinoline on his chair and drops to his knees, making good on that repeat performance from start to finish.

When I open his office door, I'm a little sweaty and definitely flushed, but oh-so-sated. I accidentally kick something on the floor.

"What's that?" Ronan grabs me by the hips to keep from knocking me over since he bumps into me from behind when I bend to retrieve it.

I hold it up for Ronan to see. "Air freshener?"

"Weird. I don't remember leaving that in the hall, but clearly I'm on the ball. Oooh, and it's festive scented." He releases a spray into his office. It smells like a cinnamon roll. It's probably a good idea since it helps cover the latex and sex.

He walks me down the hall and I come to an abrupt stop when I spot Lars behind the bar, cutting lemon wedges. Ronan bumps into me from behind. "Oh, hey!" My voice has that high pitch associated with surprise and embarrassment.

He pauses his chopping to tip his chin in our direction. "Hey."

"Lars? How long have you been here?" Ronan sounds more annoyed than embarrassed.

"Long enough." A wide grin spreads across his face.

"Oh my gosh," I mutter as Ronan ushers me down the hall toward the back entrance.

Once we're out of hearing range I turn to face Ronan. "He heard me."

"Us. He heard *us*." He rubs his jaw.

I throw my hands up in the air. "I thought you said we were alone!"

"We were." He glances at his wristwatch. "Looks like we got carried away with the foreplay."

I twist his wrist so I can check the time. "It's ten! We were in there for an hour!"

He shrugs. "I was hungry, and you didn't seem to be in a hurry."

I poke him in the chest. "This isn't funny! What if that had been Gramps and not Lars?"

"Gramps doesn't leave the house before eleven these days."

"Not the freaking point and you know it."

"Babe, relax. Lars isn't going to care, and it wasn't Gramps so we're safe."

"But he probably heard me coming and saying...things!"

"I'm sure he didn't press his ear to the door. He probably passed by, heard some noise, got cheeky with the spray, and steered clear."

"You can't know that."

"Well, he better hope that's what he did. Look, I'm sorry. Next time we'll wait until after closing before we get freaky in my office."

"What makes you think there's going to be a next time?"

Ronan cocks a brow and smirks. "Because you loved that just as much as I did."

I don't respond to that, because he's right; I did love it. "I have to get back. Callie is probably wondering where I am." I turn to stalk off, but Ronan grabs my arm.

"Hey. Don't walk away angry." He pulls me in for a hug and presses his lips to my temple.

"I'm embarrassed, not angry," I mumble against his chest.

"I love the sound of your orgasms," he murmurs in my ear. "I love the way you moan my name. I love that you're not quiet about what feels good for you. It's sexy as hell."

"And now I'm really leaving. We can talk more about that later. When we're not at work and have to function for the rest of the day."

He gives my hip a squeeze and releases me. I stand outside in the cold January morning for a couple of minutes to allow the sweat to dry and the heat in my face to calm before I go back in and apologize for taking as long as I did. Not that I regret it all that much.

As January rolls through, I do everything I can to pull in more customers—fun new cupcakes, bachelorette parties, cupcake-decorating classes in the evenings—but I'm still struggling to compete against D&B's super cheap prices and their endless marketing money. I manage to find a great part-time baker to help alleviate some of the strain on my time and demands. Financially it's going to be a bit of a struggle for a while, but I can't reasonably run a business on no sleep.

On the downside, hiring a new baker means I have to find a way to reduce other costs. I end up cutting back on Callie's hours. It's the beginning of a new semester and the workload is heavy so she's not heartbroken over it, but it still doesn't feel good.

The new part-time baker is great about helping to get the shop open, but cutting back on Callie's hours means I'm working just as many as I was before. There have been a few occasions when I've been able to enjoy sleeping past five in the morning, usually with Ronan, but if business doesn't pick up soon I'm going to have to put an end to those altogether.

The only saving grace seems to be our cohosted events. I'm grateful that Tori is planning her stop around one of those events, because those tend to be the busiest nights. She always makes her appearance a surprise, but based on her previous stops over the past week, Ronan and I predicted she'd be coming our way this week, and we were right.

She stops by during one of my comedy nights and Ronan's live bands. Of course, that morning I got a call from the best of the three comedians saying she had the flu and there was no way she could get up onstage without a bucket and a toilet. I was prepared to host it with just the two comedians, but Lars said he had a friend who was hilarious and would love the opportunity.

His friend was hot, which was a bonus, and had a pretty big following on social media so I took a chance, shuffling the acts around so he could go last. As it turned out, his pretty face was the only palatable thing about his act. It was more frat boy humor than anything my clientele would find funny, so he was met with some embarrassingly pathetic chuckles and not much else.

To make matters worse, Tori has the pleasure of witnessing it firsthand. If she'd shown up at the beginning, when everyone was crying with laughter, it would've made the final act seem a little less awful, but since she's missed the best part, it's taken the shine out of the evening. She stays for a drink and samples the cupcakes, expressing how much she loves the décor and the concept.

She's certainly done her homework, asking about my family and why I chose to go out on my own with a low-key local vibe instead of catering to celebrities. I explain that my heart is in baking and that I wanted the opportunity to prove myself, which she seems to appreciate.

She heads over to The Knight Cap while I close up. I'm feeling disheartened. I know B&B is a great place with an awesome atmosphere, and usually my entertainment is top notch. Tonight we were packed, not an empty seat in the house, but if I'm honest with myself, The Knight Cap has something special—beyond the axe throwing, which I hate to admit is really fun.

One night when I stayed to help him behind the bar during a cohosted event, Ronan convinced me to leave on the steel-toed boots and give it a shot.

Watching Ronan demonstrate how to throw and then getting all up in my personal space so he could correct my form became its own brand of foreplay. Every time I hit the target, he'd praise me, and if I missed he'd step in and give me pointers that consisted mostly of him adjusting my stance. After a while I started missing on purpose, and eventually he caught on. That night ended with me pressed up against the wall, legs wrapped around his waist while he groaned about how sexy I looked wielding an axe. Obviously, I'm kind of in love with the whole thing now.

It's hard to compete with Ronan's incredible charisma, not to mention the history and romance connected to The Knight Cap.

And Tori is certainly not immune, considering the dreamy look that came over her face when she mentioned Ronan. I can totally relate, because it's the same look I wear all the time around him. I finish cleaning up, send my servers home, and make sure everything is prepped for the morning. In the quiet that follows, I take a quick look at the books. I'm not entirely sure what the point is, since I already know I'm balancing on a fine line these days.

Even more discouraged, I close up and head over to The Knight Cap to check out how Ronan's night is going. Of course the band is on point and the crowd is going wild. I spot Tori over by the bar, chatting it up with Ronan. Every once in a while, she throws her head back and laughs at something he says.

Tori is a stunning, perfect woman. She's camera ready and a successful entrepreneur who travels the world. She's smart, savvy, and gorgeous. Yes, she has a high-profile athlete boyfriend, but there have been some rumors lately about trouble in paradise, and Ronan is a professional flirt. It might be harmless, but I'm a little sensitive after the way my night has gone.

Lars appears beside me from out of nowhere and hands me a shot. "You gotta stop trying to kill her with your laser beam stare."

"Huh?"

"Tori. You look like you want to destroy her. He's not flirting. He's just chatting and really fucking oblivious." Lars is smirking.

"I know he's not flirting." I toss back the shot.

"Your chill is at zero, though. I mean, I know you two got it bad for each other, but I didn't realize it was this bad."

"I don't know what you're talking about." I'm mentally preparing myself to go over and say hello without also saying or doing something stupid. I want to tell Lars his comedian friend sucked, but I figure I'm in too much of a mood not to be a total jerk about it, so I decide to save that for later.

Lars snorts and hands me a cocktail. I don't know where he's keeping the cocktails, or the shots, but I'm not about to say no to them. "Whatever you say, Blaire. Give him a few more minutes before you go over there and stake your claim. I know you're together and stuff, but he wouldn't sabotage you, so you should extend the same courtesy."

"I wouldn't sabotage Ronan!" I say, indignant.

"Not intentionally, but you've got that look in your eye, like you want to catfight her. And I think it's human nature to protect what's yours."

"That's rather insightful. Although, I've never actually been in a fight, and I don't want to get into one with the person who has the potential to help put mine or Ronan's business on the map."

"I don't mean that you'd actually fight her. I think you're more likely to do or say something that could mess up your chances when you're feeling this territorial, so it's best you just hang with me until she moves on." He drapes his arm over my shoulder and gives it a squeeze. "He's going home with you, and that's really the only thing that should matter."

Tori doesn't seem to be in any hurry to move on, and I'm tired and prickly, so I decide home is a better option than spreading my bad mood to Ronan when he's clearly riding the high tonight.

"I'm going to head out."

"You want me to give Ronan a message?"

"That's okay. I'll text him that I'll see him tomorrow."

"You all right to drive?"

"I just had that one shot, and like three sips of this." I pass him my mostly full cocktail.

"You're sure you want to leave?"

"He needs his focus to be where it is, and I don't want to be the clingy girlfriend."

I leave out the front door instead of going through the bar and using the service entrance, mostly so Ronan doesn't see me. I get what Daphne was saying when I first started sleeping with my competition and how it would complicate things. She wasn't wrong. I don't want him to lose, but I also want to win. It's a weird spot to be in, and right now I could really use the positive press to help bolster business.

I shoot Ronan a message when I get home, letting him know I stopped by, but that he and Tori were talking and I didn't want to interrupt, so I'll see him tomorrow. I throw in a couple of kissy-face emojis to make it seem upbeat and not like I'm a jealous girlfriend, or mopey, when in reality I'm both.

I change into a comfy sleep shirt, get my dress ready for tomorrow, and decide I've had enough of today. I brush my teeth, grab a glass of water, and climb into bed. I've just turned off the light when my phone buzzes, not with a message, but a call, from Ronan.

I debate letting it go to voicemail, but I decide that would be a jerk move. It's not Ronan's fault that my last act wasn't great and his band was. Or that he's ridiculously attractive and charming and women go gaga over him. Myself included.

I accept the call. "Hey."

"Hey, yourself. You took off without saying good-bye. I thought I was coming back to your place." There's no accusation in his voice, just a hint of disappointment.

"You were busy with Tori, and I didn't want to interrupt."

He's silent for a moment. "Everything okay?"

"Yeah, just tired after a long day." It's more of an omission than a lie.

"Is this you uninviting me over tonight?" And now there's hurt to go with the disappointment.

I should give myself the night, especially with my mood, but I'm feeling selfish and needy. "Of course not, I always love having you in my bed. I'll leave the door unlocked so you can let yourself in."

"I'll be there in fifteen."

I'm still staring at the ceiling, no longer quite as exhausted as I was when I slid between the sheets. I know I'm going to be tired tomorrow as a result, but my brain is too busy to settle.

When the door to my bedroom creaks open I flick on the lamp beside my bed and whisper "Hi."

"Hey, yourself." I watch as Ronan strips down to his boxer briefs, warmth spreading through my limbs as any residual tiredness fades away, replaced with want. As soon as he joins me in bed, I pull his mouth to mine and lose myself in him.

Half an hour later I'm tucked into his side, my head resting on his shoulder, fingertips tracing the tree limbs that climb his shoulder and morph into birds taking flight. It's a gorgeous, intricate tattoo.

"The band was great tonight," I say softly.

"They were. I was impressed. How was the rest of comedy night?" He'd stopped in during the first act, when everyone was laughing their heads off.

"Started great, fizzled out at the end."

"Oh no, I'm sorry, babe." He presses his lips to my forehead and tips my chin up. "What happened?"

"The last act was a dud. I should have cut it at two when Betty canceled, but I figured it wouldn't hurt to give someone new a chance. I think Tori being there unnerved the guy and he just kind of shit the bed."

"Maybe it's not as bad as you think."

"It is. Or was. It's okay. I'm glad your night went well, though."

"Me, too, but I don't like that yours didn't." His sincerity makes me feel conflicted. I want him to succeed, but I want my own success, as well.

"It would've been nice to make a better impression on Tori. I could really use some positive press and more customers."

"Your place was packed tonight."

"It was, but you know how quiet it's been when we don't

have cohosted events. I don't want to cut Callie's hours more, but if things keep going this way, I might have to."

His brow furrows. "It's that bad?"

I backtrack, not wanting to rain on his parade with my dark cloud. "I'm just being preemptive. I can't afford to go too far into the red, so I have to cut costs where I can." Not to mention I've been pulling out all the stops in anticipation of Tori, and that means spending more than I probably should have.

He's quiet for a few moments. "I have an idea."

"I'm all for one of your ideas because I'm fresh out."

"Why don't we have a street event?"

I adjust my position so I can see his face better. "How do you mean?"

"So when we cohost events both of our businesses see higher returns, right?"

"Definitely."

"What if we apply the same principle to all the restaurants and shops on the street? We could involve everyone and have a big weekend event with a focus on small businesses. We could plan it for Valentine's."

I perk up at the idea. "Like a Love Is in the Air event?"

"Exactly. It could be good for all of us, and a nice middle finger to Dick and Bobby's for screwing it up for the rest of us."

"I love this! And Valentine's is pretty much my favorite!"

"Why am I not surprised?" Ronan tucks my hair behind my ear, smiling wryly. "We can start canvassing tomorrow and see what kind of interest we have. I'm sure we're not the only ones who've been impacted by D&B, and there's no way in hell I'm going to let them steal your dream from you."

My heart stutters, and my worries take a back seat, at least for tonight, because I know we're in this together. Or at least I hope so.

@buttercreamandbooze:

We go together like cupcakes and buttercream.

BEST BAR AWARD GOES TO...

Blaire

It turns out that every single small business on the street is interested in being part of the event. The bars and restaurants are feeling the effects of D&B and everyone agrees that the cross-promotion certainly can't hurt.

Ronan sets up a meeting at The Knight Cap, where we come up with a weekend-long themed event that will take place in the middle of February, piggybacking on Valentine's Day celebrations. I'm grateful that Renata, my new baker, has managed to slide into the role fairly seamlessly. Sure, there have been a few hiccups, but she's got great vision and is a master baker, so I can be assured she'll be able to handle the demands that are coming our way.

Daphne came up with an idea to set up a photo booth outside of Buttercream and Booze to showcase the event. Ever since the bachelorette party she's been getting loads of bookings for weddings, engagement parties, and birthdays. Since Valentine's

Day thrives on romance and couples, it's a great way for her to get more visibility and meet some potential new clients.

It definitely doesn't hurt that the local newspapers and TV stations have picked up on the event, which helps us spread the word. Business has picked up again—not like it was before D&B came in, but at least I'm not quite as worried about having to cut more of Callie's hours. For now.

A few days before the Love Is in the Air event, my phone chimes with an alert about a new video from Tori's YouTube channel. Over the past few weeks she's made her way through the top ten bars, narrowing it down to five. I watched the one she put up the day after she visited B&B and The Knight Cap. She was kind enough to edit her video to highlight the few funny moments from the final comedian—there weren't many—and focused more on the fun, fresh vibe, the themed drinks and cupcakes, and my eclectic sense of style that was reflected in the ambiance of the café.

I consider calling Ronan before I watch the video, but Daphne's here, setting up her photo booth and taking pretty pictures for the upcoming Valentine's Day extravaganza, so we crowd around my phone as I cue up the video.

"Ready?" Daphne asks.

I nod and we both cross our fingers as I hit Play. Of course Tori takes her sweet time talking about all the amazing bars she visited while she was touring the Pacific Northwest. "I'll admit, it was a tough competition and there are some amazing bars out there. I'm going to post a top ten on my site because narrowing it down was such a challenge, but there is one bar that really stood out among the rest!" She pauses for effect. "It's not just the food or the ambiance that makes one bar stand apart, it's the whole package, and my winner has it all. A charming, homey environment, the most amazing selection of craft beers, delicious food, fabulous entertainment and a seriously charismatic, smokin' hot owner." She fans herself dramatically.

"He won," I murmur and Daphne squeezes my hand.

"The Knight Cap is the whole package and more, which is why it's getting the Tori Taylor seal of approval and the title of The Best Bar in the Pacific Northwest! I can't wait to celebrate this win with Ronan Knight!"

The video goes on to show some highlights from her visit to The Knight Cap. Ronan was wholly captivating, and Tori was happy to wax poetic about the bar, the vibe, and the gorgeous owner.

"I'm so sorry, Blaire. I know how much you wanted this." Daphne slings her arm over my shoulder and gives me a side hug.

"Thanks. I guess at least if I had to lose, he's the one person I don't mind losing to?" It's more of a question than anything, because as happy as I am for Ronan, I'm disappointed for me.

"You're still allowed to be sad about it, though. You're a big part of the reason his events were so successful, especially the karaoke, and your customers were always in his bar after, not really the other way around."

She's right. While we both benefited, Ronan was the one who got the most out of our deal, and now he gets the benefit of all the extra promotion. "The Knight Cap has a history and a story I can't really compete with, though."

"And you did amazing, despite that." She taps the comments where Tori has posted a link to her top 10 favorite bars in the Pacific Northwest. Buttercream and Booze has taken the number two spot, right under The Knight Cap.

It's positive promotion no matter what, but I still give myself a minute to be disappointed, especially since we were just so close at the end, and if my final comedian hadn't sucked, I might have stood a chance. I remind myself that it's not Ronan's fault that my original act got sick, or that his cousin offered a poor replacement. It still really sucks, though.

"I should probably go over and congratulate him."

"Probably, but if you need to eat a pint of ice cream later and be sad about it, I'm your girl, okay?"

"Thanks." She hugs me and fixes my hair before she lets me head over to The Knight Cap.

It's barely ten thirty in the morning, but I find Ronan behind the bar, tossing back shots with Lars.

His huge grin widens when he sees me, and he motions to the TV above the bar with Tori's vlog playing out on the screen. "Babe! Did you see?"

"I did. Congratulations on the win." I slip behind the bar and he scoops me up, spinning me around.

When he sets me down, I grip his arms to keep from toppling over. His wide smile falters. "I'm sorry it wasn't you."

I curve my palm around the back of his neck, determined not to put a damper on his win. "Don't apologize. If I was going to lose to anyone, I'm glad it's you."

He drops his head, his lips finding mine. He tastes like tequila. "I wouldn't have won if it wasn't for you. Without the cohosted events, I wouldn't have stood a chance. I wish there could be two winners."

"Well, that would cheapen the award." I smooth my palms over his chest. "Does Gramps know yet?" I've taken to calling Henry that all the time now. He pops by the bakery quite regularly to say hello, and also for cupcakes. He makes me promise not to tell Ronan about his little addiction.

"I haven't. Should I call him? Or maybe I should tell him in person? Probably in person, right?"

"Definitely in person." I smile at his excitement.

"Yes. Good call. You'll come with me? I want you to come with me. Can you leave Callie in charge for an hour?" He kisses me again, making it impossible for me to answer.

When he finally pulls back, I assure him that I can most definitely come with him if that's what he wants. I pop back over to B&B to let Callie know she's in charge for a bit.

Ronan meets me out back and holds out his keys. "I'm too amped to drive."

I chuckle and get behind the wheel, marveling at how smooth the ride is compared to my SUV. It takes twenty minutes to get to Gramps's place, and Ronan talks a mile a minute, his excitement infectious and adorable. "We should have a big party to celebrate, shouldn't we? Do you think to-night is too soon? Can we get something out on social media that quick, or should it be tomorrow? Is that too close to the street party?" He taps the armrest, pausing only long enough to suck in a breath. "Maybe it should just be a staff thing, you know, to show my appreciation for all their hard work in helping make this happen? Oh! I should call the band and tell them. If they're not busy, they could play a set tonight!"

"I think we can totally get a party together tonight as long as you're not looking to have it catered, and we can keep it going through the weekend as a celebration of the win."

"Do you think Daphne would be interested in taking pictures?" Ronan asks. "I'd be happy to pay her."

"As soon as we get to Gramps's I'll message her and see if she's available. And I think you can have a separate staff party to acknowledge how much you appreciate them after the event this weekend. You could even close the bar to the public one evening and have the entire thing catered. And yes, definitely call the band and see if they're available."

"I really don't know how I would've done all of this without you." He squeezes my hand and brings his phone to his ear.

By the time we get to Gramps's house, Ronan has secured the band for tonight. It's not a stretch since they were already booked for the entire weekend event. I fire off a message to Daphne and before we even get to the front door she's already agreed to take pictures, but she's adamant that she doesn't need to be paid. I'm not sure Ronan will let her get away with that, but Daphne has always been exceedingly generous, so he might have to find another way to compensate her, like free beer and food. He knocks before he lets himself in with the key. The low drone of the TV filters through to the foyer.

"Gramps?"

"Ronan? What're ya doin' here at this time in the morning?"

"I have some exciting news," he calls out.

"I'm in the living room watching *The Price Is Right*!"

Ronan holds up a finger and drops his voice. "Give me a sec. Sometimes he likes to lounge around in his underpants and it's not a pretty sight."

"Standing by."

He peeks around the corner and then gives me a thumbs-up so I follow him into the living room.

Gramps's gaze bounces from Ronan to me and back again. "Oh, praise the lord!" He makes the sign of the cross. "Ya heard me prayers, Dottie. It's finally happening." A massive grin breaks across his face. "Yer gettin' married!"

"Uh." Ronan and I exchange questioning glances. "No, Gramps, we're not getting married."

Gramps's face falls. "Yer not?"

"We've only been dating for a couple of months."

"When ya know, ya know, though." Gramps's eyes round again and then narrow. "Ya better not have knocked Blaire up or I'll whup yer ass, boy."

"Okay, first of all, you will not whup anyone's ass, let alone mine, and secondly, no, I did not knock Blaire up."

"Oh." He slumps back in his chair. "Well, whatever the news is, it can't be that great, now can it?"

"You were ready to give me an ass whupping for knocking Blaire up two seconds ago and now you're disappointed I didn't?" Ronan sounds amused.

"I figure if you knocked her up, then you'd have to do the noble thing and marry her."

"Well, I might if it wasn't the twenty-first century. People have kids without getting married all the time." He turns to me. "Not that I don't want to get married or have kids. I just wouldn't expect you to suddenly want to tie the knot should I happen to knock you up accidentally."

"That's reasonable."

"Do you want to get married and have kids?"

"Now? No. But down the line I wouldn't be opposed, when the timing feels right. We can talk about this later, though. Like months from now, even." I put a hand on his arm and incline my head toward Henry, who is smiling gleefully.

"Oh, right, yeah." Ronan clears his throat. "Remember that YouTuber I was telling you about?"

"The lady with the really long eyelashes who makes all the videos that aren't the dirty kind?"

I fight a laugh.

"That's the one," Ronan confirms. "So she came through Seattle a couple of weeks back."

"That's right, I remember."

"And she stopped by The Knight Cap."

"She's not using my bar to make dirty videos."

"Gramps, we already established she doesn't make dirty videos. She named The Knight Cap the Best Bar in the Pacific Northwest. It's going to be featured on her YouTube channel, and she's partnered with Food and Drink and *The Seattle Morning Show*, so they'll be featuring us, too. We did it, Gramps! We got the bar back on its feet, and this is going to keep it standing."

Henry folds down the footrest on his La-Z-Boy and slowly pushes to a standing position. He hobbles over and pulls Ronan into a hug. "I'm so proud of ya." He smacks him on the back a couple of times before he grabs him by the arms, eyes watery, smile wavering. "Dottie would be too if she was here. I know she's looking down on you from heaven with a big smile on her face. She always believed in you."

"I know she did."

He pats Ronan's chest and turns to me, pulling me in for a hug. "You're the one who lit a fire under his ass, so I hope he's told you how much he appreciates you."

I hug him back, choked up about the whole thing, especially since I know Ronan's story and Henry's, and how much this bar means to him and this family.

Ronan tells Henry that he's planning to throw a party tonight, and he would love it if he would be able to come to the bar for dinner at the very least to celebrate.

"Are you kidding me? I'm coming right now. You kids hold on a few minutes while I get ready." His slippers make a *whoosh-whoosh* sound as he shuffles down the hall.

"I can't believe he thought I knocked you up."

I can't believe he thought Ronan asked me to marry him. "I like that he got all righteous about it."

"Yeah, well, I think fifty percent of the reason he couldn't wait to marry my grandma was so he could finally get into her pants, because back in the sixties that was how things went."

I roll my eyes. "That's how you think things went. It wasn't any different than it is now. Teenagers had sex back then just like they do now, only now it's easier to get contraception and kids actually know that standing up after sex doesn't prevent pregnancy."

"Okay, we need to stop talking about sex and teenagers and pregnancy, because it's sending mixed messages below the waist and I'm having some conflict over that."

I glance down at his crotch. "Are you aroused?"

"Not fully." He's amusingly defensive.

I poke the front of his pants. "You have a semi?"

"You said 'sex' twice and 'contraception,' and some parts of me don't realize it doesn't mean right now."

"You're ridiculous."

"I'm excited, about a lot of things, not the least of which is my girlfriend spending the night with me. Tell me you can get Callie to open for you tomorrow. I really want you to celebrate this win with me because it never would have happened without you."

"I'll talk to her as soon as we're back at The Knight Cap."

"This is as much your win as it is mine."

"This is yours, Ronan. Don't feel bad about being excited."

"I know how much this meant to you, though."

"And it means a lot to you, too, and to Gramps." As much as I wanted the win to be mine, I can't begrudge Ronan this. There's so much love here. History and connection and family. It's impossible to compete with that kind of beautiful backstory. "I can't think of a better way to honor your grandmother's memory."

Henry appears in the hallway. "What do ya think? Not too dressy for the occasion, is it?" He tugs on the hem of his suit jacket and I want to burst into tears. Like everything else in this house, it's a throwback to the nineties, and it's obvious he's lost some weight since he put it on last.

"You look perfect, Gramps. You're gonna knock 'em all out," Ronan says, his voice breaking.

Henry looks to me and winks. "Blaire, I need a woman's opinion, not this hipster jackass."

A half giggle–half sob bubbles up, but I manage to swallow it back down. "You look absolutely dapper."

"I haven't worn this suit in a while, but I figured if ever there was a reason to wear the family tartan, this is it." His smile is huge, and my heart melts for the man who stepped in and brought his grandfather's bar back to life.

@buttercreamandbooze:

We all deserve an ALCOHoliday.

chapter twenty

DON'T LEAVE ME HANGING

Blaire

The Knight Cap celebration is fantastic.

Ronan stays over at my place afterward and keeps me up until an ungodly hour in the morning. I tamp down my resentment over his peaceful, sleeping form sprawled over my mattress, dead to the world as I tiptoe around my room and try not to trip over our discarded clothes while I get ready for work.

We only have three days left to prepare for the street party, which means I have a lot of things to take care of. I leave Ronan in my bed, ruing my lack of sleep, but aware it's my own damn fault for staying out until two in the morning and then letting him persuade me to have slightly drunk marathon sex until four. My short sleep seems woefully inadequate right now.

I'm running behind this morning, so I have to rush through decorating today's cupcakes before B&B opens. I'm grateful that Callie is around to help, because I'm still in decorating mode when the doors open. The shop is bustling with morning customers and people picking up orders. I help Callie get things under control, tragically under-caffeinated for this level of on-the-ball. I can't say I'm disappointed by the number of customers we have, though. It's busier than it has been as of late, possibly because of the best bar winner announcement and the Top 10 list Tori posted on its heels.

Once we're past the initial rush, it slows down until lunch, which means I can start tackling the event prep and the eleven million questions that come with it. I expect Ronan to stop by and say hello, get his cupcake fix, and go over the last-minute stuff we need to get in order for Saturday. Except that doesn't happen.

I pop over to The Knight Cap after the lunch rush dies down, hoping to touch base with Ronan, but he's not there. Lars isn't on until the evening shift and Lana, one of the other bartenders, doesn't seem to know where Ronan is or when he'll be in.

I send him a message, asking about an ETA and when we'll have time to go over any last-minute emergencies. Two hours and another influx of customers later, he still hasn't responded so I start fielding questions on my own.

It's almost four in the afternoon by the time he rolls in, looking a hell of a lot more chipper and rested than I feel. "Hey, babe." He leans over the counter and kisses me on the cheek. He sweeps a thumb across the hollow under my eye. "Sorry I kept you up so late. You hanging in there?"

I fight that melty feeling I always get when he touches me and remind myself I'm kind of annoyed that the day is more than half over and he's been MIA. "I'm okay. Where have you been?"

"Oh, you know, running around, picking up stuff for the weekend."

"Did you get my message?"

"Huh?"

"I sent you a message hours ago." I can feel my irritation building at his less than remorseful expression.

"Really? I must've missed it. What's going on? What do you need?"

I blink at him, trying to figure out why he's suddenly so . . . off. Preoccupied? I don't know what it is, but I find it frustrating. "We have an event in two days. I could've used some help fielding questions from all the other local businesses and coordinating with them, but you were nowhere to be found."

He seems to realize I'm pissed off. "I'm sorry. I didn't mean to leave you hanging. I was taking care of last-minute stuff. Who needs questions answered?"

"No one anymore, for now."

"Fantastic. You're always so organized. This is going to be smooth sailing until Saturday." He pats his pocket when his phone starts buzzing. He checks the screen. "I gotta take this. I'll stop by later." He kisses me on the cheek again, grabs the cupcake I plated for him—like the sucker I am—and disappears out the front door, his phone at his ear.

He doesn't stop by later, though. And when I drop by The Knight Cap again to see if he's around to go over the fine details, I discover that he left a couple of hours ago to take care of some *things*, according to Lars.

"Do you know when he's going to be back?" It's already after nine and I've been going all day. I'm barely functioning on the limited sleep I managed last night.

Lars shrugs. "Dunno. He left in kind of a hurry and said he'd try to be back before closing."

"He'd *try*?" I parrot. "What the hell could he be doing at this time of night?"

Lars gives me an apologetic look. "I honestly don't know. He's been holed up in his office most of the day, and when he's come out he's stuck around for a few minutes before he had to field another call. Do you want me to tell him you stopped by?"

I wave him off, feeling pathetic and highly annoyed. "No. Don't bother. I'll just talk to him tomorrow. I'm beat, and I need actual sleep tonight."

"Celebrations went well into the wee hours of the morning, huh?" He tips his chin up and nods knowingly.

I don't bother to respond. I'm sure my expression says everything.

"Aren't you a wild one? All sweet and pretty and proper and buttoned up on the surface, but you leave some marks behind when you really let loose?" He cocks a brow in question.

I glare at him while my face turns the same color as the

red in his plaid shirt. There were some scratch marks on Ronan's back last night and my handprint on his butt from me smacking it, telling him to go harder. The handprint was likely gone by the morning, but I'm sure the scratches are still there. "What the hell has he been saying to you?"

Lars's grin widens. "Absolutely nothing. Ronan couldn't be more tight-lipped if he tried. It was just a guess on my part, and obviously I was right. Ronan's a lucky asshole."

I laugh, unsure how he managed to turn that into a compliment. "I'll see you tomorrow."

I consider texting Ronan when I get home, but I figure it's his turn to reach out. I change into comfy clothes but don't even manage to wash my face or take my makeup off before I pass out. On top of my covers.

The next morning I'm slightly better rested and feeling less like garbage and more half-human. I have a text from Ronan about being sorry that he missed me last night, but he'll make it up to me. It's followed with a slew of emojis, including eggplants, the panting-tongue thing and a bunch of hand symbols that indicate what he may be planning to do with them.

Normally I'd think it was cute. But this morning I do not. I decide not to respond right away because I'm inclined to say something snarky and less than friendly in my current, grumpy state. Clearly the sleep wasn't enough.

As it turns out, I don't run into Ronan.

Because he's not at The Knight Cap. His car isn't in the parking lot and hasn't been there all day. I may or may not have looked outside every single hour to check.

"Okay, what's the deal?" Daphne asks when I come back down the hall after checking for the seven millionth time if Ronan is here. "I don't know what's going on, but maybe you need a cupcake and some valium so you can chill the eff out."

"I'm totally chill," I snap.

She grabs me by the elbow and steers me toward the office.

"What're you doing?"

"Avoiding a scene. In you go." She shoves me inside and closes the door behind her, barricading me in.

I fling my arms in the air. "I don't have time for this! There's too much stuff to do!"

"Take a breath, Blaire. We are ninety-five percent ready for tomorrow. It's just little things that need to be taken care of. Social media is blowing up and people are excited. But you're freaking out poor Callie the way you're snapping every time she asks you a question."

"I'm not snappy!" I close my eyes and rub my temple. "Sorry. I'm just... overwhelmed and I thought I'd get some actual help from Ronan, but he's nowhere to be found and left me to do everything."

"Isn't he next door?"

"No. He's not. He hasn't been there all day and he wasn't there yesterday."

Daphne's tone softens. "But you know where he is?"

"Running errands, apparently. The last time I actually saw him for more than five distracted seconds was two nights ago when he stayed at my place after he found out he won Best Bar." I pace my small office. It's not big enough for effective, angry pacing, though, so I'm forced to turn around after two steps and then I run right into Daphne. "What if he's using me as a means to an end? What if it was convenient to bone the chick who's super organized and loves to take control of events? What if he was having his cupcake and eating it, too!"

"Pretty sure he *has* been having his cupcake and eating it, too," Daphne mutters.

"This isn't a joke. He's been MIA the past two days and I've had to manage everything! With your help, obviously, and Callie's and his staff, but he's supposed to be here and involved and he's not."

"Have you tried asking him where he's been and what he's doing?"

"Well, he'd have to answer his damn messages for me to be able to confirm that. And now that he's won the competition and his grandfather's bar is doing well he's probably going to go ahead and open that brewery, and that'll be the end of us."

Daphne arches a brow. "You're in a pretty fatalistic mood."

"I'm being realistic. Think about it. First all the pranks, hijacking my grand opening, the freaking glitter bomb. And then we call a truce when D&B opens and start throwing all these events together. They benefit him more than they do me. And there was that time one of Tori's people came to scope things out. It was the same morning Ronan convinced me to stay at his place for breakfast."

"That seems like a pretty unfortunate coincidence," Daphne hedges.

"Except he made it to work in time to meet up with Tori's people and win them over with his charm and his charisma." I throw my hands in the air. "What about the time I found him making cappuccinos, only the damn machine crapped its pants while he was right there! If I hadn't had someone to fix it, I would've been in a huge bind on a seriously busy night."

"I didn't know about that." Daphne chews her bottom lip.

"It got fixed, but it was expensive, and then everything was fine and I forgot about it. But then Lars gives me the name of a shitty comedian on the *same night* Tori shows up. What if Ronan's distracted me with his exceptional bedroom skills and all along he's been sabotaging me! Remember how crazy it used to be in the food truck business? People constantly slashing tires, fighting over what area they were allowed to target. It was nasty. Maybe he's only been sleeping with me so he can win this damn thing and get what he wants, which is his brewery!"

"That would be a pretty calculated, somewhat sociopathic thing to do, don't you think?" Daphne sounds less like the voice of reason and more like she's just as worried as I am now.

"Well, he won the entire competition, and Gramps will fork over the start-up money for his brewery, which is always what he was working toward. And now here I am, with no win and an absentee boyfriend who's probably going to dump me." I flap my hands in front of my face as if that's going to stop the tears. "Damn it! I can't afford a meltdown right now!"

"Take a deep breath, Blaire. I get that you're upset, and all of these individual things together might seem bad, but until you've had a conversation with him you really can't know for sure, can you? And honestly, this is nothing like the food truck business, which is literally insane."

"Doesn't it seem like a pretty big coincidence that he's suddenly impossible to get ahold of right after he wins the award and we have this huge event we're trying to pull off so our businesses don't end up in the shitter?"

"Yes, I agree that it does, but I also don't want you to go off half-cocked and blow up this relationship without having the whole story."

She has a point. "I just don't want my shop to fail. I can't afford for it to fail because if it does it means my dream is dead."

"Let's not borrow trouble. You have a weekend of awesomeness planned, and we've done everything we can to promote it. Have some faith in yourself and your ability to make this a success, regardless of whether Ronan pulls through for you."

"I'm supposed to have a partner in this." And maybe that's the biggest kick in the pants for me. Because that's what this felt like, a partnership. A real one on all levels. So it hurts more than I'd like that the man who I thought was with me on this whole thing was only here for as long as I was useful and necessary, sort of like how Raphael used me to get closer to my family. In the end, my parents cared more about his skill set than my broken heart. I thought I'd been smarter this time. I thought I knew better.

"*I'm* your partner right now. You don't need Ronan to make this a success. He's great arm candy and I'm sure he's a rock star in bed, but he isn't essential to pulling this off. You've been the one to set up all the cohosted events. You made those a success."

"Well, they weren't successful enough."

"So what if you had one bad comedy act? So what if you didn't win the Best Bar title? Put that aside and focus on the here and now. You have the respect of your peers. They've come to you with every question, so remember that when you're getting down on yourself or thinking you're not enough. And honestly, if Ronan did just use you for a ride I'll happily kick him in the balls for you."

"While wearing steel-toed boots."

"Yes. Or cleats. Then he could be textured for your pleasure."

"That is not a pleasant visual."

Someone knocks on the door timidly and Daphne opens it up. "What's up, Callie?"

"Um, I'm really sorry to interrupt." She wrings her hands nervously. "But the McClellands are here and they have an order for pickup, but I can't find it in the stack."

"I'll take care of it. I didn't put it out front because it has a custard filling and needs to be refrigerated. Tell them I'll be right out," I say, much more gently than I have all day.

I push Ronan's absence to the back of my mind. I can't afford to fixate, and Daphne is right: I'm scaring Callie when I should be building excitement for the weekend.

I retrieve the McClelland order and reset my attitude. It helps put everyone else at ease, and we're all in a far more positive mood by the end of the day.

I send Callie home an hour early and post a sign that our hours will be modified for the weekend so we can stick around for all of the festivities.

The specials have already been added to the board, tomorrow's cupcakes are decorated and in the fridge, and we're well stocked with drinks and everything we could possibly need to make Love Is in the Air a success.

I pull up my Instagram account to check interaction, and the first thing that pops up on my feed is a post from Tori Taylor, which isn't all that surprising. But the fact that it's a picture of her and Ronan sitting in a cozy-looking bar that *isn't* The Knight Cap sure is not what I expect to see. And it was posted half an hour ago. So much for running errands and helping prep for the event. I'm tempted to comment on the post, but I decide it's not in my best interest to be petty where Tori is concerned.

I pop over to The Knight Cap before I head home, not because I'm looking for Ronan at this point since clearly he's too busy making plans with Tori to be bothered with the event, but because I want to touch base with the bar staff and make sure they don't have any questions.

Lars is tending bar along with Corbin, who was hired last week and seems to be a great addition to their team. He's got the whole surfer dude look going on, long blond hair, tanned, and always calling everyone "bro" and "sweetheart." The women eat it up.

Lars cringes when he sees me approach. I hold up a hand, feeling even worse based on his response to my presence. "I'm not looking for Ronan. I just want to make sure you're all set for tomorrow."

He blinks at me a couple of times but says nothing.

"Do you need any clarification on anything?" I ask.

"Uhhhh...I don't think so. I'm supposed to be here at nine thirty to help prep the bar and the doors open at eleven. I'll be serving drinks all day and managing whatever else needs to happen to make things go smoothly."

"What about the rest of your crew?"

"I think we're all good. We got your to-do list, and Lana is huge on the decorating shit." He motions to the heart garland strung all over the bar interspersed with lei-wearing cupids. The hearts are red and black plaid, to match the rest of the décor. "So I think we're okay unless something major happens tomorrow."

"Okay, great. Text me if you need anything or if there's something you're unsure of."

"Will do." A couple of college girls approach the bar.

"I'll let you get back to it."

As I turn to leave, Lars calls out, "Blaire."

I pause and give him a questioning smile.

"Try not to think the worst."

I nod, and he turns back to the girls.

It's easier said than done, though. I give in and send Ronan a message before I go to bed. I don't anticipate sleeping well, or much at all, but I figure it's worth a shot. It's well past midnight before I fall into a restless, fitful sleep. And still nothing from Ronan.

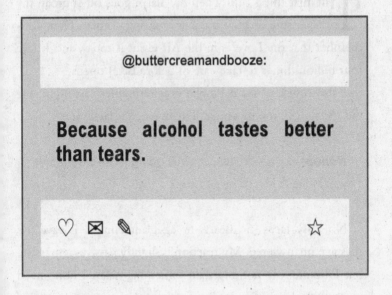

@buttercreamandbooze:

Because alcohol tastes better than tears.

chapter twenty-one

WELL THAT EXPLAINS IT

Blaire

The first thing I do when my alarm goes off is groan my displeasure at how quickly morning comes. Then I remember that the Love Is in the Air event is today, and I have four billion things to take care of before B&B opens.

I also check to see if Ronan ever responded last night. He did. At four in the morning. The message is lackluster.

Ronan: Sry it's so late, tmrw is going to be awsm, see you in the A.M.

No kissy faces, no hearts or eggplant emojis. I leave the message unanswered. My reaction is slightly passive-aggressive, but I'd rather say nothing than something nasty. I don't need to start my day with an argument.

I set the coffeemaker to brew, then shower and get ready for what I hope will be a fantastic day. The Seattle paper is supposed to come by and spotlight the local businesses participating in the Love Is in the Air pub crawl. I'm hopeful the positive press will help us all and bring to light the harmful impact big chains have when they come and undercut small businesses.

My dress boasts an adorable hearts and cupids-slinging-arrows theme. It's an old one that I embellished with a wide plaid ribbon with a cupcake, cocktails, and beer pattern tied at my waist. I also have a special apron for today.

I swallow thickly as I take in my reflection. I'd hoped that Ronan and I would've spent last night together, that he would be here to see me get ready for this event that we worked so hard to make happen.

I push aside the negative thoughts, aware they don't do me any good. I'm out the door by seven thirty. We're not opening until later this morning, but I want to be at B&B nice and early so I can make sure everything is set up and help calm anyone with event-day jitters.

I park my SUV behind the shop, surprised to see Ronan's truck there already. The moment I walk into B&B, I'm assaulted by Daphne. She grabs me by the shoulders. "You need to go next door. Right now."

I set my purse on the counter. I'm not in a hurry to see Ronan this morning. "Why are you here so early?"

"Because I couldn't sleep and because of...reasons." She tries to turn me around, but I refuse to budge. "Come on, you have to see this."

"See what?"

"I can't tell you. I have to show you."

"Well, show me later. I have lots of stuff to take care of." I glance out the window and notice there's already a crowd gathered, even though we're not supposed to open for several hours. I squint. "Is that a camera crew? What's going on out there?"

I head for the door but turn abruptly. Daphne is following so closely she slams into me and nearly knocks over a table. "Do I need to reapply my lipstick?"

"No. You're perfect. But you should lose the coat."

"It's freezing outside."

"You'll survive. I promise." She tugs my parka down my arms like I'm a toddler who needs help. Once I'm coatless, I open the door and step outside. The street has been blocked off so people are able to walk down the road and traffic won't interfere with the event. We had to petition the city councillors to make that happen.

In the middle of the street is Ronan looking damn gorgeous in his plaid shirt and black sports jacket. He's also wearing a pair of dark-wash jeans and his usual steel-toed work boots. And he's surrounded by media. There are several news crews, people from *The Seattle Morning Show*, and Tori.

"What the heck is going on?" I mutter.

"Your boyfriend is awesome; that's what's going on." Daphne squeezes my arm.

It's as if Ronan can sense my presence the moment I step out the front door and onto the sidewalk. His gaze shifts from Tori— who's standing beside him looking ridiculously perfect for this horribly early hour—and lands on me. His smile widens, and he extends a hand. "And here she is, the reason behind all of this."

"He's talking about you! Go on." Daphne elbows me in the side.

He takes a step forward, breaking from the group, and winks. "Come on, beautiful, don't be shy on me."

I give him a look, feeling my cheeks heat. He said those same words less than a week ago when he wanted to have sex on the bar of The Knight Cap. After hours, of course. Even with no lights on and the mostly opaque sign covering the front windows I was apprehensive. I gave in eventually, though. And then made him sanitize the hell out of the bar afterward while I watched, and told him he was a bad influence, and that we should maybe consider doing that on the bar in his apartment next time instead. He wondered why he hadn't thought of that himself.

"What is all this?" I ask when I reach him.

He doesn't answer at first. Simply takes my face between his cold hands—because it's frigid out here—bends down, and presses his lips gently to mine. "You look good enough to eat."

"Can you stop saying things that make me turn red?"

"Your cheeks will match the hearts on your dress." He smiles against my lips and then backs up so I can see his face. "I'm sorry I haven't been around the last couple of days, but now you know why."

"I'm confused as to what all is happening here. Is that Thom Thomas from channel five?"

"It is."

"And Claudia Carmichael from Food and Drink?"

"You're correct. Come on, let me introduce you." Ronan threads his fingers through mine.

"Do I look okay?" I smooth my hand down the front of my dress.

"You look good enough to eat, remember?" He tugs on my hand and brings me over to the group of media professionals. People I've watched on TV for years, and they're here because of Ronan. "This is Blaire Calloway. She's the reason all of this is happening."

I want to argue since he was the one who suggested the street party, but I'm suddenly shaking hands with all these influential people. Tori extends her hand. "It's so great to see you again, Blaire. I think what you're doing here is amazing. I'm a big advocate for small business owners."

"Your parents started Organically Yours," I mention.

"That's right, back when I was just a kid. I know how hard they worked to promote their business and stay current and relevant, which is how I ended up here."

"You've done amazing things for so many independent businesses," I say. Because it's true. She's always focused on new products or start-ups, giving preference to smaller companies trying to find their footing. A recommendation from someone like Tori creates buzz and awareness. It's a powerful marketing tool.

"So have you." Tori smiles like she's in on a secret.

"I'm sorry, I don't think I understand." I glance between her and Ronan.

"All of this . . ." Tori motions to the businesses setting up for the day, at the decorations that line the street.

"You're the one who made this happen, Blaire," Ronan says.

"It was your idea, though."

"I just made a suggestion. You're the one who ran with it and made it reality. I was just a bystander taking orders from the cupcake queen." He smiles down at me, his expression reflecting so many emotions. The most dominant is pride and it makes my heart swell.

"I just wanted us to have a fighting chance, and the best way to do that was to band together," I explain.

"And you were absolutely right to do that. I wanted to make sure that all the right people could be here to see it happen, so I talked to Tori."

I'm sure my confusion is clear on my face.

"Ronan thought it would be a good idea to showcase not just The Knight Cap but the entire community here, since you're all so involved with each other," Tori says. "It's amazing to see so many businesses come together instead of making rivals of each other. I thought it was a fantastic idea, so I made some calls and explained what was going on, and of course I needed Ronan's help to make it happen."

"Which is why you've been MIA the past couple of days," I whisper. I feel awful for assuming the worst, although to be fair I've had my share of being burned.

"I know I kind of left you in the lurch, but I wanted to make sure I could pull this off. That we could pull this off." He motions between himself and Tori.

Ronan forfeited his spotlight so we could all benefit, and here I was, thinking he was out to screw me over. I wave my hand in front of my face, trying to control the emotions, which apparently want to leak out of my eyes in the form of tears.

He pulls me against him and dips his head down so his lips are at my ear. "Are these happy tears?"

"So happy," I mumble against his chest. My boyfriend is the best.

There are lines out the door all day, which is fantastic. I almost pass out from shock when my family shows up late in the afternoon. My parents, aunt, uncle, Maddy, and Skylar sort of suck the air out of the place with their presence. They're dressed up like they're going to a diamond-level restaurant, but then, my family loves to make a statement. And I suppose I'm no different with the way I dress.

"What are you guys doing here?" I peel off my latex gloves and toss them in the trash. Wiping my hands on my apron, I round the display case so I can air-kiss them.

"Your boyfriend called and said you were hosting an event and that it would be great if we could come out and see what you've accomplished," my mom says.

"This place is so cute!" Maddy says.

"It really is," Skylar agrees, albeit reluctantly.

My dad pulls me in for a hug. "This really is incredible, Blaire. You've done amazing things, and all on your own."

"I didn't do it all on my own. Ronan was a lot of help with the event." Minus the past couple of days, but clearly he's forgiven for that.

"I mean with this place." My dad motions to the line of people waiting for cupcakes and cocktails—or mocktails, since there are loads of families at the event. It's standing room only, with customers ordering cupcakes to go so they can sample more vendors. "You followed your dream, and you did it on your own. I'm proud of you, honey."

I get misty-eyed at the praise and the acknowledgment that this accomplishment is well and truly mine.

My jaw nearly hits the floor when they all try a cupcake and a cocktail. Even Maddy and Skylar—although they both talk about the two-hour run plus detox they're going to have to endure because of the single cupcake they consumed.

My dad mingles with everyone, happy to tell them that he's my father and that I inherited my excellent business sense and my baking skills from him.

By the time we close the doors, the only thing that's left are a pair of lonely Death by Chocolate cupcakes.

I bring them next door to The Knight Cap, where the band has already started playing. Ronan and I are going to be dead on our feet by the time the bar closes, but we're taking a day off after all of this is over, so we should be able to catch up on some much-needed sleep and some alone time.

I spot Gramps sitting at the end of the bar, nursing a pint of Guinness. When he sees me, a huge grin lights up his face. I give him a hug from the side and shout over the noise. "Having fun?"

"I sure am. This is the busiest I've seen this place in a long time. Dottie would be proud 'a both of you." He thumbs over to the band. "But I gotta be honest, this just sounds like noise. Gonna finish my pint and head home."

"Want dessert with that?" I flip open the lid on the box.

"You don't have to ask me twice." He winks and takes one.

I leave him to his pint and I sidle up next to Ronan behind the bar. "Gramps is having a great time."

He glances down at my feet, but doesn't comment on my lack of proper footwear. "I'm impressed that he's still here. I would have thought he'd bail so he doesn't miss the late night rerun of *Jeopardy*."

"Thank goodness for DVR, I guess. Did he used to watch it with Dottie?"

"Every night at seven thirty. They'd compete to see who could answer the most questions correctly."

"Did they keep score?"

"Sure did."

"He must miss her so much."

Ronan nods. "He does. We both do. But I think I'd rather have someone to miss than never have the opportunity to witness that kind of devotion. They were each other's everything."

"Makes it tough to settle for anything less, I would think." I tip my chin up, overwhelmed by the sudden surge of emotion. I don't really know what it's like to watch a love like that. My parents are the most unconventional people I know, and the idea of finding a soul mate seemed elusive.

Lars interrupts—his timing sucks—to ask Ronan for some help behind the bar, because they're swamped and I'm monopolizing him. I change into a pair of boots and mix some drinks.

When the band finishes, the crowd slowly starts to dissipate.

"I can't believe how well this has gone." I load barware into the washer and dry off the clean ones before I stack them. "Or that you managed to get Thom Thomas from channel five here, or that you forfeited your spotlight with Tori so we could all be in it."

Ronan puts the beer steins in the freezer. "To be fair, it was Tori who pulled all the strings since she has all the connections. I just proposed the idea and she ran with it. I'm sorry I left you hanging the last couple of days, but I really wanted to be able to pull this off and give you and Buttercream and Booze the attention you deserved."

"I feel bad for being annoyed with you." And for doubting his sincerity and his loyalty. Although I was under a lot of stress, and he did sort of screw right off immediately after winning the Best Bar in Town award, so there was some room for doubt and worry.

He laughs. "Lars said you didn't look all that impressed the couple of times you stopped in here. I told him I was trying to make some things happen, but I wouldn't tell him what exactly because I couldn't be sure he'd keep his mouth shut. And I knew if I saw you I'd want to tell you what I was planning, but on the off chance I failed, I also didn't want to disappoint you. It was a real conundrum."

"I'm so sorry I was less than sweet to you the past couple of days." If I'd known he was planning something then maybe I would've calmed my tits and not been so passive-aggressive. It's a good reminder that I can't base my opinions or assumptions on past experiences and that Ronan isn't like Raphael.

"It's not your sweetness that keeps me coming back, Blaire." He winks.

I'm about to give him some sass, but Tori appears at the bar. "Do you have a few minutes for an interview? I'd love to get your thoughts on how today has been for you and the rest of the family-owned businesses on the street."

I make a move to step to the side. "I'll just give you a few minutes."

Ronan snags me by the waist before I get too far. "I think Tori actually wants to interview you, Blaire, since you're the one who orchestrated all of this."

I glance between him and Tori. "But it's your spotlight."

"I'd actually love it if you could do this together. Ronan's already answered most of these questions for me over the past couple of days while we've been getting everything together to make this happen, but I'd love to get them on camera and hear your side of things, too, Blaire. Are you okay if we go live with this? It's more organic this way, you know? Feels a lot less scripted."

Ronan defers to me. "Are you okay with that?"

"Sure, of course. We can go live." As if I'm going to pass up this opportunity.

"Great." Tori motions for her crew to get set up and three women swoop in with makeup brushes and attack her face. "Can we touch you up, Blaire?"

"Um, sure?" One of the women flits down the length of the bar and makes her way to me, brushes and makeup case in hand.

Tori taps her lip. "I think you two should stay behind the bar. I like the lighting and the backdrop is fantastic. Are those your grandparents?" She points to the picture behind Ronan.

"That's them."

She looks from the framed photo to us and back again. "It's like history repeating itself." She does a little shimmy. "This is beyond perfect."

Two minutes later I'm all touched up and when the girl moves in to get to Ronan he raises both hands in the air. "Is it okay if you don't use that stuff on me?"

Tori waves her off and she takes a seat at the bar. I make her a pretty cocktail and we plate the lone Death by Chocolate cupcake for her. She's all about product placement, making sure the coaster with The Knight Cap logo on it is situated so viewers can read it easily and that the cupcake box with the B&B sticker is equally visible and prominent.

"You two, nice and close, please." Tori makes hand gestures until our shoulders are touching. "You can put your arm around Blaire, Ronan."

He slings it over my shoulder and I wrap mine around his waist. I tip my chin up as he looks down and we both smile and laugh. He bends to press a kiss to my temple.

"Oh my God, cuteness overload," Tori sighs.

"You ready?" the cameraman asks.

Tori gives him a thumbs-up. "Okay, we're going live in, three, two, one." The camera guy focuses on Tori and she squares her shoulders. "Tori Taylor here and tonight we're celebrating Love Is in the Air with the Best Bar winner, The Knight Cap, but Ronan Knight, our designated winner, wanted to share the limelight with the rest of the family-owned businesses in the area, so they created this amazing Love Is in the Air event, and it has been outstanding! I've never had so much fun in my entire life! Ronan, tell me what inspired you to put together such an incredible day."

"Alice in Wonderland," Ronan blurts.

To her credit, Tori hardly misses a beat. "The Tim Burton remake?"

"That's what he called me the first time he met me," I supply.

"Oh? This is definitely a story. Do tell!"

Ronan and I look at each other. "Go ahead. I'm interested to hear your version of events." I nudge him playfully.

His smile widens. "Are you sure you want me to share this story?"

"Just remember whose bed you're sleeping in tonight." I bat my lashes.

Ronan bites his lip, likely to prevent his grin from growing any wider. He tips my chin up and kisses me softly. I don't think he's even in tune with the fact that he's being recorded anymore because he doesn't look at the camera.

"I'll never forget the moment I met you. God, you were just so angry and beautiful and righteous. And I never would have admitted it then, but now I can say that it was a total jerk move to start renovations and not come by and introduce myself first."

"Tell us more about that." Tori pulls his attention away from me.

Ronan blinks a couple of times and realizes he's not talking just to me but a million plus subscribers. "Uh. I'd just agreed to help my grandfather with The Knight Cap. We lost my grandmother a while back and they were the epitome of soul mates. They did everything together, including run this place. After she passed, it was hard for him to run it on his own."

Tori nods, her expression sympathetic. "You're very close with your grandfather."

"I am." He goes on to explain the deal he made with his grandfather to get his brewery capital.

"You worked here before, though, right? It was your first job," Tori adds, shifting away from the heavier topic of losing his grandmother.

"I washed dishes, bussed tables, served them—and sucked

at that part—before I finally got to tend the bar. It's all a lot different than running the place."

"And you added some new features."

"I did, and they weren't particularly convenient for my neighbor." He smiles down at me. "She came in here, all fired up about problems I was causing her."

"He wasn't very receptive at first," I add.

"Oh, I was more than receptive, and that was the problem."

I cock my head. This is the first I've heard of this.

"I didn't need a distraction. I needed to take this bar from red to black and then I could move on. That was my plan, and then Blaire happened. I've never met someone so determined to succeed. She comes from a family of restaurateurs and she's a baker. You might think it's the same, but it's not. We shouldn't have been each other's competition, but we were. Blaire is a force; she's smart and beautiful and driven and uniquely herself. And I think it took me about two weeks to fall for her, but man I tried so hard not to."

"You fell in love with your rival?" Tori presses her hand to her heart and I stare up at Ronan, trying to figure out what in the world is happening here.

His expression turns panicked, like he suddenly realizes what he's said and where. He doesn't address Tori, but he does address me. "I'm so in love with you," he says softly, with conviction.

"And I'm so in love with you," I whisper back. If I hadn't made the decision to go out on my own I never would have met him, or had the chance to fall for him.

His smile is beautiful. He dips down and presses his lips to mine. "I can't wait to take you home and show you how much I love you," he murmurs.

I'm all for that, but I'm not sure all of Tori's subscribers need to know about it. "There are cameras rolling," I say against his lips, trying my best to keep his tongue from sliding between mine.

His gaze darts to Tori and the cameraman. "Damn it. Right. I keep forgetting this is a live thing."

We all burst into laughter and Tori turns to face the camera. "I think we all know this one has a happy ending. So make sure to come visit The Knight Cap and Buttercream and Booze, and maybe you, too, will find your very own happily ever after."

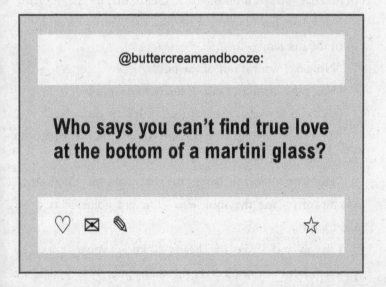

@buttercreamandbooze:

Who says you can't find true love at the bottom of a martini glass?

epilogue

I LOVE YOU MORE THAN CUPCAKES

Ronan

Three months later

Gramps hoists himself up onto one of the barstools and pulls a bottle of my homebrew out of the inside pocket of his coat and sets it on the bar. "Uncap that for me, Ronan."

I shake my head but do as he asks, then retrieve a pint glass from the freezer.

"No, no. I want it out of the bottle."

"You can't drink this out of the bottle, Gramps."

"I can do whatever the hell I want. It's my damn bar."

"This guy giving you a hard time?" Blaire sidles up beside me.

"He won't let me drink my beer out of the bottle." Gramps gives me the stink eye. "I'm not gonna start a bar fight with it."

I laugh and shake my head. "I know you're not. The problem is that we don't carry this in the pub, and if people see they might want to know what it is and you'll be drinking the only one 'cause you brought your own beer into the bar."

"Well, start serving it and I won't have to bring my own."

I shrug. "I don't have enough space to brew it in large batches yet."

"I already said I'd cut you the check," he grumbles.

I lean an arm on the bar. "When'd you say that?"

He waves a hand around in the air. "I'm old, how am I supposed to remember when. After you won that Best Bar award, I said I'd cut you a check for the start-up cost."

"Are you sure you said it out loud?"

Gramps gives me a look and turns to Blaire. "Are you listening to this? Giving this old guy a hard time, making me question my memory. It's ageism is what it is!"

"Maybe you already cut him the check and he's messing with you to make you think you didn't," Blaire teases.

I lean on the bar and fight a smile. "Whose side are you on?"

She grins up at me. "I'm not taking sides on this."

"Sounds like she's taking my side." Gramps gives her a wink and an affectionate smile. "When you putting a ring on Blaire's finger? Everyone's waiting for it, ya know."

"Yeah, Gramps, I know. Everyone needs to find some chill about it, too." I kiss Blaire on the temple. We've only been together for a few months, but I can't see my life without her. "And I've been thinking about the brewery situation lately."

"I'll miss driving in to work with you." Blaire gives my arm a squeeze.

"Well, that's the thing…Lars is a good kid, but he isn't anywhere near ready to take over this place, and I kinda like what we've got going on here." I put my arm around Blaire's shoulder and pull her in closer. "People really love what we're doing, and I figure I can put the brewery on hold until we can settle on a location."

"But that's what you've been working toward," Blaire says.

Gramps nods and sips his beer, a hint of a smile there, like maybe he knew this was coming. "The McCurdys next door have been thinking about selling. At least that's what Bertie says pretty much every time I go over to buy some cold cuts."

"If they decide to sell we could look at what it would take to convert it. Wouldn't take much to make a doorway to connect the two," I say.

"Things to think about." Gramps shifts his attention to Blaire. "Might be a good time to mention that thing *you* were thinking about. Pretty sure you might be on the same page."

Blaire gives him a meaningful look. "I'm not sure now is the time."

I look between them, unnerved that Gramps and Blaire are having conversations about whatever, apparently behind my back. "Now isn't the time for what?"

Gramps wears an expression that looks a lot like a smirk and then turns away as a couple of his friends walk through the front door—they've taken to coming out at least once a week for beers and wings—and he slips off the stool. "I'll leave you two lovebirds to talk."

"Are you going to explain what that's about?" I motion between Gramps and Blaire as he ambles over to one of the four-tops.

He's been in such better spirits lately. So happy with how the bar is doing, glad to see it full of life and people again. And honestly, so am I.

Blaire slips her arm through mine. "Come on, let's go talk in your office."

"Are you going to try to distract me with sex?"

Blaire laughs. "I could, but I won't. Especially not while Gramps is here."

I slip into the office first so I can quickly shuffle some of the papers around on the desk, hiding the ones I'm not sure I'm ready for Blaire to see yet. I close the door and sit on the edge of the desk, giving her the new executive chair. As much as Gramps loved the old one, it was falling apart. Literally. One of the arms fell off two weeks ago and it was really all the encouragement I needed to buy something comfortable.

"So what have you and Gramps been talking about behind my back?" I go for light, but I'm not sure it comes out that way.

Blaire reaches up and takes one of my hands in hers, skimming along the design on my wrist. "It was just something I mentioned a few weeks back, more as a joke than anything."

"Okay." I wait for her to elaborate, but after a few seconds of quiet, I press. "Blaire? Are you gonna tell me?"

"I just made a comment that it would be a lot easier to run

all of our cohosted events if we put a doorway between B&B and The Knight Cap." She laughs, but it's high and nervous.

I have to give it to Gramps; he really knows how to force a conversation I wasn't sure I was ready to have. I lace my fingers with hers. "Oh yeah? And what did Gramps say about that?"

She waves her free hand in the air. "Oh, you know Gramps."

"So you were just joking about that? About a doorway between our places?"

Her expression is somewhere between embarrassed and nervous. "I'm already moving in with you. It's not like you want me in your face all day every day, too. Besides, Gramps has had to manage enough change with all the renovations this year."

Last month I suggested she move in with me. It's maybe five minutes farther from the bars, but my place is also twice the size of hers and nicer, and my bed is bigger. And she actually kind of lives in a shithole, not that I would say that out loud. But it isn't great. So she's been driving stuff over by the carload.

"I'd be more than happy to have you in my face all day every day and every night." I raise our twined fingers and kiss the back of her hand. "But I totally understand if that would be too much of me for you."

"I can't ever get enough of you, Ronan. You know that. Anyway, it was just a silly idea I threw out, because it was cold and rainy and I didn't have an umbrella with me."

"What if I said I didn't think it was that silly of an idea."

She blinks up at me. "What do you mean?"

"I mean what if we joined forces permanently? I love you and I love this place, and I think we work really well together."

"So do I, and I love you, too." She gives me a gentle, inquisitive smile.

"I know how important it is for you to do this on your own, and I don't want to take that away from you, but my favorite nights are when we cohost events. And the thing I look forward to the most every day are the times I get to see you."

Blaire's fingers go to her lips. "You're serious?"

"I think we make a great team."

"Me, too." She smiles, and then her expression turns serious. "We'd have to open up a wall."

"The adjoining wall doesn't have anything but electrical to worry about, and that's easy to shift around."

She cocks her head to the side, considering. "What about the booths and the wall of photos?"

"We'd only have to lose one booth to put the doorway in, and we could have a host stand between the two."

"You sound like you already have a layout for this." She laughs.

"I might have drawn up a rough sketch and looked into a few things."

"Wait. You've already thought about this, too?" A small

wry smile tips up the corner of her mouth. "So that's what Gramps meant by we're on the same page."

"I don't want to push you into this either way, Blaire. I know how important your independence is, and how hard you've worked so you don't have to compromise your dream. I just want you to know that if you're ever interested, I'd love to do this together with you, but it's really okay if you don't like—"

She launches herself out of the chair and wraps her arms around me. "I'm interested. I know I've always talked about not compromising my dream, but I realized I really love having a partner. Having the *right* partner. I only wanted to do it on my own because no one ever thought I could, and now I know I can. My favorite place to be is right next to you. I want us to do this together." She smooths her hands down my chest. "But what about the brewery?"

"I don't want to let this go—us, the bar, the connection I have to you and this place is far too important. I came into this thinking I would make it work and then move on, but I got so much more out of it. I got you."

"And cupcakes. Don't forget about those."

I chuckle and bend to kiss her. "And cupcakes. So we're in this together?"

"There isn't anyone else I'd rather do this with than you."

"Let's go tell Gramps the good news. He's been hounding me to ask you."

"How long have you been thinking about this?"

"A while." I've thought about it since I won Best Bar. But I started falling for her long before that.

I tug her by the hand and give Lars a covert thumbs-up on the way over to the table where Gramps is sitting. Lars gives me a quick nod and pulls his phone out of his back pocket, speed typing a message.

I survey the booths close to Gramps's table, glad everything seems to have fallen into place today. Like fate has stepped in once again and thrown something undeniable in my path, forcing me to stop and see what's in front of me. Or in this case, hugging my arm and practically skipping toward Gramps.

His gaze meets mine, and anticipation churns in my gut. He and I have sat down countless times over the past several months, hashing this out, me questioning whether I'm moving too fast, him telling me I'm moving too damn slow. I've been worried about making more changes to The Knight Cap, but he's assured me that Grams would be all for it. Grams always said it wasn't about fixing broken things; it was about giving them a lift to make them feel new again.

And that's exactly what we're going to do.

Gramps pushes out of his chair, a little unsteady, just like me. "So? Do you like the idea?"

Blaire laughs and releases my arm so she can hug him. "I love it. I think it's perfect."

He hugs her back and winks at me over her shoulder. "I knew you would."

When he releases her I step in and give him a hug. "Thank you for believing in me."

"Always, son, always." His voice cracks, and I feel the emotion rising, the sadness over our mutual loss—first his son, and my father and mother, then Grams. But he gives me a pat on the back, then he takes my hand in his, giving me the last piece of the puzzle. "Now stop stalling."

I nod once and turn to face Blaire, who looks like she's on the verge of tears—happy ones, though—and I drop to one knee.

Her eyes flare with surprise, but stay locked on mine as understanding dawns. I've taken a lot of big risks today and I'm about to take the biggest one of all.

I smooth my thumb over the worn velvet box, finding strength in it. It isn't a new ring, but it's special and it has meaning, because it was my grandmother's. I flip the lid open, the diamond catching the light, and rainbows dance across the back of my hand and Blaire's dress.

"Oh, Ronan," Blaire whispers. Shaking fingers touch her lips and she smiles behind them, even as a single tear tracks slowly down her cheek.

"Blaire, for a long time I didn't want to fall in love, because the reality of losing someone you love is so hard, especially when you don't expect it. But this, being here"—I motion to the bar, and all the people in it, watching me take a huge chance on the woman I love—"and meeting you changed everything. You came slamming through that door and you made it impossible not to fall in love with you and your determination and your beautiful, creative mind." I squeeze her hand, and she squeezes back. "I want you at my side every day. I want your good days and bad. I want your fight and your warmth and your effervescence lighting up my world. I want your forever. Marry me, please."

"Of course I'll marry you."

I slip the ring on her finger and push to a stand. "She said yes!"

Everyone bursts into raucous cheers as I wrap my arms around her waist. I kiss her, probably longer than is appropriate with the number of people watching. But I don't care, and neither does she, apparently. We've found forever in each other, and now I never have to let her go.

Blaire

6 months later

"One year ago today I stepped in a pile of dog crap."

My stylist, Frangelica—yes, like the liqueur—meets my gaze in the mirror briefly and smiles. "Oh?"

Daphne snorts and takes another photo.

The cameraman steps to the right, presumably so he can pan in on my face.

"Is this the story of the first time you met?" Tori asks.

She popped in as soon as my makeup was done so she could get a few minutes with me while Fran finishes up with my hair. It's my wedding day and I'm clearly nervous since it's going to be livestreamed on Tori's YouTube channel.

"It is." I'm about to nod, but remember Fran is working on my hair.

"Oh! I've only heard Ronan's version! I want to hear yours!" Tori claps her hands excitedly.

So I tell her my version, including all the little details, the bang we thought was an earthquake, the broken unicorn glass, the way I lost my ability to speak and string together logical sentences because he was so disarmingly handsome and ridiculously composed. I recall how annoyed and flustered I was, so much so that I stepped in the dog poop I'd marked with a flower and forgot about. Recounting the story helps settle my nerves.

So much has happened in the past year, but the last six months have been an amazing whirlwind. Lars recorded Ronan's proposal and shared it on social media after I said yes. From there things went a little crazy, especially with the incessant requests from people who wanted to see us tie the knot live.

So we agreed to let Tori do the honors, in part because of her role in bringing us together. Yes, there were other variables and factors at play, but if we hadn't been competing against each other, and then eventually banding together to outdo D&B, we may not have fallen in love. Shoddy plumbing shut D&B down after the Love Is in the Air event, and they ended up relocating to another end of town. The building across the street has been turned into a software company with fifty new employees, which means more business for us.

Which means The Knight Cap & Cupcakery is thriving.

When we opened the wall between B&B and The Knight Cap we needed to find a way to blend the two very distinct, very different themes. Instead of a complete overhaul, we found a way to work the plaid into my side and the whimsy of cupcakes into his without emasculating it entirely.

My family shows up as I finish the story. There's a whole lot of hugs and hands flapping in front of faces to ward off the tears. My parents have really come around in the past year, offering support and praise without trying to take over. Although Ronan is pretty good at standing his ground and politely telling them to back off. I've even gotten better at it, too.

Eventually we shoo everyone out of the back room—it's not really made for more than two or three people—so Daphne can help me into my dress.

My dress isn't quite the typical bridal gown. It's far more representative of me and Ronan and where we met, which is here. It's champagne colored and the entire bustier top is red and black plaid. It matches Ronan's tux with his red vest and plaid tie.

"Ronan is going to lose his freaking mind when he sees you in this dress," Daphne mutters. "Let's hope he can make it through the reception instead of dragging you into the office."

I snort indelicately, as though the idea is completely ludi-crous. "As if." I can feel my face going red, especially since my mom is also in the room with us.

"Not according to Lars," she mumbles.

"What did you just say?"

She gives me a serene smile. "Hmm?"

I poke her in the shoulder. "Since when do you and Lars gossip about what Ronan and I do behind closed doors?"

Her smile turns into a smirk. "You mean closed *office* doors, which happen to be right across the hall from the stockroom."

I don't get to grill her about it because there's a knock on the door, but I make a mental note to give Lars hell for telling Daphne about the office incident. He was supposed to take that to the grave.

Daphne opens the door for my dad. "Care Blaire, you look gorgeous." He pulls me in for a huge hug and for once I don't hate that nickname. He holds me at arm's length, eyes watery, a sad smile on his face. "You ready for this?"

"I've never been more ready for anything in my life." And it's true. I can't wait to marry Ronan, because then we can officially start our forever. I slip my arm through his. "You ready to walk me down the aisle and give me away?"

"Never, but I can see how much you two love each other, so I'm willing to put my own feelings aside on this one." He winks and gives my arm a squeeze. "I don't really feel like I have any words of wisdom to impart to you where marriage is concerned, all considering."

I lean my head on his shoulder. "You taught me that love doesn't always fit into a neat little box, and I'm a better person for it. Plus, normal families are boring."

He chuckles and bends to kiss me on the cheek. "I'm glad he loves you enough to deal with the rest of us."

"We're kind of a package deal, aren't we? Now let's get out there so I can marry the one that I want."

The wedding march starts—bagpipes, of course—and we walk down the short hall, turn left at the end of the bar and there's Ronan.

His hand goes to his chest and he tips his chin up to the ceiling; his eyes fall closed for the briefest moment and he murmurs something that makes Gramps squeeze his arm. Of course he's Ronan's best man.

As I make my way down the aisle, past our family and friends and Tori and the camera crew, I feel like I'm falling backward through time, Alice traveling to Wonderland, to the moment when Henry and Dottie found their forever in exactly the same place, on exactly the same day, sixty-three years ago. History sometimes repeats itself in the most magical ways.

When I finally reach Ronan, my dad kisses me on the cheek and I take Ronan's hand. He looks magnificent and happy and a tad nervous, and like he's on the verge of tears. So am I.

"God, you're beautiful." He squeezes both of my hands. "You look like you were made for me."

I squeeze back. "That's because I am."

And I know without a doubt that Ronan is mine. That we'll stand beside each other through all the good times and the bad, that we'll argue and cry and laugh and love.

He's the icing to my cupcake. My happily forever after.

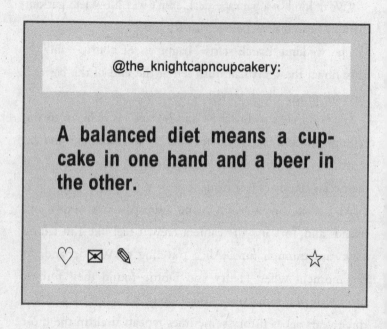

@the_knightcapncupcakery:

A balanced diet means a cupcake in one hand and a beer in the other.

ACKNOWLEDGMENTS

Hubs and kidlet; you are my rocks and I'm incredibly lucky to have your love and your support. Mom, Dad, and Mel, you're amazing cheerleaders and I adore you.

Deb, you are always there to lift me up when I need it, to make fun of me when I'm being dramatic and ridiculous, and you never fail to celebrate my victories, no matter how small they are. You're a once in a lifetime friend and I'm so lucky to have you.

Kimberly, I'm so grateful for your friendship and your incredible business brain. Thank you for being such a force to reckon with.

Sarah, I am beyond blessed to have you in my corner; you are the keeper of my sanity, and I adore you. Hustlers, thank you for being such an endless source of support and friendship.

Tijan, you're such a warm hug and a gentle soul, thank you for being you.

Leigh, thank you for always being a voice of reason when the doubt kicks in.

Huge gratitude to Leah, Estelle, and my team at Forever for

all the amazing ideas, support, and enthusiasm for each new project. I'm lucky to have such wonderful, innovative women to work with.

Sarah, Jenn, Hilary, Shan, and my team at Social Butterfly, you're an amazing group of women and I adore you. Thank you for everything you do.

Sarah Musings, you create such gorgeous graphics, thank you for sharing your talent with me.

Gel, you are a graphic wizard, and I adore your creative mind and your out of the box thinking. Thank you for bringing my words to life.

Beavers, I'm so grateful for all of you. You are my safe space and the place I go to when I want to laugh and share my excitement.

I have so much love for the incredible women in this community who are my friends, colleagues, teachers, and cheerleaders: Deb and Katherine, Tijan, Marty, Karen, Teeny, Erika, Shalu, Kellie, Ruth, Kelly, Melanie, Leigh, Marnie, Julie, Lou, Laurie, Kathrine, Angela, Holiday's. Thank you for being such influential people in my life. I'm so fortunate to have all of you.

To my readers, bloggers, and bookstagrammers: Thank you for loving books and believing in happily ever afters.

Prepare to fall in love with
Helena Hunting's *Meet Cute*

'You can't go wrong with *Meet Cute*' *Bustle*

PRAISE FOR *MEET CUTE*

'Perfect for fans of Helen Hoang's *The Kiss Quotient*. A fun and steamy love story with high stakes and plenty of emotion'

Kirkus Reviews

'[A] smartly plotted and perfectly executed rom-com with a spot-on sense of snarky wit and a generous helping of smoldering sexual chemistry'

Booklist

'If a "rom-com in book form" is what you're after this spring, you can't go wrong with *Meet Cute*'

Bustle

'*Meet Cute* is entertaining, funny, and emotional'

Harlequin Junkie

'As charming as its title, but it's also so much more … Fans of Jasmine Guillory's The Wedding Date and Helen Hoang's *The Kiss Quotient* will love *Meet Cute*'

The Washington Independent Review of Books

'Meet Cute is a novel where you will laugh and cry – sometimes, on the same page. It is a story of kindness and affection, sassiness and tenderness, where joy and sorrow are intermingled. You don't want to miss this book'

Frolic

Be charmed by Helena Hunting's
The Good Luck Charm

PRAISE FOR *THE GOOD LUCK CHARM*

'Fabulously fun! Lilah and Ethan's second-chance romance charmed me from the first page to the swoon-worthy end'

Jill Shalvis, *New York Times* bestselling author

'*The Good Luck Charm* is an absolute delight ... Ms. Hunting crafted an entertaining and sexy story with a relatable cast of characters. Fans of Emma Chase, Christina Lauren, and Jaci Burton will love *The Good Luck Charm*'

Harlequin Junkie

'Hockey talk, more than one steamy scene, and a hero and heroine who have a genuine respect as well as a fiery passion for each other make this romance an all-around winner'

BookPage

'Writing with a deliciously sharp humor, Hunting shoots and scores in this exceptionally entertaining contemporary romance'

Booklist

'Hunting sparkles in this well-plotted contemporary'

Publishers Weekly